ALSO FROM TENEBROUS PRESS:

Crom Cruach
a novella by Valkyrie Loughcrewe

Lure
a novella by Tim McGregor

One Hand to Hold, One Hand to Carve
a novella by M.Shaw

Your Body is Not Your Body:
A Body Horror Anthology from Trans & Gender Nonconforming
Voices
edited by Alex Woodroe with Matt Blairstone

In Somnio: A Collection of Modern Gothic Horror
edited by Alex Woodroe

Green Inferno: An Ecological Horror Anthology
edited by Matt Blairstone

**More information at
www.tenebrouspress.com**

Brave
New
Weird
the Best
New Weird Horror
Vol. 1
edited by
Alex Woodroe

Published by Tenebrous Press. Visit us at
   www.tenebrouspress.com.

First Printing, February 2023.

Print ISBN: 979-8-9859923-2-8
eBook ISBN: 979-8-9859923-3-5

Cover art and design by Matt Blairstone.

Formatting by Lori Michelle.

Printed in the United States of America.

TABLE OF CONTENTS

Dedicated to all the readers who are searching for something beyond this world, and the writers who aren't afraid of giving it to them. May you both find so much more than you bargained for.

—AW & MB

AN INTRODUCTION TO NEW WEIRD HORROR

(excerpted from "The Weird of Tomorrow" by Alex Woodroe, originally published in The Tentaculum, November 2022)

"I WANT TO propose this thought: a story's genre is not an adjective that characterizes it, like *dark* or *small* or *heavy*.

No, I want to propose that every story's genre is its living, breathing, growing body. I want to propose that it has limbs, and that it moves, and evolves, and that it joins with other story-bodies in writhing, swirling Genre flocks that we can sort of follow through their ages and predict to a small degree, but that never take the exact same shape twice. Flocks that every story-body contributes to and changes. I want to propose that the flocks don't define the body, but all the bodies make up the flocks.

And, most importantly, I want to propose that New Weird—with or without Horror—is far from the cemetery of glorious but forgotten corpses all the authorities make it out to be.

I've got a vested interest in this, to be wholly transparent. New Weird kept me company through some of the most trying times of my young life, and likely shaped a lot of the author and editor I turned out to be. Now that it's my turn to publish authors, I found myself drawn to the same comforts, and in my need to find words for the bodies of what I was reading in my submissions, I named their flock New Weird Horror.

Because I don't believe in expiration dates. I believe in evolution, and adaptation, and the irresistible force of a generation's gut instinct to return to their spawning grounds."

WEIRD PILGRIMAGE

A Note from Publisher Matt Blairstone

BRAVE NEW WEIRD paints a technicolor picture of the State of the Weird Horror Scene in 2022; and if I may be so bold, the Scene is looking pretty goddamn healthy. This volume showcases a sprawling web of publishers visionary enough to release these gems in the first place, and the artists bold enough to write them. You may recognize some of these names, but definitely not all; we certainly didn't!

Scoff at our audacity if you like, but I defy you not to emerge from this inaugural volume of *Brave New Weird* with no less than half a dozen writers you weren't previously familiar with who will be burned eternally into the Weirdest crannies of your brain.

This volume isn't for the meek; only the Bravest and Weirdest should consider crossing this threshold. But if you count yourself among that number, know that you will be among kindred; part of a sacred fellowship; an exploratory pilot into the Unknowable, the Unsettling, the truly Weird. You might not recognize their faces—and those faces might shift on a dime, may melt into the scenery, may even become your own—but trust me, they recognize *you*.

You are one of them. You are of the Weird.

Do not panic. Breathe deeply. Let it settle along your throat, coat your insides, become your new identity.

Now, take the first step.

BANHUS

M. E. Bronstein

WELL BEFORE ALICE learned to call him "Word-Eater," he found her dating profile and asked, *Do you know what alice means in Italian?* She didn't. So he told her: *anchovy!!*

Much later, Alice would also learn that the Word-Eater was hunting for brainy women who spoke languages he hadn't yet eaten.

They met at a bar a few days later. The Word-Eater drew a little tin out of his pocket, set it on the table, and slid it toward her like a black velvet box. Alice knew what the tin contained even before she read the label and she laughed until her gut twitched in complaint.

Alice said, "Di kats hot lib fish."

The Word-Eater waited.

Alice explained, "That's Yiddish. 'The cat likes the fish.' I forget how the rest goes—something like, 'But she doesn't want to wet her paws.'"

"Meaning?"

Meaning: The cat wants what she can't have? The cat is lazy and will not struggle for a meal? Who is responsible if the cat starves but the cat herself?

The Word-Eater asked her to repeat the phrase in Yiddish; he mimicked her and absorbed her syllables, made them his own.

***

The Word-Eater's easy confidence felt impossible and so alluring. Even his pauses were loud, persuasive; she could almost hear the semicolons. Alice wanted that command over language and its absence.

He taught her new words and where they came from. She repeated after him. *Taffeta* was derived from a Persian verb that meant "to twist" or "to weave." The Word-Eater liked weaving-words, like *text* in English (from *texere*, also the root of *textile*). He liked food words like *candy, anchovy, carrot*.

The Word-Eater drew a circumflex (^). He explained: "We call it a *carrot* because of some conflation between the Latin word (*caret*: 'it lacks,' 'it is missing') and the pointy vegetable (carrot)." Alice liked that—a root in two senses. He asked her, "Caret?" a lot when she seemed sad. His way of asking what was wrong, what was missing.

They had been seeing each other for just a couple of months when the Word-Eater begged Alice to take a few days off work and come to the lake house where he stored the words of all the other women. He didn't talk about the women or their words, though. He said he had inherited the house from his grandparents, who were a convenient combination of dead and generous. Alice was just a couple of years out of school and lived in a tiny studio; the idea of so much space belonging to one person felt unreal.

The house turned out to be an old Victorian with two floors and an attic, decrepit and elegant. Two stained glass windows framed the front entrance and glittered red and yellow, candy-bright. Thin lines arced across the white-painted walls, scars threatening to open and peel. The doors were all bloated with damp, their brass handles and locks corroded, hard to shut and harder to reopen.

The Word-Eater had mentioned someone named Vira who was eager to meet Alice; the way he talked about her, Alice assumed she was a childhood friend or a close relative. Vira turned out to be a cat. She kept prowling around Alice and whining for attention. Alice was allergic to cats, a fact she tried and failed to hide during her first evening as the Word-Eater's houseguest.

When the Word-Eater caught on, he drove into town to buy her some Claritin and said, "No more suffering in silence, Anchovy. You have to tell me what's going on."

In college, she had only been on a couple of dates with boys who were sweet and dull, with weed-fogged eyes, who asked her if she would like to go out again, and she said yes, she'd like that, and then never answered their text messages. The Word-Eater was a decade-ish older than her and felt like a different, more knowing species. He kissed her, inspected and catalogued her parts. He traced the shape of her collarbone and asked, "Do you know why it's called a *clavicle*?", which none of the college boys ever would have wondered (and if they had, they'd have told her without asking).

"No," she said.

He explained that it was kind of a misleading word. It sounded like *clavis*, meaning "key," but really came from a diminutive derived from *clavis*: *clavicula*, "a tendril," "a vine," or (sometimes) "the bolt on a door." Like bodies were ruined palaces crawling with ivy, their bones full of creaky old hinges and locks.

The house smelled of rising bread and garlic in oil. The Word-Eater poached eggs in red wine for their first dinner. Plums drooped from a tree in the yard; the next day, he baked a clafoutis studded with scarlet half-moons. Alice's mother used to call any man who could cook a "keeper"—another misleading word, since it sounded like the man was the one doing the keeping, rather than the one to be kept.

While the Word-Eater went out for groceries, Alice lingered in the house. The floor overhead whined as though beneath someone's footfalls. The attic, the Word-Eater had told her, turned chatty when the wind roamed through it.

Alice sat on an old sofa before a cold and empty fireplace and listened. Some of the house's chatter echoed down the flue.

There was a bit of drapery, an old scarf or shawl, pinned to the wall above the hearth where most people might have put a mirror or a painting. Alice approached and pinched the cloth. Decayed lace and silk and lusterless sequins that reeked of rose water and mothballs. Whose? His grandmother's? A little torn piece of paper fell from its folds onto the mantlepiece. Only one word on it— maybe a signature. It started with a *T*; farther on, two ruffled *F*s plumed across the paper. Then, the line trailed off.

The front door squealed open, slammed shut. Alice caught a glimpse of the Word-Eater overladen with groceries. He yelled, "Hello, Anchovy!" as he slipped into the kitchen, and her hand clenched around the note—he was being nice and making dinner for her and why had she been mucking around with the decorations on his walls? She could hear him whistling as he unpacked ingredients. Alice turned back to the shawl, wasted a silly minute trying to restore the note to whatever fold it had fallen from, but it kept drifting out again, like it wanted her to read it. She left it on the mantlepiece.

The roof groaned.

"Alice!" came a cry from the kitchen. Oil spat in the distance and radiated something warm and pungent.

Alice joined the Word-Eater.

"What're you making?"

Tomatoes and olives simmered and popped in a skillet. An empty anchovy jar sat on the countertop by the Word-Eater's elbow. The musk of the sauce curled Alice's hair as she leaned over to taste.

"Puttanesca," said the Word-Eater. "You know what that means?"

Alice had a guess, thanks to a college Spanish teacher who had liked to teach them curses sometimes. Italian couldn't be too different. "Wait. *Puttana* . . . ? Is that 'whore'?" she said.

"Bingo!" said the Word-Eater. "Good girl. Do you know the story behind it? *Stories*, I should say. There's one legend that the whores of Naples would cook this—because of the smell. To lure the sailors to their beds as they came back ashore . . . "

"And you're cooking my name in it?" She pointed at the empty anchovy jar.

The Word-Eater chuckled and took his time answering as he stirred the sauce.

"Just a joke," he said.

Later, they ate and laughed and drank red-black glasses of Barbaresco. The Word-Eater's hand reached for Alice's, kneaded her knuckles.

It could be nice for this to become a pattern. Weekends away together, more of his cooking, his words.

Then, he leaned over, dabbed at her collarbone with his napkin, though Alice hadn't been conscious of soiling herself. A low growl rumbled in the house's depths and something cool chilled the skin near Alice's throat. She touched her neck, her chest.

A lock clicked and turned in her bones while the Word-Eater collected their plates and took them to the sink.

And then her ears popped, static muffled her gaze, and Alice drooped off her chair and onto the floor. Her cheek settled against the wood grain, her breath filled the cracks in its surface.

"Anchovy! You okay?" said the Word-Eater. He crouched beside her, pressed a hand to her forehead, like he meant to take her temperature.

Instead, he pushed.

She sank through the floor, down, down.

It was hard to say how long she spent sinking and fading; her body and its weight in time stopped mattering. Her voice, however. Her thoughts and words spread and settled. The house took her in. It chattered a greeting.

***

Alice was sent to stay with her grandmother whenever her mother couldn't handle her (so, more often than not). Her grandmother would say weird things that Alice later learned were sloppy translations of Yiddishisms. "You should grow like an onion, with your head in the ground and your feet in the air," was an elaborate way of telling someone to go to hell.

She said, "Der mensch tracht un Gott lacht." Man plans and God laughs.

Klop dir kop in vant. Beat your head against the wall.

Gay kocken offen yom. Go take a shit in the ocean.

Alice stopped speaking after her grandmother died. When she did take up talking again, it turned out to be harder than she remembered. She spent so much time in her head choosing the right syllables and marveled at people whose words fell out easily.

The Word-Eater murmured, "No, not that. Let's get back to that grandmother of yours. Tell me all the things she said."

Too bad Alice had never learned her language properly; that annoyed the Word-Eater. He stamped on the part of the floor where she had disappeared, as though to rattle new and delicious words out of her, the words she owed him.

Alice slipped through wood and paint and concrete.

The house chattered, the wind speaking through its rafters, its gables. And how terrible, not to be alone in it. There were other women everywhere, encoded into the house's every wrinkle and corner, their skin brittle, their hair lank. They muttered in their sleep, in faded dialects of Italian and German, Persian and Sanskrit, Vulgar Latin—a mock Babel. After so much time, their dream-talk had gotten stuck in moldering wood and rusted pipes.

The other women savored their curses like candies but spoke kindly to Alice, audibly saddened that she had joined their ranks.

One of them stayed caught in the glittering shawl she had once worn. Another paced back and forth through the attic. Still others muttered like mice behind the walls.

They told her to keep some words for herself. Not to give them to him, no matter how much he needled. Hide them somewhere safe.

"But it's not even my language," thought Alice. "It's my grandmother's. It's not mine to hide."

They told her, No, it's yours too. Hold on to it.

Alice asked, "How long have you all been here? Are we stuck forever? Why has he done this?"

The house went quiet.

***

Outside, summer faded. The house grew cold.

Alice dreamed of her grandmother, whose cooking she hated but ate out of stubborn loyalty. No grandmotherly cookies, but blintzes plump with acrid cheese, pale chunks of fish in jars. Mildness and subtlety never figured into her grandmother's palate or vocabulary, and she was so very loud where Alice had always been sweet and docile. What would *she* have done if he'd made the mistake of trapping *her* in the house instead of Alice? She would scream and shout. She would curse him. She would break the house and spill out of it.

The other voices stirred. They said that, yes, curses could eat holes into the house. They could burrow through it like termites, pick at it like woodpeckers. They said, We can get out—sometimes, briefly. But the house always takes us back in.

They sounded reluctant to tell her this. Didn't want Alice to wound herself with hope.

Still—to be herself again, if only for a little while. To be something more than a voice and half-remembered language.

"Grow like an onion," thought Alice. She could not remember the words in Yiddish, except that *onion* was *tsibele*.

Alice sank and dreamed of the Word-Eater bent over like an old cartoon ostrich with his head buried—not in sand, but in the cold cement of the cellar—and green ribbons of leaf sprouted out of the nape of his neck. She tried to remember. *Vaksa, vaksen?* She gripped her dream of an onion's leaves and pulled and pulled until a moldering skull popped free. Browned teeth like decayed corn kernels leered at her.

Beat your head against the wall. Grow like an onion. Her curses could make a hole, an avenue out, if only for a little while. If only she could remember it right.

Vaksn zolstu—

"Vaksn zolstu vi a tsibele—!"

Alice threw her curse, the skull, and it cracked against something—

An old iron wood stove in the corner.

Alice was Alice again and ached all over. She had stopped sinking and spreading through the house's innards. She tested her arms and legs, but it had been so long, they didn't feel like hers anymore. Alice leaned upright on her elbows. An angry hurt thundered through her bones and at first, all she wanted was to disappear again and will everything away. But no. Time to move. To get out of here.

She sat still and listened for a minute—maybe two. Heard nothing save for Vira mewling for food in the distance. And so, Alice got up and hobbled to the stairs that would lead out of the cellar. He must have left for a bit. She could slip out, feel the autumn air. If only her legs would quit shaking and carry her.

She stopped in the kitchen first, bent to the faucet and drank what felt like a river's worth of water.

Then, the click of a lock. Not in her bones, but the front door.

It had been raining recently, and the wood was swollen and resisted him.

Alice grabbed the first blunt object on hand: a very heavy cast-iron skillet. She slipped into the hall, considered avenues of escape. The window? No—the frame was stuck, wouldn't budge. Alice stumbled upstairs instead, just as the door finally yielded behind her—she heard him scraping his boots against the doormat. On the second floor, adrenaline fueled her up the rickety stepladder to the attic.

He called out, "Alice? You there?"

Alice stood on top of the attic's trapdoor and clutched the skillet.

A knock on the wood beneath her feet.

"Alice," said the Word-Eater's muffled voice, "what are you doing? Carrot?" He meant, Caret? What's wrong, what's missing?

The Word-Eater talked through the door. Alice had been sick, and he was taking care of her, keeping her safe. What had gotten into her? What did she think was going on here?

"Come on, Alice," said the Word-Eater. "Enough of this. You should be resting."

Time to come out.

Alice stepped off the door and let the Word-Eater push it open.

His head surfaced through a square of brightness, and for a moment, Alice hesitated. But then Vira, beautiful Vira with her noxious fur, mewled somewhere out of sight. Alice could picture her winding up the attic stairs, nudging the Word-Eater's leg, eager to be fed.

And as soon as the Word-Eater turned, Alice hefted the skillet—whirled it down on his skull as hard as she could during that whisper of a second while he shooed away the dumb cat.

***

She dropped his body in the lake. (Who was the fish now?) Later, she wished she had kept his head. She could have filled his skull with onion seeds and buried it and so made the curse come true.

Alice spent that night in the house. The Word-Eater's sounds and smells—bread and brandy—went on clinging to the walls, the curtains, the pages of his books. But so did the voices—the voices Alice had come to know while she spent months sinking through the house.

And so she could not go—not yet. Not while they went on muttering so very audibly behind the house's walls. But were they right? Would she sink back into the house, just like them, if she lingered here? Surely killing the Word-Eater changed things; maybe she could help them break out, too, now. Or had they been stuck too long, become irrevocably embedded?

At night, Alice squeezed a pillow and stared at a long crack in the paint that cut the bedroom ceiling in two.

The Word-Eater had a degree or two in Historical Linguistics and some other related field. Or so he'd said (it could get hard to keep track of all the things he'd said and done and said he'd done). He had grown up speaking Italian and spent his youth orbiting the Mediterranean, "picking up" Latin's neighbors and descendants, then rattled other branches of the Indo-European language tree until they yielded him some fruit too.

"I'm a word-eater," he had said—with such a proud, dimply smirk that she didn't feel the warning in his declaration.

And this was the storehouse where he put all the words for safekeeping.

A low and lurking noise hunted through the dark.

Alice rose, traced the sound through the walls until she had to crouch, and found a hole where the molding met the floor. Her fingertips brushed against something pointy—long and thin and cold—and she flinched backward. A mouse? No—Alice yanked the thing out of the hole.

A carrot.

Caret?

A word, a root, poking out of the house's crevices.

Maybe that was when it occurred to her: she had never heard the Word-Eater speak his other languages at length; he had only spoken them in bits and pieces and used English to define and contain all the other words and roots that he knew. His English was nothing more than a creaky old house, an overloud container of other languages.

***

Alice waited for daylight, then found a terra-cotta pot for the carrot. She patted soil around it and remembered the Word-Eater, an imminent corpse twitching at the bottom of the attic stairs, Vira licking the blood as it pooled out of his head. Alice sat cross-legged by the hole in the wall and studied it. She ate her lunch there and scattered bread crumbs by the hole, as though to tempt more words out like hungry mice.

And then:

Alice smelled anchovies.

Alice smelled *like* anchovies?

There was an important difference between those two sentences, but Alice couldn't figure out which one wanted to be more to the point. Noses are not very discriminating about the niceties of literal versus metaphorical expression, direct objects and subject complements.

Oh no—was it taking her back, making her into language again? Did she really have to be Alice the anchovy? Couldn't she just be Alice?

"Not yet," muttered Alice to herself, to the house, to who knows what. "Please not yet . . . Oh God, oh yuck." She rushed to the shower.

A banging and muttering in the pipes echoed and bounced off the bathroom tiles. A faraway chant, resonant even when obscured by hissing water and steam. Alice turned the tap off, shivered, and listened.

"Anchovy," said the voices. And something else after that.

Alice exited the shower with shampoo still in her hair, ran to the kitchen and wrote on the dry-erase board on the fridge. She copied down the chant while her marker squeaked in protest. Her writing wept as she dripped on it.

And then Alice stared at what she had written atop the palimpsest of the Word-Eater's neatly composed shopping lists. She bit her lips to keep her teeth from chattering.

anchovy werewolf virago puttanesca banhus candy clavicle taffeta carrot

The note that had fallen out of the shawl—the signature. *Taffeta.* A twisting, a woven word. And the threads of the house's language warped all around her. A soft and tangled nest. It wanted to take her back into its weave.

A more benign noise whined at her feet. Vira.

While the cat bared her belly and a purr rumbled beneath Alice's hand, Alice wondered how to let the words out—let them scream.

She ached, tormented by their weird drip feed of syllables overburdened with meaning. It was like she had turned into an erudite hamster stuck in a cage, hungry for morsels of language.

"I am not a hamster," she told Vira. The cat purred. Alice sneezed.

BANHUS

Hamster comes from a word meaning "corn weevil." Hamsters are not corn weevils. But both like burrowing, eating. (*Rodent* has a similar heritage; it comes from *rodere*: "to gnaw. Erode.")

Then: a strident little whimper.

Alice ran to the hole in the wall where she had found the carrot. She got there just in time to watch a shadowy slip of something—a mouse?—wriggle its way through the hole. Alice pressed her ear against the wall. Heard more voices, trapped and muttering and scratching. Rodent-like words, an infestation gnawing through the house.

Vira followed her, mewled at the wall and its noises. She rubbed her head against Alice's leg. "Hush," said Alice. Vira hissed instead.

***

The Word-Eater had once said they needed a word for etymology's opposite, for words that have died but shouldn't have. A study of dead words' ghosts, rather than living words' roots. Some words (and languages) are like haunted houses: abandoned but rich with old echoes. *Banhus*, for instance. An Old English word for "body"— literally translating to just what it sounds like: a "bone house."

Alice spent days pressing her ear against wood and plaster, but the voices would not come out.

They were waiting, too. Waiting for her to sink through the floor again and rejoin them. But didn't they understand that the Word-Eater was dead now? That had to mean something. Were they *still* doomed to haunt this place without him keeping them there?

She would have to listen harder, remember how to communicate with them. Maybe that way, she could lead them out.

But the longer she lingered, the more her skin crinkled and scaled like a fish's, and when she ran a finger across her arm it came away slick with oil. A salty stink followed her everywhere. She couldn't tell if it came from her or the house. Or both.

Alice followed the house's noises upstairs, where they whispered off in too many directions to follow at once. Like a root system of voices that spread softly beneath the floorboards, behind the walls.

"What did you say," whispered Alice, and the house offered her nothing coherent in response. Just overlapping threads of chatter.

She went up, knocking on the wall all the way. "Hello?" she said again. "I know you're there. Please talk to me. I won't hurt you. I just want to talk—to help."

Alice banged a fist against one of the wall's many long seams, like an answer would fall out of it.

"What did you say!"

Caret, said the wall. (Which is to say, it said nothing, it lacked.)

Alice found a pencil and wrote the chant atop the seam in the wall, treated it like an underline, because she didn't want *that* word to be its final word; she needed to fill the gap with something. The wall felt strangely delicate beneath her hand, like she could reach right through it if she wanted and tear the house's guts out.

"Anchovy?" said the voices.

"I," said Alice, which was the right answer to that, after all. But she didn't know what else to add. Why didn't she ever have the right words when she needed them? Nothing makes sense when you're haunted by words and the words are already haunted, when bodies are houses and houses are bodies, when the borders between things crack.

"Virago?" said the voices, and Vira whined in response.

***

Alice had misheard the Word-Eater the first time he called the cat by her full name. Like most good students of classical Latin, he pronounced the *V*s like *W*s, and so Alice heard *Virago* as *werago*, like Vira was some kind of werewolf or other were-creature Alice hadn't heard of before.

The Germanic *were* in *werewolf* means "man" and is related to Latin *vir*, which is also the root of *virtue* (understood as a manly quality). A virago is a warrior, a mannish and brave woman. Or an angry and troublesome woman.

Old conversations dripped through the house; fell on sheets of notepaper, on the dry-erase board; filled up the walls with shaky graphite.

"Got something to say, Vira?" asked Alice, crouching before the cat. A low feline growl reminded Alice that Vira could not say anything. "Or something to show me? Will you help me—help us?" Alice held out her hand, and a wet little tongue tested her fingertips. Vira's whiskers tickled, like ants crawling across her skin.

12

The cat's volume increased. Grew insistent. Like she wanted to be fed. She wound herself in a circle around Alice's legs and then looked toward the attic.

"Okay," said Alice, and she followed Vira as she bounded up the stepladder.

Night had started to fall, and it was dark in there, and Alice couldn't see right. The floorboards were dusty, not rippled and cool as water beneath her feet. A gabled ceiling peaked overhead, and a narrow skylight let in a bone-white sliver of moon.

Vira continued to mewl and whine, and Alice followed her to a corner of the attic and felt through the dark until her fingers came across tin cans, little towers of cat food. And then, as she explored, something else. Glass. A jar.

Alice wrenched its lid off and let out someone's pickled scream. She felt like an anchovy dissolving in oil—her body losing its old weight and meaning. She was becoming like them again. But at least she would not be stuck in this place anymore—none of them would.

Where were the others? The rest of the voices the greedy Word-Eater had trapped in the house?

Alice followed Vira and tore things open, broke them, and their collective shouts howled at the moon.

***

The house became a thing of broken eggshell, all its rich words a mess that spilled and spread.

Whenever anyone (mostly drunk teenagers on Halloween) went inside, the house muttered and snickered in response. Cracks riddled its walls and its white paint glittered, sweated a faint oily sheen. A faraway stench of salty sea, fat bubbling over a fire. The stained glass windows broke, the toothy red glitter that lingered in the frames still candy-bright—*candy* comes from a word meaning a "fragment" of something in Sanskrit—and the fragmented house had a new kind of loudness now, riddled with holes and narrow yet strident wind tunnels. It had become a kind of musical instrument, a giant woodwind.

Dodder and ivy crawled out of the house's shattered windows and open doors, twined out of seeds nestled within every broken lock and hinge. Outside, shreds of cloth dangled from the trees like colorful catkins. A little white bulge and ribbonlike shoots of green sprouted in the plum tree's shadow (an onion surrounded by rotting brown-and-purple fruit).

Noises roamed across the lake at night, like a pack of wolves out hunting, their howling and hungry sounds eager to devour the moonlight. Old meaning stretched out at last and echoed.

USER WARNING

Charlotte Ariel Finn

THE FIRST THING you did was throw up.

The internal pharmaceutical implant did what it could to mix up antacids and anti-anxiety medication out of internal stores and stray hormones in your body. But a miracle maker, it was not. And so you knelt by that ancient cold porcelain toilet that you kept around because tearing out the plumbing would do too much damage to the fixtures and paneling of your home.

After last night's meal and something that looked like blood, after your stomach gave everything it couldn't allow any more, you check your notifications again, to see if there was a mistake. It's as familiar as swallowing by now, given the years you've had the neocortex. You hesitate a little, like a kid who hasn't learned how peek-a-boo works yet; the deeply irrational part of you thinks, maybe if you don't check, it won't be real.

But you check, and it's real. The message from HaveIBeenPwned is real.

One of your neural backups was just uploaded to the Internet.

***

After the shock wears off, you put your neocortex in safe mode, leaving yourself outside the touch of wireless neural backup for the first time in eighteen months. You expect to feel fear, but you don't. It'd be like being scared of dehydration while you were drowning. A lack of backups is not your problem right now.

With your brain in safe mode, you go digging through your old banker's box full of electronics for something you can fashion into

15

a crude means of accessing the Internet. An old wireless card, a keyboard from that brief flirtation with DVORAK, that old external holograph you use for when you need to diagnose a problem with a display.

You boot up and the first thing you do is change your local wireless password; thankfully, no one who knows it is anywhere close to your house. What you had before was seventeen extremely rare words long, but that doesn't matter; you remembering it means that now they all know about it.

That solved, you then log onto the provider for uSync Neocortexes. You used the hardware but not the firmware, but check anyways to see if there's a noted issue with the hardware. Tens of thousands of words of legalese stream by your eyeballs; your own fluency with the language isn't good enough to know if they have covered their asses enough.

You have no leads, and so, with some heaviness in your heart, you go to the software forum for Jucci, the programming collective that makes the software in your neocortex. It's a lot more easily modified than uSync's default backups and regulatory behavior; it also has a steeper learning curve.

You wonder for the first time if maybe, despite the degree on your wall, if maybe it was too steep.

They are already talking about the hack. There are a lot of theories as to how it could have happened and no one's taking responsibility. There's some idle speculation as to how to invalidate the data, but everyone knows the central problem: trying to take data off the Internet is like trying to take water out of the ocean. And translating the human psyche into data meant it was inevitable that this would happen.

There are people there who proclaim that well, yes, this is a serious breach and all, but be honest, if it had to happen to anyone, it might as well have happened to you, right?

They're banned. Eventually.

You log off and try not to cry.

***

You spend your morning changing every single password that you have.

All your old backup phrases are useless; everyone now knows

16

your favorite author, your favorite movie, your first crush. You contemplate going back to carrying around a tabula recta, because yes, carrying a piece of paper with random characters on it is a pain, but is it that much worse than this?

As you rebuild your digital security, you get a message from Cleo, who tells you that she knows where the hack is hosted, and where people are discussing it. With morbid curiosity, you open a parallel session and see for yourself.

Without the actual neocortex and the very specific configuration of your neurons, they can't actually simulate your brain that easily. (Yet.) But they have already begun trawling through the memories they can decode. You read reaction posts full of that corrupted image of a soda can that looks like it's laughing painfully, as people go over all your private shames and failures. That time you wet the bed when you were sleeping over at a friend's. That time you plagiarized a joke. That time you lied when you said your favorite movie was the four-hour cut of In Paradise, Nobody Laughs when it's actually a superhero movie starring an actress you had a crush on.

They laugh at the time someone slipped something into your drink at a party, and they denigrate the hazy memory of Sophie as she gets you out of there before anything can get worse.

The neocortex alerts the pharmaceutical implant, and it does what it can, but you know.

There's no fixing this.

***

You no longer have a job when lunch arrives.

Some anonymous citizen sent a thorough list of all the sites you visit when you're in the mood for a certain kind of erotica; your employer reads them off to you and takes your silence as confirmation. Of course, they are very open-minded, *very* open-minded, of course they know it's all pretend. But it's a messed up kind of pretend, isn't it, and in contrast to everyone else's pretend, it's now a public pretend instead of a private pretend, and your access to the work servers has been revoked.

At the least, they have no grounds to sue, since you were very diligent at booting into safe mode during work hours and not thinking about work outside of work hours. Still: better safe than sorry. They are going to be spending their afternoon revamping their security as well, which of course, is just what they don't need. Why did you have to do that, they ask. Why did you have to get one of those things.

In the middle of this conversation, a stranger pings you on the social network you do all that pretending on, and asks if you would be into that very specific kind of pretend.

You're meaner to them than they really deserve.

***

That afternoon, more anonymous messages roll in.

There's the ones you expect; the ones that say you deserved it because of all the shit you tried to stir within the community, with your writing and your advocacy and the criticisms you've had for how the community handles things. None of them admit that your memories exonerate you in the public dispute you had with Dr. Feine, of course.

You don't cry. Not yet.

Some of them are messages saying that they knew you were always faking it, sending you a compiled list of every time you doubted the gender identity you arrived at. You remember, freshly, each and every time you did exactly that.

You don't cry. Not yet.

You check the forum and someone is already working on You v1.1—bullshit posturing, of course, hacking a brain image on that scale would take tens of thousands of hours of work. But he seems pretty dedicated to his new hobby. He says that he has friends who are pretty into it too. Says he can't wait for simulation tech to get better so that he can have fun with the copy of you from six months ago. He has a lot of ideas.

He says that version 1.1 of you will smile more.

You don't cry. Not yet.

Someone posts a crude deepfake of a memory you had, where you were naked and looking in the mirror and admiring the progress you were making; they've inserted themselves behind you, wearing a tactical balaclava, their gloved hands reaching for your throat.

You don't cry. Not yet.

As you're finishing up the last of your changed passwords, as

18

you're finally eating something you cooked on the stove because right now you don't trust anything with a wireless connection to the Internet, you get a message from someone telling you that they really enjoyed how you felt at your mother's funeral. How the speech you gave was heartwarming and that they know—they have confirmed—that the emotion you felt was genuine.

And that is what does it.

Then, you finally cry.

***

The local mutual aid network's head organizer says that this will all be solved once we've achieved full socialism.

He talks at length about how once everyone's basic needs are met, there will no longer be any incentives to steal someone's brain images, because the secrets within won't be valuable anymore. That once what he, and you, have advocated for becomes the way people live, what you're going through won't happen to anyone else.

As he talks, you idly look him up. He seems sincere, is the thing; he seems to honestly believe this. He wants a better way of life for everyone, and so do you. But he did defend Dr. Feine that one time, though he later changed his mind. And he does have an account on the forum currently tearing your life apart in a very literal sense. You don't have anything concrete. But you wonder.

You wonder how, considering how well off the forum in question's userbase is, if seeing to the basic needs of everyone will really solve the problem. Capitalism sure isn't solving it, of course. But that doesn't mean anything else can.

Then you remember that your bills don't care about your feelings and that your implant needs a restock, and so, you swallow your pride and nod along as he goes into the speech he's practiced.

Then you wonder if he'll ever find out what you really think of him. But thankfully, you haven't done a backup since booting into safe mode.

You think about toggling it off, but . . . not yet.

***

That evening, Sophie calls you in tears.

It's not your fault, she says. She knows it's not your fault. You didn't tell a soul about it, just like you promised. But you remembered, and your neocortex backed up the memory, and now, everyone knows, so whether or not it's your fault, her life is still in tatters.

You can still remember that day, the day she cried into your arms as she told you something she never told anyone before, or anyone since. About why she refused to testify. You remember holding her, and you remember not agreeing. But you remember saying "I understand," and you remember saying it enough that you began to actually understand.

But as you hold onto that memory, you know that it's not just yours and hers anymore. Now it belongs to anyone with an Internet connection. There will be stories written about you soon. And well, they'll have to talk about some of your memories, won't they. Otherwise they'd just be dancing around what a violation this is. And in talking about them, they'll be making sure that they spread that much further and that much wider.

And meanwhile, Sophie confesses that she no longer feels like she can trust you with anything while that thing is in your head, that she can't share anything in confidence because she no longer has any. It's not you, it's the implant. She swears, it's the implant.

You say you understand, and you cry, as your oldest friendship dissolves into dust and you can't do a thing about it.

***

By the time midnight hits, you're looking up transhuman collectives.

A few people out there have anticipated this problem, that neural uploads could never be fully secure and would necessitate a change in social order. So they built a collective where there is an explicit expectation that you cannot trust all secrets to stay secret forever, and they have built their community around that.

You do the research. They seem okay. No major incidents. They are understandably resistant to outsiders; who wouldn't be, given that they've given up on even the pretense of privacy over their own memories and thoughts? The few videos of them make them seem charming and affable, and you wonder if it's just because everyone in their community is pointing a camera at everyone else all day, every day. Who wouldn't learn to be photogenic?

The big catch is, of course, that you couldn't be in contact with anyone outside the collective; everyone in the collective has agreed to be an open book, and without the consent of those outside, it's unethical to form any kind of meaningful relationship with those whose privacy is at risk.

You think about turn-of-the-century literature about the digital divide, about a world divided neatly in two, between the digital haves and the digital have-nots, and you wonder if that's just the nature of the beast.

You don't find an answer. You just wonder.

***

You finish this journal, and you're still in safe mode.

While you're in safe mode, all uploads are restricted; in the event of catastrophic failure, you'll be restored from backup from the day before writing this.

You think about that, and as you write, you think about trauma.

You ask yourself if it's really ethical to subject a future version of yourself to the memories of this day, considering how often throughout the course of the day you've fantasized about taking a drill to the part of your skull that feels a little colder than the rest. You can spare them ever having to remember all of this. Just stay in safe mode forever.

You also ask if it's ethical for that other version of you to wake up one day with no idea of how, or why, their life has so radically changed. If the version of this that they'd go through, all over again, would be any better. You can prevent that from happening. Simply turn off safe mode, even once, just long enough for an upload.

You ask if it's better to forget the trauma, or let it live on forever. And you contemplate the old fear of death, awoken by seeing your mother's body wither away, and you ask yourself if she'd have gotten one of these things. And you'll never be sure, because she's gone forever. Meanwhile, you—once the technology of backup bodies catches up with the state of backup minds—could choose to live forever.

The toggle for safe mode is easy. Pressing the toggle under the skin while reciting the passphrase. Impossible to turn on, or off, by accident. Turn it back on, and you return to being immortal, and that means you remember today for all your infinite days. Leave it off, and let yourself go through this for the first time, again and again forever. Or wipe your backups and make peace with knowing that one day, you'll never experience anything ever again.

You think about Hell, back when you believed in it, and how what scared you the most was how it never ended. And you think about the first time you stopped believing in Hell, and contemplated death—contemplated ceasing to be, forever.

And you still haven't decided which one's worse.

And you stop writing this journal, and prepare to find out.

THE BEAR ACROSS THE WAY

Emily Rigole

I **PAID NO** more attention to the bear than I would have any new neighbors. Despite what my husband might tell you, the fact that he was a bear played into my curiosity very little. It was his behavior that concerned me. The same behavior that would have concerned me of any new member to our community. And if people had listened to me a little earlier, instead of tiptoeing about trying not to—God forbid—offend the bear, then maybe all this could have been avoided.

For one thing, he kept very odd hours. I only saw him in the early hours of the morning when I made coffee for Greg or late in the evening as I turned out the lights. I thought this very strange behavior indeed, but I would have been willing to leave it at that, if not for the other thing.

That was the sound. Usually, I could block it out with chores or television, but at night it came clear. A humming that seemed to rise out of the earth below the bear's house and infect my dreams. I would have preferred it to be music. At least there are things you can do about loud music. Certain calls you can make. But what can you say about that alien hum? Even Greg looked at me as if I were crazy each time I brought it up.

Oh, but he was a darling of the neighborhood. He had guests most every evening. I watched them through the kitchen blinds as I prepared dinner. Joan and Terry and Marcia and Don. The women brought him pies and the men clapped his back as if they were old friends. When they finally left, long after sundown, it was with smiles and flushed cheeks. And always they left with a little glass jar.

This jar was the greatest mystery. At first, I thought it was a small flashlight, because of the way it illuminated everything around it. But then I saw the light seemed to emit from whatever was in the jar. I pulled Greg over to see, wondering aloud about radiation.

"You know, we could always go and find out." He would say. I think he was teasing, but I had excuses prepared just in case. For months I escaped the bear's den. But summer turned to fall and fall wilted to winter and finally fate caught up with me.

***

It was sometime after Thanksgiving. Greg came back from a morning run, his cheeks red with cold. He was smiling, some private joke on his lips, but it fell when he saw me. I knew then. He had spoken with the bear.

"It's just once a week, Shell." He said. "It's the neighborly thing to do."

That was easy for him to say. He had agreed to a task he did not have to perform. The bear was going to sleep for a long time and he needed someone to watch over his house. My wife stays at home, Greg offered. She'd be happy to help.

"And look, here's your reward." He presented me with a small, cloth-covered shape. I took it and the cloth fell away, revealing a tiny glass jar of gold. He laughed at the face I made. "It's only honey after all."

***

We went to the bear's house that night. I brought no pies.

"Come in, come in." He said as he opened the door. It was meant to be warm but his voice was horrible, like churning rocks. "I cannot tell you how grateful I am for this."

It was cozy enough inside. A healthy fire glowed in the hearth and the air smelled faintly sweet. There was not much in the way of furniture, but the pieces he had were rustic and wood-carved. I might have been comfortable if not for the hum. I could hear it very clearly now, droning through the floorboards. I looked to Greg, but if he heard, he showed no sign.

The bear himself was massive. He walked on his hind legs and hunched to fit in the room. His eyes were small and shrewd, his claws long like fossilized fingers. There was no teddy bear warmth to him, but he dressed as a teddy bear might, in a nightgown and cap. It was somehow more beastly than if he had been naked.

"I don't think we've met," He rumbled in my direction. "I'm Abernathy."

"Shelley Lowell."

"A pleasure."

Blessedly, he did not hold out his paw for me to shake.

"As you can see," he said, "I require little, so I hope it will not be much trouble for you. I will sleep here." He led us to his room, which was empty save for a mass of pillows in its center. "You need not worry about waking me. I am a deep sleeper." He made a huffing sound that might have been a laugh, then led us out to a door across the kitchen. The closer we got, the louder the humming grew. The door itself seemed to pulse with the rhythm of it. Whatever was on the other side, I knew it was the source.

"But this is why I asked you here." The bear said, gripping the handle in his claws and pulling. The hum exploded. A burst of static that rattled my bones.

"What, uh . . . what have you got down there Abernathy?" Greg asked, peering down the staircase the door had revealed.

"My greatest treasure," he said. "The hive."

***

There was no light in the cellar, only a small window, but there was no need for one. The honey produced its own light. It lit up the nests so they appeared as bright misshapen stars, clumping in the corners and hanging from the ceiling. I stepped forward. The air was so alive with bees that it seemed to speak with the beat of their wings. No longer a hum but a full-throated song. This was the heart of my nightmares and yet, now that I was here, it compelled me. My blood thrummed with its music.

"They should take care of themselves," the bear said slowly, as if entranced. "They've enough honey for the winter months, but if it fades, you must take more from my stores and feed them. They will die without it."

I do not know how I left that strange space. A part of me thinks I am there still, suspended in honeyed amber. I remember floating back up the steps, collecting our things and saying goodbye. I

25

remember the shadowed silhouette of the bear, standing in his doorway, paw waving.

"Good night my friends, I will see you again in spring."

And I remember that when I dreamed that night, it was of stars.

***

I knew it was unnatural, but I could not stop thinking of that golden place. Perhaps it was some sort of test the bear set up for me. Perhaps, knowing what I would do, he engineered all this from the start. Whatever the case, thoughts of the hive came to me in every empty moment. I counted the days until my return.

The day came a week later. I walked into the house half-giddy and half-shy, casting a cursory glance around the den, the kitchen. I peeped at the sleeping hulk of the bear in his room. He was nothing but a brown mound, swelling and deflating with each breath. Like a dragon over its hoard of gold. That makes me the knight come to reclaim it, I thought as I descended to the hive.

I lost hours there, sprawled on the floor, gazing at the fat stalactite nests. The bees whirred above me in the dark. I caught flashes of their furred bodies, saw their shadows move against the nests, but I did not see all of them—not even a fraction. They were a fathomless presence, like standing before the ocean. I found myself not wanting to leave.

As winter set the bees slowed. They bundled in their nests, dimming their light. It felt lonely without them filling the air. One day, I walked to one of the nests, looking inside. The slabs of honeycomb glistened like squares of butter. My mouth watered.

My hand moved faster than my mind. I broke off a piece of the nest and brought it to my lips. I had never tasted anything like it before, sweeter than sugar and headier than wine. I could drink rivers of it and never feel sick. Before I knew it that entire nest was a husk in my hand. I went home and ate dinner. I kissed my husband. But I could not chase that perfect taste from my mouth.

***

It became a habit. I picked the nests that seemed smaller, more separate than the rest. The ones I thought would not be missed. Whole afternoons I spent, licking the honeycomb clean. Then I'd lie down and let a great satisfaction settle over me. I did not notice the lights growing dim, until one day I entered the hive to be greeted with only darkness.

The bear had said to take honey from his stores, but I knew that would be no good. The air was dead. If I took a step, a carpet of insect bodies crunched beneath my feet. There was no going back from what I had done. I fled, and did not return.

***

The bear will be reasonable, I thought. He made this hive, he can make another. There are more bees in the world. But my heart whispered misgivings. None like those, it said. The bear will wake and when he does, he will come for you.

Weeks passed and the frost cracked. Green buds spotted the trees. I woke one morning to sun streaming through the windows and birdsong. I took a moment to bask in it, the bear and his hive an ugly memory melting in spring sun.

Then, the world broke.

It sounded like a storm, like an earthquake. I turned to Greg and saw my fear reflected in his eyes. He ran to the window.

"It's Abernathy," he said, racing outside. I went to the window. The bear was there indeed. He stood in the middle of the street, beating his chest and roaring murder. Venom flew from his lips and he attacked whatever was in his path. I felt each strike, every snapped mailbox and smashed car. I knew it was meant for me.

I fell to the floor. Greg kept a rifle in the closet, but I didn't know how to use it. There were knives in the kitchen, but if I got close enough to the bear to use a knife then I'd already lost. I could do nothing but hide. I squeezed under the bed, wincing, breath ragged, and waited for the walls to come crashing down around me.

They never did. Instead, I heard sirens. And voices. Car doors being opened and shut. The bear bellowed until it choked, the sound crumpling into something like a sob. Then: Pop, pop, pop. Three solid blasts, one right after another, like firecrackers. I did not hear the bear again after that.

I crawled out from the bed, legs shaky, and wandered outside. The whole neighborhood was there. They were speaking to each other in hushed voices, looking around warily. I followed their gaze until I saw the bear.

27

His body was twisted, arms and head bent at ugly angles. His red tongue lolled on the asphalt. His eyes were open, the same black holes I remembered, but his cheeks seemed dark and matted. As if with tears. The ground was black and wet where he lay.

I found Greg. He wrapped an arm around me and pulled me close to him.

"You were right, Shelly," he said softly, stroking my hair. "All this time, he was just a wild animal."

And then I realized what everyone was saying. He seemed so nice, they whispered, but you can't trust a bear. These friends who had dined with him, who had laughed at his jokes. They knew nothing of the hive, or the honey. To them it was just a beast behaving as beasts do.

A weariness landed on my shoulders. I looked into my husband's eyes, shining with shock and betrayal. I could have told him everything, but then that shock would be pointed at me. And besides, if it had not been the honey, then it would have been something else. I leaned into his arms and sighed.

"Well," I said. "That's just how bears are."

EN EL PATIO DE LA CASA DEL CALLEJÓN

Tania Chen

THE HOUSE AT the end of the street has an abandoned fountain on the ground floor patio. It is littered with leaves and bruised flowers, fifty-year-old dust and dirt clogging metal poles that sustain a Statue, lanced through its granite limbs: two arms, a tail and spine.

(It breathes in through stone gills;
behind two sets of eyelids
it flutters its eyes and
breathes out.)

There was, once upon a time, a tree that fed the fountain with oranges and limes. It suckled from infancy the sweet-sour nectars and grew, limbs stretched out like bougainvillaea branches.

There is a man that lives in this house, decayed. Misery and decrepit bones alongside sixty-year-old flaws and fears clog the arteries, that sustain that rickety denture; that creeping heart.

This man hates the Statue; he thrills in its decay and revels in its abandonment. And so the granite fades under the sun and rain, the pipes rust, flaking off reddish strips as water makes sluggish attempts to circulate.

And the Statue knows it.

It has laid silent for so long, generation after generation. This house is an inheritance, stolen from his sister. Unceremoniously waiting for time to aid his theft, entrenching himself in the bowels of this house: its winding staircase and spacious patio, its wilting garden and decaying Statue.

The dried ink on dotted lines wakes it.

(it breathes in   draws itself upwards,   slinking out of the sea of leaves and neglect that has become its home.)

Behind, it drags its tail; with hands, it claws across the stone, and the yellowed grass, desperate for a taste of clear, cool water. The long metal spikes hold its head, its limbs entrapped. It wails, high pitched and rage-filled.

The Statue loves only women. It remembers this: once upon a time a woman swept the patio—she prayed daily, left flowers and honey, peeled oranges and lit candles. When the grass was green and the trees hung heavy with the fruit of that faded memory, the woman's hair spilled like ink at the edge of the fountain. Her eyes grew marble black and empty as they looked up at the Statue in supplication. She'd always been told that for love to grow it must be cultivated, methodical; this love is not, it is a relentless storm of summer that turns a desert into an ocean.

The Statue remembers the woman with the sweet smile that swept the patio every morning until her brother threw her out and stole everything.

(it drags its tail along the red tiles
of the parlour floor,
past the eyes of other dented statues
that hold the sun and moon.

Up the steps made grey with dust;

Up along urine stained carpets.

Up until the velvet red curtain starts—

where it makes its way into the bed
claws curled in the tapestry
claws curled into what lay behind them.)

The man's shock robs him of his voice before the statue collects: his life for all those he ruined. *You're dead*, he says, with no regret and endless resentment, splayed out on the carpet. His head caved in, the sight of the beams in the ceiling fading to black. There is a sound of moving stone, like an avalanche before his world ends.

His last thoughts are of himself, and the bone-deep terror of knowing that the house is no longer his to have. The narrow hallways and secret dining room will belong to his sisters once more.

***

There is a house where a nameless, miserly man no longer lives. Where flowers bloom in season and the sea-salt air permeates through its untamed vine covered gates. The entrance is littered with orange peels, outlining a path to its patio where a fountain sleeps.

At the end of *El Callejon de la Sirena* lies a house thought decayed. A house owned by a statue with a voice of the deep.

IN HASKINS

Carson Winter

EVERYONE, BOTH THE young and the old, went about their lives as usual on the day of the Mask Festival. The downtown streets were covered with colored leaves and Mr. Burkett still waved at children and swept in front of his storefront. Mrs. Farley still clucked to Mrs. Durant on how the new teachers at the old school would not and could not teach their children anything. And the policemen still ate lunch at the Morrison Deli on Main. Normality ruled with benevolent routine. But still, as the leaves fell, and the stage was erected, the people of Haskins braced quietly for their most insistent tradition.

At the fairgrounds, Jennifer arrived early to help set the stage. Her eye sockets hung loose and rubbery around her blue eyes. She was the first Jennifer to have blue eyes. The mane on top of her head was coarse and tawny. Flies buzzed in her stomach and she was thankful she was Jennifer because Jennifer always had to stay busy. Cindy was already there, cross-legged and cutting orange leaves out of construction paper, looking prim and sweet in her blue dress.

She nodded to Cindy as she found a pair of scissors. When Cindy did not return the movement, Jennifer decided that her eyelets must be misaligned.

"Hey," she said, gaining her attention.

Cindy looked up from a pile of construction paper. "Good morning," she said between ragged breaths. She always complained of being overheated. "Are you excited?"

Cindy's voice was low this year, deep. She was tall and

muscular, but Jennifer always gave her credit for her commitment to Cindy's primary traits—innocence and geniality. They were best friends.

"Yes, in a way," she said.

Cindy's scissors made ripping sounds as they ate through the construction paper. "Are you worried?"

She was talking about Rance and Rance was a key aspect of Jennifer. They fit together like pieces of a puzzle. Jennifer was a cheerleader and Rance was the high school quarterback. He had a shock of blond horsetail hair on the top of his rubber scalp. His mask was loose and shook back and forth like a great Jello mold when he spoke. They were to be married, the day after the Mask Festival.

She froze for a moment. "No," said Jennifer, wondering how much of herself she should share. "Rance and I will be very happy."

"Of course."

"We'll be very happy," she said again. Because right now, she was Jennifer, and that is something Jennifer would say.

The stage was decorated with cornucopias and browning sunflowers—symbols of the season. Orange and brown paper leaves decorated the backdrop, frozen in mid fall. The people of Haskins shuffled in quietly, some enthusiastically. Others came with an expression of boredom, of toe-tapping impatience. Haskins was a small town, but it contained all sorts.

Jennifer snuck down from the stage as twilight struck and the big sky above the small town glowed with gold and crimson ribbons. The people were drinking their ciders, wiping the grease from the lips of their masks as they devoured turkey legs through the slits that made up their mouths.

She found Rance sitting on a hay bale, his legs resting on a large pumpkin with a blue ribbon. She said his name and he reacted in mock exaggeration, pretending to fall from his spot. Rance had always been a jokester—for the last three dozen years, at least. Before, he was cruel—a bully—but time had softened his demeanor. He was now something of a class clown. Even in Haskins, times change.

"There she is, my beautiful." He stood up and touched her waist. He was shorter than her and the way he looked up into her eyes made him seem like a child looking up at the stars in the night sky. She could see him, his eyes behind the rubber curves, big and brown, pointing up to an endless sky with infantile delight.

They mashed their faces together, crumpling into each other as their masks folded into sweating slabs of rubber. Their tongues found their way out of their mouth-slits, tasting each other's flesh.

They held on for as long as they could. Rance found his head on her shoulder. He would not say what he wanted to say, but she could hear the choke in his voice all the same. She could divine his meaning.

She pulled apart from him and looked down, grabbing his half-drank cup of cider for a sip. "We're getting married tomorrow," she said.

He swallowed, a noise that seemed to echo behind his mask. "Yes, I know."

Behind them, past the tents and merchants, folks began to gather. A horn blared.

"Could we just—"

She stopped herself. It was not Jennifer speaking.

Rance sniffed and took her by the arm. "We should head up," he said. "They'll start without us."

They pulled each other through the crowd and stood to the far side near the stage where they could see Mayor Granger adjusting his cufflinks. He preened in the expected manner, debuting a new suit with extravagant embroidery for the occasion. Mayor Granger was always wearing the finest clothes.

"Alright, yes," he began. "Okay, well, here we are. This is the Mask Festival. The Festival of Masks. An old tradition, a very old tradition, indeed." Mayor Granger's speech ran out of steam before it began, as it often did in the last year, so instead of continuing, he straightened his silk tie and smiled. "Let's begin," he said, finally.

Through the wings of the stage, two farm boys with rubber jowls pushed a wooden cart with a large pumpkin on top of it. Granger clapped his hands and let out a nervous sigh. The two boys hoisted the pumpkin's top off together, struggling under its weight.

Jennifer and Rance held hands as they watched Mayor Granger close his eyes and reach into the pumpkin. When his hand came back with two slips of paper, the festival began.

"Connie and Delmont," he called. "Please come up to the stage and make your exchange."

A small woman with a snug mask trotted up on stage, she carried with her a wicker basket of flowers. She curtsied before the audience. On the other side, a mechanic in overalls with long black hair stomped with heavy boots to the center of the stage. They turned to each other and bowed, then walked to the rear of the stage, their backs to the audience. With both hands they removed their masks, then, without looking, held them out to the other. The new Connie's mask was so tight that her features seemed to pop out of the eyelets. Delmont was slight and wiry, but the wearer had begun to learn his movements, raising his feet in great destructive arcs. The crowd cheered and the new Connie skipped heavily back into the crowd and disappeared.

Before long, Mayor Granger's name was called too. His change was extravagant, of course. He danced to the back of the stage and when he came back his voice grew more resinous, his stature more assured. The old Granger disappeared into the crowd wearing Jim Brown's face and drinking sweet liquor with Jim Brown's loud friends.

Jennifer held Rance's hand until he had to leave for the stage. He met with Susan Hickens, a girl a year below them, and they swapped faces. When Rance came back to Jennifer, he was taller. Susan held her face in her hands as she was embraced by her family. For just a moment, Jennifer saw her look back at her, the black holes of her eyes an implacable enigma. She was always known to be shy.

The new Rance put his arm around her—in a way that was so unlike the old Rance that it made her skin crawl. She told herself that it was okay, that they were to be married and that this was a perfectly apt display of affection. It was only that—Rance used to hold her hand. He did not usually wrap his arms around her casually, she was used to feeling his fingers between hers. She wriggled out of the embrace and grabbed his hands, demonstrating the protocols of their relationship in a discreet way. His hands were rough and large. He turned his head toward her, bright hazel eyes hidden behind eyelets. She thought she detected a nod of understanding. He held her hand and watched the stage.

Mayor Granger dug his hand into the pumpkin and came out with two slips of paper. He squinted his eyes, one hand tugging a finger into his eyelet, spreading it so that he could read. "Cole Drewson and Jennifer Maisey. Come on up!"

Her heart shivered, palpitating in erratic bursts of electric anxiety. She unhooked her hand from Rance and felt a chill. She looked at him briefly, to see his eyes, but they were not the eyes she knew. She seemed to float to the stage, dragged along by an inevitable leash. Mayor Granger took both of their hands and raised them. He was adding to the spectacle, he was making decisions. She reflected that this was indeed in line with Granger's character, and she wondered why no one considered taking the hands of those on the stage and raising them before. It added a sort of spectacle to the event, and historically, Mayor Granger was spectacle incarnate.

Granger joined their hands and for just a moment, she felt as if the hand in hers was Rance's. The Rance *she* knew. But the palm in hers was sweating and Rance never sweated from his hands. She and Cole walked to the back of the stage—an eternity—and she looked straight ahead as she took off her mask.

Cole was doing the same beside her.

She wondered if he felt the same rush she did when she removed it. *I'm still Jennifer I'm still Jennifer I'm still Jennifer*, she thought. Her face was naked and she was still Jennifer. She panicked. Her heart kicked her sternum. She did not feel any different. She liked being Jennifer. She was still her. Jennifer was who she should be, and why now should Cole get to be Jennifer? Why now should *she* have to be Cole?

She tried to catch her breath and reach some sort of compromise with herself as Cole pulled off his own mask and held it out to her.

Her body failed her. It had become too accustomed to the ways of Haskins. She reached out with her own mask and they exchanged without looking at each other. She pulled on Cole Drewson's face and felt the sweat and stink of another human and she began to pray—that she would *be* Cole, that she would forget what it was like to be Jennifer, what it was like to love Rance, her Rance.

They both turned around and Cole Drewson waved weakly to the audience and went down the opposite side of the stage. Jennifer found Rance and they put their arms around each other and embraced.

In the back of the fairgrounds, Cole found himself in the men's room, staring at his new face. Long jawed, with a mustache. Stubble dotted his chin. A trucker hat covered his black hair. His creases were long and deep like knife cuts.

Behind him, a boy he could not see left a bathroom stall and walked out the door. When he was alone in the surgical teal bathroom, Cole whispered his old name.

****

The next month was a period of adjustment for everyone. Cole woke up in his new home and learned his old habits. His wife, Pauline, was a quick study. She would cower in fear whenever he entered the room, although she would do so in a pathetic, approval-seeking way.

Cole was more lethargic, less vigorous in his anger than usual, but he made his threats, he spat between the lips of his mask and cursed. He drank the same beer, although he had not been able to drink as much as he used to. Most nights, when trying, he fell asleep in the white light of the television while Pauline stepped lightly out the front door to meet their neighbor.

When he'd wake, he'd go to his job at the plant, where he learned to speak crudely with the other men at work. His tone was high and girlish but they accepted him with backslaps and unhinged laughter.

He did not feel like Cole, but he did appreciate that the others felt like he was playing his part. Cole was a difficult role, he demanded a certain physicality that was difficult to match at first. And although, behind the rubber of his face, he still felt like Jennifer, he was beginning to appreciate the inherent violence of his new identity.

He'd begun to get comfortable slapping Pauline when he was angry. The first hit had been a surprise to them both, but it was very much in line with what Cole would do. She looked up at him, having fallen to the floor and rubbing her cheek, and she looked almost appreciative.

"Don't look at me like that," he muttered.

The incident happened after he came home late. He told her he'd gone to the bar, but really he'd gone down to the old high school to watch the football game. He'd brought a bottle with him. It was gone by the time he got back. She only had to ask him where he'd been and it was enough. It took only a second for his rage to show its face.

After, of course, he felt sick. As Pauline hid the rest of the night, he became preoccupied with the dimensions of his mask. He drank until he fell asleep.

Cole was not known as a sports fan, but it was certainly not so out of sorts for a drunk and a wifebeater to enjoy football. Cole considered this to be an aspect of the Cole character he could develop. What are games but an excuse to drink? What violences could he commit to Pauline when the home team lost? At first, it seemed strange for Cole to go see the local team play every Friday, but then as his work friends came around, it didn't seem so strange at all. And besides, if Rance could now put his arms around Jennifer rather than hold her hand, why couldn't Cole like football?

"You like that cheerleader? The one with the legs?"

Cole shook his head. He did not care for the cheerleaders. He was not looking at them. His eyes were always on the crowd, looking for a young girl with brown hair that always fell in front of her mask. But Susan Hickens was shy and he didn't know why he thought she might decide to come to the game.

He took off his hat and rubbed his mane of hair. He punched the side of his head impotently.

"Y'okay, Cole?"

"Yeah, fine. Watching the game."

Rance, the quarterback, completed a thirty yard pass and the crowd erupted in unhinged ecstasy. Cole put his hand on his head and said, "I'm gonna head out. I wanna go fishing in the morning."

His friends booed and waved their bottles in mock-disapproval, but fishing had been another recent addition to Cole's canon, and he was allowed to leave. He balled his fists in the cuffs of his coat, cursing under his mask, stealing glances at the field. *They were going to be newlyweds*, he reminded himself. He got into his car and rubbed at the rubber covering his face. He rubbed it into himself, tried to make it melt into his flesh.

When he got home, he greeted Pauline by cracking her jaw.

She threw her hands up in front of her, but her eyes showed the same twisted sort of glee she always shared whenever Cole played his part well. She braced for the next hit and when she got it, her head snapped back into the cupboard behind her.

Blood flowed from the slit of her lips. He heard whimpering from inside of her mask. Cole stepped over her body to get a beer from the fridge.

She got on all fours, she was trying to stand. "Cole," she started.

He wound up and kicked her in the ribs. She dropped back to the floor, moaning as she gripped her sides.

Cole stood over her, sweating. In a shaky voice, he said, "Don't ever call me that again."

When she tried to speak again, he stomped down on the back of her neck until he felt something crack.

"I'm sorry," he said. "I'm sorry."

Her legs were shaking, twitching.

"It's just—I'm not Cole."

They stopped moving, and because he was supposed to be Cole, he could only do what Cole would do, so he stomped his boot down hard once more; again and again until her spasms ceased.

Cole had never killed anyone before. There would be side-eyes and gossip, as Haskins generally appreciated its townsfolk to maintain the status quo—but Cole was always a violent man. This was as true an ending to Pauline's story as any, he told himself.

He placed his head against the hard wood of the pantry and tried to think. *Yes, this was a fine ending. True to character. People had died in Haskins before. Not many, but it has happened.*

The body would be discovered eventually, perhaps by a mailman or a friend of a friend. He would be locked up when it was discovered, but he felt no real urgency regarding these truths. He would perhaps have days, maybe weeks to continue on unfettered. Cole sat down beside Pauline and stroked away the hair on her mask. Blood leaked through its nostrils. It was not a pretty mask: it was far too large on her, as most masks were.

Cole wondered what would have happened if he had been Pauline. If Cole would have killed him in the kitchen, if he would have been so sniveling and grateful as the world blackened around him. He yanked on her hair and saw a bit of skin, real skin, beneath. The idea of it was so alluring, so mysterious. He pulled again to free her head and he pulled until Pauline's face was limp in his own hands, stretched into a long liquid yawn. Cole turned her head, the head of a young man with light brown hair buzzed short. His face was covered in bruises, a kaleidoscope of greens, yellows, browns, and purples. Cole took off his own mask as well and rubbed his fists into his eyes. This is not something Cole would do, he realized, crying harder. He was not Cole.

***

After work, he and his buddies went to the game like they always did. Such was their lot. They all drank, but by now Cole was used to drinking. They didn't realize he was drinking less, but then again, it didn't matter how much he drank because drink pervaded his being. He smelled perpetually of whiskey. And no one questioned whether Cole was drunk, because of course he was. He's Cole. And just as everyone assumed he had been drinking, no one asked about his wife. Because Cole never talked about her anyways. It just wasn't done.

"You lookin' at those cheerleaders, Cole?"

"Too old for me," said Cole, his voice flat. "I like 'em young,"

His face was pointed toward the announcer's box. He was squinting as his friends howled.

"Oh yeah? How young?"

"Real fucking young."

They liked that. They screamed in joy. And as they screamed, he squinted his eyes to see the shy girl with brown hair keeping score a world away.

When the game ended, he waved them off. "I gotta go fishing in the morning," he said.

The crowd was clearing out and he disappeared within them— several hundred rubber faces adorned with wigs and eyeglasses. The girl was climbing down from the announcer's box and he started to quicken his pace. Susan was unassuming, her back turned toward the fence, ready to slip out unnoticed now that her obligation had finished. Cole jogged lightly, not so fast as to draw attention—just the pace of a man eager to get home.

She passed through a split in the chain link fence and began walking down the sidewalk with her nose in a book. Susan was always reading. Cole followed, a block back at first. If anyone was watching, they'd see him fumbling with his keys, looking for his car.

Susan lived near the school, the ward of bookish parents with large rubber noses and glassless spectacles. She spent most of her time at home and she was no doubt eager now to return. Susan portrayed this well when she first heard Cole shout her old name.

"Rance," he said. "Wait."

She stopped, moving her shoulders as if she were breathing deep, frightened. She turned at a glacier's pace, her mask turned downward toward the pavement.

"I've got to get home. It's late."

"It's not late," said Cole.

"I've got to go."

"We were supposed to be married."

"I'm Susan," she said. "We don't talk. You're too old to talk to me. I'm just a girl."

Cole ground his teeth, sweat dripped into his eye. He thought of Pauline and her face of mashed cherries. "I want you to come home with me tonight, Rance."

"No—I really can't—"

"It's Jennifer. I'm still Jennifer, Rance. Please, come with me. This is me speaking, I want you to come with me because I still love you. We're supposed to be married."

"Rance and Jennifer are getting married next year, the day after the festival. Not us." Her voice quivered when she said it.

Cole was a fast man, quick—a coiled spring. And when he bound toward Susan, she froze. That was a very Susan thing to do. She was not good under pressure and she was so much smaller than Cole.

He wrestled her to the ground and did what came most natural; an open hand pressed to her mouth, then a stranglehold around her neck. He felt her soft, sweating flesh. "Please," he said, whispering through her nostril holes, "come with me."

***

Like in any small town, a death causes an uproar.

A dead girl on the side of the road, bleeding out her mask.

And just like in any small town, time marches on.

***

"You don't usually have people over, is that true?"

The two had never been here before, a fact they seemed self-conscious of—still, they remained as chipper as they could, considering. They pointed at the elk's head on the wall and asked Cole if he hunted. They complimented Pauline on the furniture, their aesthetics as well as comfort.

Pauline bowed extravagantly, an ironic affectation. "The house was such a mess before. We're trying to be better about that."

Through the kitchen doorway came Cole, holding a tray of cocktails. "Please, help yourself, plenty more where that came from." He lowered the drinks on the table and poured himself a glass of club soda.

"You're not drinking?"

"Oh no, I'm a monster on that stuff. I'm turning a new leaf. I found God, I guess. The grain spoke to me. The seeds were sown. The old scarecrow came home to tend to the blackbirds in the field. All that jazz, you know?"

Pauline rubbed his shoulder, she kissed the back of his head. "He's been doing really good. Great."

There was a moment of silence, a pregnant pause. Pauline reached a hand out to their guests—a man and a woman, with large noses and glasses. "Awful what happened to Susan."

The man nodded solemnly and Cole huffed in sympathy. Snow began to fall and the gray light outside penetrated every inch of their humble home.

"Haskins isn't perfect," said the woman. "But then again, no place is."

They stared at each other, through each other for a long moment. Pauline's brown eyelets shined like glossy caramels by the fire as she took Cole by the hand and held it ever so tight.

THE IMPERFECTION

Mae Murray

MIRA WAS IN a hospital gown, looking at her phone. The girl with the bleach-blonde pixie cut had been tantalizing in her OKCupid photo, but when they met last week, she noticed the deep-pitted acne scars peppering her jawline and the glaring red spots on her cheeks and between her thick brows. These imperfections made her no less attractive to Mira, but they proved a distraction in conversation; one that left her questioning whether or not she should block her profile now.

"Mira Shelby?" The door cracked open, warmth from the hallway wafting into the cold room. She'd been sitting on a padded table covered in crinkly white paper, her skin washed out under a fluorescent light. Her hairy legs were bare over thick woolen socks, feet dangling above the floor. She was jolted out of her intense focus on scrolling, and her thumb instinctively struck the BLOCK button on the fake blonde's profile as the rheumatologist entered. Well, that was that. Done and done. Ghosted.

"It's actually Shebly. B-L-Y," Mira said, shifting on the itchy paper that bunched up under the weight of her thighs.

"Ah, I remember you now; I remember your hair. It was a different color last time. Not green . . . "

"More like teal," Mira said, though her eyes were on the open folder in the doctor's hands.

"Yeah, teal. That's one of my favorite colors. My car's teal, you know."

"*So* cool."

She hated the small talk, the prelude to bad news, the stalling that showed the doctor had been in a hurry, hadn't read her test results before this very moment. Or, God forbid, he was trying to make a connection; a paltry show of effort in a time when no one had time for anyone anymore.

"So, we did your ANA panel last week; your antinuclear antibodies. We also took urine. We found a few crystals, nothing to worry about. But your ANA was positive; that means there's a presence on the cellular level. It binds to the nucleus, damaging and destroying those cells. We see this in most autoimmune diseases." He let it sink in for a breath. "This doesn't necessarily have to indicate disease, but for you . . . You came in reporting fatigue, rashes, hair loss, pain. The nurse noted swelling of the fingers and paleness in your extremities. That combined with a positive ANA and no other organ involvement . . . "

Mira was listening, but her eyes drifted to the anatomical illustration on the wall. It was the outline of a man, skin flayed from muscle. The ribs were skeletal and housed organs, blackened by text; symptomatology, diagnostic criteria, potential treatments and mortality rates. Blown up wide in a corner of the poster was a drawing of a cell. Inside the cell, fluorescent green shapes festered like radioactive fried eggs.

" . . . Systemic Lupus Erythematosus. The rash on your nose and cheeks is a tell-tale sign; we call it a butterfly rash."

"Am I going to, like, die?" Mira drew her eyes back to the doctor, noticing the mole on his lip for the first time.

"No, no. Not anytime soon. There's no cure, but there are treatments available now that we didn't have 50 or even 10 years ago. With diligence there's nothing stopping you from living a long, relatively healthy life." He closed the file in his lap and began scribbling on his prescription pad, great illegible swoops. "But you really should quit smoking."

***

Outside, Mira stroked her hair back into a loose bun at the nape of her neck and pulled a baseball cap over her bangs. She lit a cigarette and started walking, her new prescriptions in a white paper bag, twisted up and tucked against her body with the crook of her elbow. She was scrolling her phone again, the buzz of it going off every now and then in her palm; a match on OKCupid, or a call from work asking why she was half an hour late.

User jaymasays caught her eye; a thin social media influencer-type with a caramel balayage, her lashes doll-like and thick with extensions, her lips a permanently plastered pout, puffy as pillows. In her photo she was smiling, the light catching her eyes in dazzling crypts of honey and green. There was an instant attraction coupled with the knowledge that Mira couldn't possibly be this girl's type. A quick search on Instagram confirmed it. There she was, holding a bouquet of flowers against the backdrop of a farmer's market. And again, whimsically grinning under a wide-brimmed sun hat, her eyes closed as a crowd of music festival-goers huddled around the main stage. Despite the forces at work that would keep girls like Mira and Jayma apart, some stronger force was at play; when she swiped right, they were a match.

Mira shot off a quick message:

mira-cle-im-alive: sorry if this is weird, but you are so fucking pretty.

***

"How was the appointment?"

Harrison was Mira's coworker, a punky high school senior who had scored his first job at Starbright Cafe by being the owner's third cousin twice removed—or something like that. Despite the nepotism, he was a good worker, a hell of a dishwasher, and he didn't know how much they were being underpaid so he was happy all the time. And considerate. And Mira's friend, despite their 12-year age difference.

"Kind of a joke," Mira said, wrapping her apron around her waist while Harrison clocked her in on the iPad Velcroed to the cash register.

"How so?"

"Well, I'm riddled with disease, so there's that. I've got Lupus."

"Like George Costanza from Seinfeld Lupus? Like *literally* Lupus?"

"Yeah. Like House, 'It's never Lupus' Lupus. Well, this time it's Lupus, motherfucker."

"I never watched House."

"Don't. Seinfeld is better."

"Seinfeld is always better."

The cafe was empty this time of day. A Tuesday afternoon, after the lunch rush, after all the suited gym rats in the nearby office parks crawled out of their cubicles like ants to sugar, looking for their midday fix. Harrison leaned against the counter, his phone flat on the surface between the blueberry scones and the double-chocolate chip muffins.

"What are you on, Grindr?" Mira had pulled out a saran-wrapped cucumber, waving it at Harrison's nose.

"Nah, I'm seeing how long you have left to live."

"Funny."

"I really am looking up Lupus. What'd the doctor tell you?"

"Not much. He gave me a pamphlet to read at home. He was in a rush."

"Sounds about right."

Mira unwrapped the cucumber and began peeling the skin slowly, sloughing it off onto the cutting board in thin ribbons. The water seeped out across the surface of the counter, the ribbons of skin curling into spirals. She had the fleeting inclination to do the same to the raised rash on her wrist, burning with itch from brief exposure to the sun. She pushed the thought away, would not allow herself to be pulled into the sensation of her sickness; not just the pain, but the fear of something uncontrollable at work inside her.

"Did you know they call it Lupus because some guy in the 1200s said the rash you get on your face looks like a wolf bite?"

"Nope."

"So you're practically a werewolf."

"Shut up."

"I will when you shave your legs."

Mira smiled, first at Harrison and then at the customer darkening the open door. She made a quick motion at Harrison to swap places with her. The man coming in was a regular, an interior designer who liked his latte just so, and preferred when Mira made it.

"Haven't seen you in a while," she said, ringing up his order before he ever opened his mouth. She'd already poured his milk and set the espresso to drip.

"My husband and I just got back from Paris." He was white-haired and short, stocky, wearing a scarf and a coral button-up that brought out the bright splotches of burst capillaries across his nose. Mira forced herself not to stare at the tangle of blood vessels.

"Sounds nice. I've always wanted to go."

"You've never been? Oh, you should really go."

The man took his latte. The man smiled politely. The man did not leave a tip.

"So much for Paris," she said once the man had turned the corner outside the door. They were walled in by towering brownstones, old slums that had been remodeled for the upper class and went for a few million a pop. The man lived in one, while Mira's pain was constant and sharp and not worth the ten dollars an hour.

"Hey." Harrison bumped Mira's shoulder lightly. "Are you okay, for real?"

***

She didn't let herself cry about her diagnosis until she got home that evening, until she'd showered the day away. Laying on the futon in her studio apartment, she balanced bags of ice on the tops of her swollen feet.

She'd taken great care not to look at herself in the mirror, something she'd stopped doing, for the most part, just after her 30th birthday. Each glance at her reflection made her feel more aged than the last; the circles darkening her eyes hung beneath her bottom lashes like inverted gravestones, and her crow's feet crinkled even when her expression was slack and stoic.

A single wiry gray hair had appeared at her grown-out roots, springing up like a stem from seed and defying her tweezers. She could not twist, could not pull the thorn from follicle, could not destroy the evidence that the sickness raging in her blood had taken a toll in the months leading up to her diagnosis.

All the other post-punk scene girls she knew had already gone on to marry, to wear oversized cardigans and beige skirts and to birth red-headed babies and to bake fresh bread. Somehow their aging had only made them seem more mature, but never old. Mira felt she had been left without youth or maturity, and was instead something grotesquely unfeminine. It was only in these quiet moments alone that she let the pain in her bones move her to tears, imagining them bulging—for that's how the pain felt to her. Pulsing, burgeoning.

She lay her head back on the metal bar that served as the arm of the futon, covering her eyes with her arm while the other crossed over her chest. Her fingertips slipped under her shirt collar, smoothing over her skin in search of blemishes like braille. She found a bump in the skin, a pimple the size of a small freckle, and tore it up from under the thin membrane of her epidermis with the blunt half-moon of a fingernail, setting the hole to bleed.

***

She hadn't slept well in days, if not for worry, then for the twisted ache at every hinge of her body where bone met bone. On the third day, she called in to work; she couldn't walk, she said. She couldn't even make it to the bathroom, she said. She didn't elaborate that she'd been peeing in a takeout container beside her bed and dumping it out the window, squinting her eyes against the garish light of the sun hanging in the pale New England sky.

She was in the midst of a 'flare,' the pamphlet said. She'd been here before—many times, in fact—before she was ever officially diagnosed, wondering if the onslaught of physiological symptoms were just an extension of her fears around sickness, around death. She had rubbed her jaw and throat raw checking for swelling of the lymph nodes, swelling of the thyroid gland, anything that might indicate cancerous growth. Now she knew it wasn't cancer, wasn't some tangible lump, benign or metastasized, but something completely unseeable to the human eye. Blood eating blood, bone eating bone.

The one thing her current state provided was an indefinite pool of time in which to wade through those awkward first conversations with Jayma.

jaymasays: I like your style. What kind of dye do you use?
mira-cle-im-alive: thanks! it's mermaid by manic panic
jaymasays: Nice! Are you vegan?
mira-cle-im-alive: huh?
jaymasays: Manic Panic is a vegan company, isn't it?
mira-cle-im-alive: oh yeah! totally forgot. i'm not vegan though. sorry if that's a dealbreaker!
jaymasays: I'm not vegan either. Manic Panic just paid me once to post about their brand. I put a purple streak in my hair and everything.

mira-cle-im-alive: wow. living the dream. if i got paid every time i dyed my hair . . . alas, i'm just a lowly coffee slinger
jaymasays: Don't say that. Imagine if you didn't do what you do? The road rage would be insane
mira-cle-im-alive: honestly in boston i'm not sure the caffeine makes it any better :-P
jaymasays: Lol!

The conversations went like that, the back and forth of a relationship starting in the shallow end and becoming deeper over time; insecurities revealing themselves, family histories uncovered like the lifting of a veil. Jayma had had a privileged life on the surface, had never wanted for anything—except to be seen. In many ways, she had gotten what she wanted: thousands of Instagram followers and brand endorsements, amateur photoshoots edited to look like every other influencer's Insta-grid. Her brand was a meaningless piece of art in a staged Ikea living room, a picture frame featuring Smiling Generic White Woman With Plant.

The day Mira's fears about Jayma were assuaged, Jayma had sent Mira a photo of herself without makeup, bare-faced and freckled by days spent in the sun. That much was real. There was a birthmark at Jayma's temple; a dark, wine-stained thing that seemed to seep from her skin like blood on cotton, something shameful and covered by her hair. Mira spent her sick days and nights dreaming of kissing it, heartbeat quickening every time she opened the photo on her phone. That much was real. That much was very real.

***

"Hey. Mira, helloooo?" Harrison plucked the phone out of Mira's hand and ran-skipped to the sink behind the counter, out of view of customers. It was her first day back after her Lupus flare, body unsteady from dark and the dead weight of being bed bound, so she didn't give chase, only followed him back and held out her hand with brow lifted.

"Nope. Not until you tell me who you're talking to. Jayma, isn't it?"

Mira smiled, rolling her eyes. She was so tired, but Harrison's youth—for that was the true difference between a healthy 18 and a chronically ill 30—could always make her smile past the bitterness.

"Yes, it's Jayma. We're meeting up after I get off."

"Aren't you supposed to get off *after* you meet her?"

"Stop!" She pushed his shoulder with a short, almost breathless laugh. He handed over the phone.

"You aren't wearing that, are you? You've got butter on your t-shirt."

Mira looked down. Butter had seeped into the fabric, creating a permanently wet-looking oil stain.

"Shit."

"Don't worry, I have an extra shirt in my bag. It's a button-up. Jayma's high femme and you're more dykey anyway. It will be perfect and less confusing for the straights at whatever 5-star restaurant she's taking you to."

"We're going to Chipotle."

"Tacos." Smirk. "You have a pimple on your forehead, by the way. No worries. I have concealer in my bag, too."

***

By the time she reached Chipotle, the pimple was an angry bleeding monster with a face of its own. She hadn't meant to pick at it on the bus, peeling away the concealer and the head of it so the gummy pus jammed under her fingernail. She hadn't meant to pick the pus from under her fingernail with her teeth, move the grit around her tongue and over the roof of her mouth before swallowing it. She hadn't meant to, but that is what she did.

The cold of the rainy night had chilled her to the bone, the ache of her disease setting in again. She picked at the pimple as if the act could soothe that pain, distract her from it, swap one for the other, begging and borrowing in a hellish, never-ending and lacking negotiation between body, blood, and brain. The ache persisted. And now her forehead was bleeding.

Chipotle was packed, bursting at the seams with hot bodies pushed in against each other in a line that wrapped around the perimeter of the room. The tables were mostly full, and the ones that weren't had smears of guac and queso on their shiny silver tops. It wasn't the grandest, but it was what Mira could afford.

She was in line a few minutes before she realized Jayma was

already sitting, her face angled down and lit by the ghostly glow of her phone, scrolling and scrolling.

No one ever looked the way they did in their pictures. The caramel in Jayma's hair was dull and brassy, and Mira was surprised to see deep purple circles under her eyes that could rival her own. She had the fleeting thought that most of the men she had gone out with on OKCupid would be disappointed at the sight of Jayma—cheated somehow—as they had been when they met up with Mira in dive bars and bowling alleys. Mira knew this because they had expressed as much. They thought she'd be taller or thinner or less queer, and they had barely veiled contempt for her upon sight. She didn't feel that way about Jayma.

"Jayma?" Mira put her hand lightly on Jayma's shoulder. When she looked up from her phone, her hair fell away from her face, revealing the stain—the size and shape of Mira's thumb.

***

"I'm sick. I'm in so much pain."

"Shh. It's okay. I don't mind topping. Lay back. Let me take care of you."

"No one's said that to me in a long time. Maybe not ever."

"Well, it's about time, don't you think?"

***

Jayma lay on her stomach, arms under her pillow, eyes open and staring at Mira with a soft smile. Mira traced the line of Jayma's spine with her middle finger, tickling the peach fuzz of her freckled skin. The act was a thinly veiled search for imperfections, her fingertips feeling for bumps; for clogged follicles or rough edges, for rash or knot. She leaned over Jayma's body, bringing the light of her phone screen to a barely perceptible snag in the otherwise smooth surface.

"You have a blackhead." Mira pulled and pinched the skin to make sure. "Want me to get it?"

"Oh my god. Ew. I mean, yes, but ew." Jayma looked over her shoulder, a mix of amusement and embarrassment on her face. Mira liked the way her mascara clumped after sleeping.

Mira squeezed the spot between her thumbnails until the pore opened and burst with a little snake of impacted oil and hair. Left

51

behind was a hole in the skin the size of the eye of a needle, the tiniest empty mouth. While Jayma had her head turned, Mira put the contents of the blackhead on her tongue and swallowed like a salty little pill.

"Did you get it?" Jayma sat up, her hair falling over her shoulders in an unkempt, wavy mass. "Let me see."

"I dropped it."

"Gross. Now it's in the bed."

"Yeah, with all our other shed skin cells. And pubic hair. And juices."

"Don't say juices!"

"Juices. Juices. Juices!"

Mira had never laughed so full-bellied and unselfconscious with another.

***

Mira stared at her own hands in the dim light of her bedroom. The shadows played tricks on her now. Her rheumatologist called it brain fog; a strange state in which words could not come easily and thoughts slipped through her grasp like water from a pitcher, poured and up and away in zero gravity. In her mind's eye, her cells were wolf-heads, snarling in her blood, swelling and fighting the vein like a rope round their necks. The wolf-heads gnashed at her kidneys and made her have to pee, over and over throughout the night. They were the source of the crystals in her bladder, and the reason why her stomach burned when she ate, the reason her stool was pale from lack of bile and her skin was red with rash. It wasn't a wild animal inside her, but an entire molecular strain of wild animals, roaming and feeding and shitting in her body, contaminating and eroding it.

She picked at the pimples on her arms. She pried them up, indiscriminate between clogged pore and healthy skin. The spots swelled into bleeding pox speckled so thickly the skin looked ragged in the shadows, and in the morning she cried at what she had done.

***

Mira wasn't getting any better. The doctor did blood work every two weeks. The medication just wasn't helping. The wolf-heads were still raging in her blood. She began infusion treatments; half a day sitting in a reclining hospital chair sandwiched between cancer patients young and old, a needle in a green vein on top of her hand. No one spoke to one another or smiled or looked up from their phones. The sickest patients dozed wrapped in blankets, their faces swollen or sunken or somehow both. There was no joy in this place.

Her nails scritch-scritched at her arms, now completely raw.

"I wish you wouldn't do that," Jayma said, standing before Mira, angling her phone to capture the light coming from the window behind the recliner. Mira appeared infrequently on Jayma's Instagram in shadows, in saccharine squares holding Jayma's hand, the infusion needle visible by design. *Send good vibes to my sweet love. #LupusWarrior.*

"It's a nervous habit."

"I know, because it makes *me* nervous."

Mira's eyes felt strange, vibrating in their sockets as the infusion rushed through her bloodstream flushing out the wolf-heads. She could taste saline in the back of her throat, could feel the tickle of salt in her nose.

"I saw a spot on your shoulder earlier, I want to check when we get back to your place. It could be a mole, but I just want to make sure."

"I don't like it when you pick at me. It reminds me of those videos of monkeys eating lice off each other's backs."

"I just want to make sure it's nothing serious. It could be cancerous for all we know. Or just a blackhead or pimple."

"I know you're trying to take care of me, but I don't like it."

"I don't like it either, but what if it turned into something crazy like a big cyst? Those things make tunnels deep in your skin if you don't catch them early. You could become one big cyst, you know."

Jayma laughed, then Mira laughed. The sound was haunting and hollow in a room so brightly lit against all the pale faces fighting death.

Back at her apartment, Mira popped the pimple on Jayma's shoulder, kissed and sucked the hole until a bruise-colored blemish appeared, a temporary tattoo.

***

Jayma didn't know that Mira's picking had given her scars. They peppered her back in a constellation of discoloration, a map made flesh that led to nowhere, a map Mira could trace with her middle finger. It was more difficult to find the imperfections then, once so much scarring had been done, each little raised bump now a false alarm. Mira often picked those scars raw over again for nothing, sopped up the blood with a q-tip. No wolf-heads inside Jayma, none that she could see.

***

Harrison stood at Mira's apartment door, knocking hard. His dad used to do that, jolt Harrison into overdrive with a potent burst of adrenaline from the sudden sound of a fist slamming on door. Such an unpleasant memory, yet he couldn't stop himself from the same insidious playfulness.

"Hey, bitch!" Harrison called, a term of endearment. "Bitch, at least answer your door if you won't answer your phone. I came all the way here!"

The truth was, Harrison was worried. Mira hadn't shown up for work today or the day before. It wasn't like her not to call. He checked Jayma's Instagram feed. She hadn't posted in three days, not to her grid and not to her stories. He said as much to the building's super before returning with cop and a key to open her door.

They recoiled immediately at the smell, putting their forearms over their noses.

***

Mira sat on the cold checkered tile of the bathroom floor, hunched over her leg, which bent at an odd angle to gain access to the back of her thigh. Her fingers were dark with blood, some dry as cracked paint, some coagulated, oxygen exposure dulling its shine, gummed up under her fingernails where it had turned black as dirt.

"Mira?" Harrison's voice quaked in his throat as he approached, lowering himself to his knees in front of her. Her fingers still worked at her skin, deep in a burrowed hole in her leg that squelched when she stuck her finger inside to dig ever deeper. She did not look up at him, just worked with a fanatical flare that

54

made it difficult to tell if the sound of his voice was accessing the part of her brain that would recognize it. "Mira. Oh my god."

The cop's radio came static-to-life. He was already back in the living room, muttering to dispatch. "Yeah, suspect's name is Mira Shelby. We're gonna need an ambulance. I'm about to search the apartment . . . "

"Hey, bitch." Harrison put his hand on Mira's shoulder, squeezing gently. "Where's Jayma?"

The sound of Jayma's name seemed to draw her eyes from her work, finger stopping knuckle-deep in her flesh as she met Harrison's gaze. Her own was wide-eyed, almost startled, a deer in the face of a great and unseen predator.

To answer his question, she stuck out her tongue as far as it could go, wide and flat and curling down her chin. On the center of it, a rubbery piece of wine-colored skin torn in a ragged shape by Mira's own teeth. Then, she drew it back inside her mouth like a lizard, gulping.

"I think I got the fucker," she said, breathless. "The thing inside."

BLAME

Warren Benedetto

from: LinkedIn job-listings@linkedin.com
to: Kristie Griffin kristiegriffin99@gmail.com
date: Aug 20, 2021, 6:13 PM
subject: Today's job listings

Hi Kristie,

Here are the latest job listings from the companies you follow:

AudioSnap.com
  • Software Engineer *(posted 2 weeks ago)*

For more listings like this, visit LinkedIn.com.

***

from: Mitchell Sanderson mitch@audiosnap.com
to: Kristie Breslin kristie@audiosnap.com
date: Aug 23, 2021, 12:06 PM
subject: Audio corruption

hey kristie, nice meeting you just now. sorry for the confusion . . . i didn't realize we had hired anyone for that role yet. anyway, welcome to the team! i hope you brought your bikini, because i'm going to throw you right into the deep end. Rob (CTO) is on my ass about an audio glitch that has been affecting our voice chats. we just pushed some codec updates . . . maybe one is borked? idk. anyway, please take a look when you get back from lunch.

Mitch

Mitchell Sanderson
Engineering Manager
AudioSnap.com

****

from: Kristie Breslin kristie@audiosnap.com
to: Mitchell Sanderson mitch@audiosnap.com
date: Aug 23, 2021, 12:42 PM
subject: Re: Audio corruption

Thanks, Mitch! Looking forward to getting my feet wet. Hopefully I'm not in over my head. :-)

I created a JIRA issue (AUDIO-149). I'll let you know what I find.

Kristie Breslin
Software Engineer
AudioSnap.com

****

AUDIOSNAP JIRA
AudioSnap / AUDIO-149

DETAILS
Type: Bug
Priority: Urgent
Status: Open
Created by: Kristie Breslin kristie@audiosnap.com

DESCRIPTION
Customers are complaining about unusual background noise during voice chat. Variously described as droning, weeping,

whispering, cross-talk, etc. Recent codec update may have introduced a bug.

****

from: Kristie Breslin kristie@audiosnap.com
to: Mitchell Sanderson mitch@audiosnap.com
date: Aug 23, 2021, 3:19 PM
subject: Re: Audio corruption

Hey Mitch,

FYI, the codec was a dead end. No issues filed on their GitHub, so it's probably a bug in our stack somewhere. I'll keep you posted.

K.

****

AUDIOSNAP JIRA
AudioSnap / AUDIO-149

COMMENTS
Kristie Breslin (just now)
Attaching audio recordings from customer complaints for further analysis:

- *helpdesk-issue-39520.mp3* : "Whispering in background of call."
- *helpdesk-issue-39566.mp3* : "Weeping noise during group voice chat."
- *helpdesk-issue-39590.mp3* : "Background droning sound."
- *helpdesk-issue-39621.mp3* : "Sounds like someone is crying."

****

Mitchell Sanderson
This is the very beginning of your direct message history with @mitch

Kristie: hey, you around?
Mitch: for you? always. lol.

Kristie: so, i pinged angie in customer service and had her send me the recordings of the voice chats
Mitch: smart girl
Mitch: you, i mean
Mitch: not angie
Mitch: she dumb. ;-)
Kristie: i definitely can hear the problem
Mitch: that's . . . good?
Kristie: well it's easier to fix a bug that i can hear, so yeah
Kristie: anyway, whats weird is the noise is basically the same in all the recordings. if it was a compression artifact, it would be different for each call. but it's always the same no matter who's talking or what they're saying.
Mitch: what's it sound like
Kristie: listen
Kristie: *attached helpdesk-issue-39590.mp3*
Kristie: you hear it?
Mitch: it sounds like crying
Kristie: yep
Mitch: wtf
Kristie: don't know yet. will let you know when I do.

****

Angie Martinique
This is the very beginning of your direct message history with @angie

Angie: hey you. got another one of those complaints just now.
Angie: *attached helpdesk-issue-39633.mp3*
Angie: give that one a listen. it's a little different than the others.
Kristie: define different
Angie: it still has the crying or whatever, but there's also like this voice underneath
Kristie: listening . . .
Kristie: holy f
Angie: i know, right? it's creepy as hell
Kristie: what's it saying?
Kristie: sounds like "which will get it"
Angie: i heard "bitch i'll hit it"

Kristie: lol
Angie: hahahaha
Angie: it's like one of those audio illusions where people hear what
they want to hear
Kristie: totally
Angie: you figure out the problem yet?
Kristie: meh. not really.
Angie: any clues?
Kristie: a few. still trying to connect the dots. every time i think i
know what's happening i find some new detail that completely
changes the picture
Kristie: like, i think i'm drawing a bird, and then i'm like "wait,
maybe it's a frog"
Angie: wow sounds super fun /s
Kristie: that's why they pay me the big bucks
Angie: alright, well don't work too late
Angie: watch your six if you do
Kristie: my six?
Angie: your back
Kristie: . . . ok?
Angie: mitch can get a little handsy sometimes. dude watches too
much Mad Men if you ask me.
Kristie: oh hell no
Kristie: i will cut him
Angie: hahahahaha that's my girl

***

Kristie-Breslin-PC
~/Desktop/AudioSnap/branch/AUDIO-149

```
$ GIT STATUS
ON BRANCH AUDIO-149
CHANGES TO BE COMMITTED:
    NEW FILE: RAPIST.TXT
```

***

BLAME

from: Kristie Breslin kristie@audiosnap.com
to: Security security@audiosnap.com
date: Aug 25, 2021, 9:09 AM
subject: Unauthorized PC access

I was just checking my git status, and I saw this (screenshot attached). See that RAPIST.txt file? I didn't create that. All my changes were committed before I left last night. Which means someone accessed my computer sometime between when I went home at 1 AM and now. What do I do?

Kristie

****

from: Security security@audiosnap.com
to: Kristie Breslin kristie@audiosnap.com
date: Aug 25, 2021, 9:42 AM
subject: Re: Unauthorized PC access

Looks like you were the last person to leave last night, based on the keycard logs. Nobody came in or out after that. You sure you didn't just forget that you created that file, babe? ;-)

Jasper
Infosec Lead
AudioSnap.com

****

from: Kristie Breslin kristie@audiosnap.com
to: Security security@audiosnap.com
date: Aug 25, 2021, 9:54 AM
subject: Re: Unauthorized PC access

No, I didn't just *forget* that I created that file, babe. Somebody accessed my computer last night, and it wasn't me. My name is Kristie, btw.

****

from: Security security@audiosnap.com
to: Kristie Breslin kristie@audiosnap.com
date: Aug 25, 2021, 10:01 AM
subject: Re: Unauthorized PC access

Fine KRISTIE. Bring your laptop down and we'll take a look.

Jasper

***

Kristie: what is it with the men in this company?
    Angie: what did he do
Angie: did you cut him? lol
Kristie: no, not mitch. jasper from infosec. fucking weirdo.
Angie: oh HIM
Angie: the neckbeard is strong with that one
Kristie: that fedora has seen better days, lemme tell ya
Kristie: i can smell it from here
Angie: hahahaha
Angie: be careful or he will try to make you his waifu
Kristie: /giphy barf
Kristie: this is why i'm gay
Angie: lololol
Angie: so what happened?
Kristie: somebody accessed my PC after i left last night
Kristie: created a new file in the branch where i'm working on
    that audio bug. RAPIST.txt
Angie: holy shit
Kristie: i know, right?
Angie: what was in it?
Kristie: nothing. it was empty. which makes it even weirder.
Angie: you sure it wasn't him?
Kristie: him who? jasper?
Angie: i mean, he does have root access to every computer in the
    company, so …
Angie: he can basically do whatever he wants
Kristie: why though? just to mess with me?
Angie: maybe it's his weird way of getting you to talk to him?
Kristie: oh god. kill me.

BLAME

***

```
// ADD NEW AUDIO CHANNEL, UP TO MAX_CHANNELS
ADDNEWCHANNEL : FUNCTION(NEWCHANNEL){

    IF (THIS.NUMCHANNELS <= MAX_CHANNELS){
        RETURN AUDIOSNAPLIB.ADDCHANNEL(NEWCHANNEL);
    } ELSE {
        THROW NEW ERROR(TOO_MANY_CHANNELS)
    }

    // HE LIES.
}
```

***

Kristie-Breslin-PC
~/Desktop/AudioSnap/branch/AUDIO-149

```
$ GIT BLAME AUDIOSNAPLIB.JS
```

***

Kristie: i'm freaking out right now
Angie: oh no. why
Kristie: so i just got back from lunch and my computer was already logged in
Angie: uh oh. senpai strikes again.
Kristie: i noticed a file had been modified, so i did a git blame. check it out.
Kristie: 800a806f (Greta Griffin 2021-08-25 13:23:10 266) // He lies
Angie: what's a git blame
Kristie: sorry. git blame is a command that shows who was the last person to edit each line of a file
Kristie: someone edited the file at 1:23 PM while I was at lunch
Kristie: and added a comment that says "He lies"
Angie: the hell?
Kristie: who is Greta Griffin

Angie: she was the programmer on the project before you started
Kristie: well she obviously still has access
Angie: i don't think so
Kristie: she has to. she's the one who edited the file. like literally 10 mins ago.
Angie: that's not possible
Kristie: why?
Angie: because she's dead
Kristie: omg
Kristie: what happened
Angie: killed herself
Kristie jfc are you serious
Angie: we should talk. meet me outside?

****

from: Kristie Breslin kristie@audiosnap.com
to: Mitchell Sanderson mitch@audiosnap.com
date: Aug 25, 2021, 2:35 PM
subject: Harassment

Hey Mitch,

I hate to be the squeaky wheel, but I'm having some problems and I need your advice. Somebody has been changing files on my machine without my knowledge. Last night, they created a file called RAPIST.txt that I found this morning when I came in. Now, I just got back from lunch and another file was changed while I was gone. I feel like someone might be messing with me.

Do you have time to chat sometime today? Thanks.

Kristie

****

Mitch: saw your email. got a sec to chat now?
Kristie: yep
Mitch: great. okay if I record our call for HR?
Kristie: of course
Mitch: *is calling you*

BLAME

***

Audio transcription between Mitchell Sanderson (@mitch) and Kristie Breslin (@kristie)

Mitchell Sanderson
Hey, Kristie. Thanks for hopping on. You okay?

Kristie Breslin
Yeah, I'm all right. I mean, I'm a little freaked out, but –

Mitchell Sanderson
Sure, of course. I would be too.

Kristie Breslin
So, what do you think I should do?

Mitchell Sanderson
Well first, let me say that I'm really sorry this is happening to you. Whatever it is, we'll get to the bottom of it. You have my full support. And anything we discuss is confidential. Cool?

Kristie Breslin
I appreciate that.

Mitchell Sanderson
Great. So, I'll be honest. This isn't the first time we've heard concerns about Jasper.

Kristie Breslin
I didn't say anything about Jasper.

Mitchell Sanderson
No, right. I know. I'm just saying. He can definitely come on too strong sometimes. He's just, you know, he's kind of awkward. Big guy, hasn't been around women too much. But I promise, he's harmless.

Kristie Breslin
Okay . . .

Mitchell Sanderson
I think the main thing I want you to know is that it's okay to take it easy a little bit. Give yourself a rest. I appreciate you staying late to figure out that audio bug, but it's not worth sacrificing your health for it. I can have someone else look into it.

Kristie Breslin
My health is fine.

Mitchell Sanderson
Sure, I get it. You're a trooper. I just don't want you to get too burned out in your first week.

Kristie Breslin
Really, I'm fine. I can handle the hours. But I'm not sure what that has to do with what I emailed you about.

Mitchell Sanderson
Well, I talked to Jasper–

Kristie Breslin
You did?

Mitchell Sanderson
Not about your email! No, no, sorry. Let me be clear. Not about your email. Just about the unauthorized access to your computer. He brought it up to me.

Kristie Breslin
Uh huh.

Mitchell Sanderson
Anyway, he mentioned that, you know, there wasn't really anybody else who accessed your computer at the times you said. He checked the security footage and everything.

Kristie Breslin
And you're just going to take his word for it?

Mitchell Sanderson
He's worked here for, what? Thirteen years? So, yeah. I trust him.

Kristie Breslin
Oh. Okay. So, what . . . ? I just dreamed it? Maybe I sleepwalked into the office and started editing files in my sleep?

Mitchell Sanderson
I'm not saying that.

Kristie Breslin
Maybe that's what happened to Greta Griffin too? She just sleepwalked off the roof?

[Silence. 00:11]

Kristie Breslin
Mitch? You still there?

Mitchell Sanderson
– hear . . . [unintelligible] . . . driving–

Kristie Breslin
Hello? Mitch?

[Call disconnected]

***

Are you sure you want to delete "mitch-kristie-20210825.mp3"?

This item will be deleted immediately. You can't undo this action.

CANCEL | **DELETE**

***

Kristie: that motherfucker
Angie: what did he say?
Kristie: oh, nothing. just tried to blame me. told me to take a break, that I was working too hard
Angie: well, are you?
Kristie: oh no. not you too.
Angie: I'm just saying, it has been a long week. maybe you should take off a little early.
Kristie: why is everyone treating me like i'm made of glass
Kristie: i'm fine

***

```
// ADD NEW AUDIO CHANNEL, UP TO MAX_CHANNELS
ADDNEWCHANNEL : FUNCTION(NEWCHANNEL){
    // HIS FAULT
    // HIS FAULT
    // HIS FAULT
    // HIS FAULT
    // HIS FAULT
}
```

***

Kristie-Breslin-PC
   ~/Desktop/AudioSnap/branch/AUDIO-149

```
$ GIT BLAME AUDIOSNAPLIB.JS

86254460 (GRETA GRIFFIN 2021-08-26 02:07:10 258)
    // HIS FAULT
86254460 (GRETA GRIFFIN 2021-08 26 02:07:10 259)
    // HIS FAULT
86254460 (GRETA GRIFFIN 2021-08-26 02:07:10 260)
    // HIS FAULT
```

BLAME

86254460 (GRETA GRIFFIN 2021-08-26 02:07:10 261)
    // HIS FAULT
86254460 (GRETA GRIFFIN 2021 08 26 02:07:10 262)
    // HIS FAULT

***

Kristie: is there anyone else in infosec besides Jasper?
Angie: yeah, there's a whole team
Angie: they all report to him though, so . . .
Kristie: /giphy goddamnit
Angie: still having computer problems?
Kristie: you were friends with Greta Griffin, right?
Angie: work friends, yeah
Kristie: what was she like?
Angie: hella smart. ballsy. kinda hot, it a nerdy sort of way.
Kristie: did she seem depressed at all? before
Angie: no, that's what made it so surprising. she was totally fine.
Angie: just got a new puppy
Angie: just moved in with her girlfriend in park slope
Angie: she was happy
Angie: at least she seemed like it
Angie: obviously she wasn't
Kristie: if I tell you something, do you swear not to tell anyone?
Angie: of course
Kristie: let's go for a walk

***

from: Amazon.com auto-confirm@amazon.com
to: Kristie Breslin kristie@audiosnap.com
date: Aug 26, 2021, 3:44 PM
subject: Your Amazon.com order # 111-8508406-3189834

Hello Kristie,

Thank you for shopping with us. We'll send a confirmation when
your item ships.

DETAILS

Xiomi Micro Security Camera w/High Sensitivity Microphone
Arriving: Tomorrow, August 27
Order Total: $23.57

We hope to see you again soon.

Amazon.com

***

from: Willis Cole mailroom@audiosnap.com
to: Kristie Breslin kristie@audiosnap.com
date: Aug 27, 2021, 9:10 AM
subject: Amazon Package

Hi Kristie,

Your Amazon package has arrived.

Willis

***

Jasper: did you see what she installed at her desk?
Mitch: no, what?
Jasper: security camera
Mitch: seriously?
Mitch: /giphy facepalm
Jasper: dude. literally *nobody* touched her computer.
Jasper: i swear, she changed those files herself
Jasper: where did you find her anyway?
Mitch: i didn't
Jasper: well, she's nuts
Jasper: bat
Jasper: shit
Jasper: crazy
Mitch: i know i know

***

BLAME

from: Angie Martinique angie@audiosnap.com
to: Mitchell Sanderson mitch@audiosnap.com
date: Aug 27, 2021, 11:25 AM
subject: Kristie

Hey Mitch,

I'm a little worried about Kristie's mental health. She has been working crazy hours trying to figure out that audio bug, and I think she's starting to crack a little under the strain. She told me yesterday that she thinks the bug is actually being caused by the ghost of Greta Griffin. Like, literally, a ghost is changing her code. That's not normal.

I just thought you should know.

Angie

***

from: Mitchell Sanderson mitch@audiosnap.com
to: Angie Martinique angie@audiosnap.com
date: Aug 27, 2021, 11:38 AM
subject: Re: Kristie

oh man, that's bad. thanks for the heads up. i'll talk to HR and see what they think we should do. i hate to let her go, but we obviously can't have that kind of crazy around here.

mitch

***

r/AudioProcessing *Posted by u/kristiegriffin99*

Can somebody help me extract and analyze a specific background noise from a series of audio and video recordings?

I have a couple of voice chat mp3 files, as well as a couple of security camera mp4 video files. To my ear, it sounds like they all have the exact same sound in the background, despite being recorded at different times in different places on different devices by different people. That's impossible though, right? Bonus points to anyone who can actually figure out what the voice in the background is saying.

audiodoc *1 min ago*
DM me. I can probably help.

****

kristiegriffin99: any luck
audiodoc: yeah, that's definitely crying, and it does seem to be the same person on all the recordings
kristiegriffin99: even on the security camera footage?
audiodoc: yep
kristiegriffin99: and you're sure it's the same sound as on the voice chat recordings
audiodoc: absolutely
audiodoc: maybe it's the girl
kristiegriffin99: what girl?
audiodoc: in the video
kristiegriffin99: there's no girl in the video. it's just my empty desk the whole time.
audiodoc: look again
audiodoc: in the reflection on the office window
kristiegriffin99: hang on
audiodoc: you see her? standing next to the desk?
kristiegriffin99: oh my god
audiodoc: weird, right?
audiodoc: could be someone behind the camera. hard to tell.
audiodoc: or could be a ghost lol
audiodoc: anyway
audiodoc: you still there?
audiodoc: hello?
audiodoc: all right, well . . . speaking of ghosting hahaha
audiodoc: btw i'm pretty sure i know what the background voice is saying
audiodoc: it's clearer in the video than the voice chats

BLAME

audiodoc: sounds to me like it's saying "mitchell did it"

***

Mitch: i'm running out to get food. want anything?
Jasper: nah im good thanks
Mitch: you sure? i can expense it since we're working late
Jasper: say no more fam
Mitch: i'm thinking mexican. the usual?
Jasper: si
Jasper: swing by my office when you get back
Jasper: i found something interesting about that kristie girl
Mitch: like what
Jasper: more red flags than a chinese pep rally
Mitch: /giphy kill me
Mitch: who hired her anyway
Jasper: um
Jasper: you?
Mitch: not me
Jasper: who did then?
Mitch: probably Rob? idk
Jasper: well he should have done a background check
Jasper: the girl has issues
Mitch: she has been asking about greta
Jasper: yeah i heard
Jasper: did she know her?
Mitch: dunno
Mitch: i hope not
Jasper: so what you are you going to do?
Mitch: gotta run
Mitch: let's talk when i get back

***

WALMART
SAVE MONEY. LIVE BETTER.

ST# 01453 OP# 567890 TE# 23 TR# 03111

PRODUCT: CAMILLUS CARNIVORE X MACHETE
SERIAL #: CM778976

```
SUBTOTAL: $26.82
TAX 8.000%: $2.14
TOTAL: $28.96

ACCOUNT #: XXXX XXXX XXXX 9983

CHANGE DUE: $0.00

08/27/2021 8:42 PM
```

***

AUDIOSNAP.COM KEY CARD ACCESS LOG

Fri Aug 27, 2021 8:54 PM : Kristie Breslin [ENTER] Main Lobby
Fri Aug 27, 2021 8:55 PM : Kristie Breslin [ENTER] Elevator 1 [UP TO] Floor 4
Fri Aug 27, 2021 8:55 PM : Kristie Breslin [ENTER] 4th Floor West

Fri Aug 27, 2021 8:55 PM : Mitchell Sanderson [ENTER] Main Lobby
Fri Aug 27, 2021 8:56 PM : Mitchell Sanderson [ENTER] Elevator 1 [UP TO] Floor 4
Fri Aug 27, 2021 8:56 PM : Mitchell Sanderson [ENTER] 4th Floor West

***

AudioSnap Tower Security
Date: 2021-08-27 9:01 PM
Caller: Mitchell Sanderson | 212-555-4932 | 4th Floor West

Front Desk
Security. This is Nick.

Mitchell Sanderson
[unintelligible]

Front Desk

I'm sorry, can you repeat that?

Mitchell Sanderson
[unintelligible]

Front Desk
I'm having a hard time hearing –

Mitchell Sanderson
[whispering] Mitchell did it.

END OF CALL

***

Jasper: yo you back with the food yet?
Jasper: im starving

Jasper: holy fuck
Jasper: did you hear that?
Jasper: sounded like screaming

Jasper: you there?

Jasper: hello?

***

AUDIOSNAP.COM KEY CARD ACCESS LOG

Fri Aug 27, 2021 9:03 PM : Jasper Heinz [EXIT] 4th Floor East
Fri Aug 27, 2021 9:03 PM : Jasper Heinz [ENTER] 4th Floor West

***

911 CALL
Q=911 Dispatcher
A=CALLER

Q: 911, where is your emergency?
A: Yes, hello? 911?

Q: Yes, sir. Where is your emergency?

A: AudioSnap tower. The address is, um . . .

Q: It's okay, I've got it. Tell me what's going on there.

A: I don't know. There's so much blood.

Q: Are you injured?

A: No, it's not mine. Oh, god. I'm going to–(vomiting noises). I'm sorry. (vomiting noises)

Q: It's okay, just try to remain calm. I've got a unit en route. What floor are you on?

A: Fourth floor. West.

Q: And how many people are injured?

A: I don't know. There's no body.

Q: There's no body?

A: No. Just blood.

Q: Okay. And what's your name?

A: Jasper Heinz.

Q: Are you an employee there?

A: Yeah. Oh my god. Mitch. (weeping)

Q: Who's that? Mitch, you said?

A: Yeah. Mitchell Sanderson. I'm in his office.

Q: All right. Is there anyone else there with you?

A: Just me and him. We were working late.

Q: I mean, is there anyone else with you right now? Are you sure you're safe?

A: I . . . I don't know.

Q: Okay. I want you to go ahead and lock the door to the office until officers arrive. Can you do that for me?

A: (unintelligible)

Q: Say again? . . . Sir? . . . Sir, are you there?

CALL ENDED

✱✱✱

AUDIOSNAP JIRA
AudioSnap / AUDIO-149

DETAILS
Type: Bug

Priority: Urgent
Status: Resolved
Resolved by: Kristie Breslin kristie@audiosnap.com

***

AUDIOSNAP.COM KEY CARD ACCESS LOG

Fri Aug 27, 2021 9:09 PM : Kristie Breslin [EXIT] 4th Floor West
Fri Aug 27, 2021 9:09 PM : Kristie Breslin [ENTER] Elevator 1
    [DOWN TO] Floor 1
Fri Aug 27, 2021 9:10 PM : Kristie Breslin [EXIT] Main Lobby

***

NEW YORK POLICE DEPARTMENT
Incident Report

Case #: 12-0386
Incident #: 75240
Date Reported: Friday 08/27/2021 21:04
Date Occurred: Friday 08/27/2021 21:00 (approx.)
Incident Type: Homicide

Date Written: Monday 08/30/2021 14:21
Officer Name & Rank: KELSEY, JONATHAN (PO)

Narrative:
PO Kelsey responded to the AudioSnap Tower (4th Floor West) after being dispatched to investigate a 911 emergency. Upon arrival, PO Kelsey secured the scene then began his investigation. No bodies were found, nor was the 911 caller present. Based on the volume of blood at the scene, PO Kelsey concluded that multiple homicides had likely occurred.

Upon reviewing security footage from the scene, PO Kelsey noted several audio anomalies that warrant further investigation: the sound of weeping, as well as the repeated whispering of a phrase sounding like "witch will get it." Expert analysis is pending.

Keycard logs indicate the presence of an individual named Kristie Breslin at the time of the murders. However, there are conflicting reports about whether anyone by that name was ever employed by AudioSnap. CTO Rob Davenport maintains that no such employee exists; others interviewed by PO Kelsey insist a woman calling herself Kristie has been working in the office for at least a week. Residential records indicate a Kristie *née* Breslin living in Park Slope, Brooklyn, but attempts to contact her have been unsuccessful.

An item believed to be the murder weapon, identified as an 18-inch Camillus Carnivore X Machete, was retrieved by PO Kelsey from a dumpster in the South alley behind the building. A Walmart receipt for said weapon was also found in the dumpster. Credit card records indicate the weapon was purchased using a card belonging to Greta Griffin, a former employee of AudioSnap.

PO Kelsey noted that the South alley was the scene of an incident to which he had responded three weeks prior: the death of Greta Griffin (Case # 12-0299 Incident # 68323), who fell from the AudioSnap Tower roof. Although the death of Ms. Griffin was initially ruled a suicide, additional forensic analysis now indicates the presence of semen in her genital area, raising the possibility that she may have been sexually assaulted before her death. Given the relationship between Ms. Griffin and the suspected victims in this case, and the use of Ms. Griffin's credit card to purchase the murder weapon, the Griffin case is now being reclassified as a possible homicide. END.

***

from: LinkedIn job-listings@linkedin.com
to: Kristie Griffin kristiegriffin99@gmail.com
date: Aug 30, 2021, 6:10 PM
subject: Today's job listings
Hi Kristie,

Here are the latest job listings from the companies you follow:

AudioSnap.com
- Software Engineer *(posted 3 weeks ago)*
- **[NEW]** Engineering Manager *(posted today)*
- **[NEW]** Infosec Lead *(posted today)*

For more listings like this, visit LinkedIn.com.

LOW TIDE JENNY

Bitter Karella

LOW TIDE JENNY sat in her folding deck chair on the beach, stationed right where the sand met the ice plants, staring out at the black ocean with her eyeless sockets hidden behind oversized sunglasses. Her red bikini top was faded, slopping off her deflated tits, and the few strands of hair that still clung to her skull made Babs think she had probably been a blonde in life, though Babs couldn't begin to imagine when that was.

No one ever saw Low Tide Jenny move, but Babs assumed from the pattern of her appearances that she must have a sense of humor since she mostly appeared when tourists were on the beach. That meant she appeared less and less as the years went by—Santa Carcossa's status as a vacation destination had been fading since the 1950s and especially since they shut down road access in Sectors L through R. Still, nothing made Babs' day more than explaining to some bewildered snow bird who'd wandered in off the boardwalk, face pale and hands clammy, that *oh no, that's just our Low Tide Jenny, she's harmless, don't worry about her*.

"She loved the beach when she was alive," Babs would say as she folded a "Santa Carcossa est. 1868" sweatshirt across the counter and rang up the sale. "After she passed, poor thing, she just wanted to enjoy what she loved in life."

Babs didn't know if that was true, but she liked the sound of it and it wasn't like anyone actually knew the truth about Low Tide Jenny's origins. The locals, what few remained, just knew that she had appeared on the beach at her own whims for as long as anyone could remember, always in her red bikini and sunglasses, always sitting silent and still in her folding deck chair. Some people said she used to be a flirtatious starlet who summered at the Santa Carcossa Sands resort, until a jealous lover murdered her and dumped her body into one of the local sea caverns. When she was younger, Babs thought that version was more thrilling but now she preferred to think that Jenny's end was peaceful. It would be nice to have a peaceful end.

Jenny's long hair and perfect teeth made Babs think that she was probably beautiful when she was alive, in that bleach bottle blonde sort of way, a classic bombshell beauty. Marigold told her, when they first moved in together, that she found that beach ghost creepy. But that was a long time ago, back when Santa Carcossa didn't empty out in the off season and when the off season didn't last the whole year. When Babs closed the shop and headed home, the dunes were dark. She could see lights in the windows of one out of maybe every dozen houses. The Sands had been shuttered for decades, but its skeleton still loomed over the town in the darkness.

Marigold hated Low Tide Jenny and she hated the beach. She hated getting sand in her crevices and salt in her hair, hated the sand fleas and the wind and most of all hated the trash that would wash up, hated the oil black color of the waves, hated the brooding yellow sky, all of which triggered her hysterical sobbing and begging Babs to tell her that it would all be fine.

"Have you ever thought of leaving," asked Marigold over dinner. Babs didn't answer, she just got quiet and hoped that Marigold would stop. "There's more fires. And the sea's getting worse."

"We could go to Las Brujas," continued Marigold. "There's nothing here."

Babs couldn't give Marigold an answer and that just made Marigold mad so she stomped off and locked herself in the bathroom and eventually Babs had to go apologize. But Marigold wouldn't understand. Babs' mother used to run the shop, back in the old days, selling dreamcatchers and snow globes and driftwood mobiles. Babs had gradually replaced the old inventory over the years with personalized novelty license plates and T-shirts emblazoned with messages like "Female Body Inspector" and "I Lost my [Picture of a Heart] at Santa Carcossa." Babs kept telling herself: *I live here. There's a community here. I know there is.*

She thought back to how it used to be: The boardwalk was bustling, there was an arcade and a midway, a wax museum and an aquarium, and endless rows of chowder houses and fish 'n' chip restaurants, each one draped with whimsical fishing nets and Japanese glass floats and each one with a fiberglass statue of a bearded sailor in a yellow rain slicker, biting a corncob pipe between his teeth and holding a small chalk board that said "Today's Special: Clam Chowder w/ sourdough bread bowl." Every day's special was always clam chowder in a sourdough bread bowl. She didn't remember the names of the people, though. She should have learned them when they still lived around here.

They shuttered the shops when the wildfires tore through the hills and then the ocean turned black and the tourists stopped coming and they started closing the roads. And everyone left Santa Carcossa because they were all smarter than Babs. Maybe they won't close any more roads, Babs always said. But they always did. They always did.

The radio always had new announcements about road closures.

Marigold spent most of her time crying these days. Babs knew when she returned home that Marigold would be staring at her cellphone, sniffling and sobbing and pretending that she was trying to hide it and whining "I'm sorry, I know it makes you mad." It did make Babs mad.

"They closed the roads in Sector G," blubbered Marigold, tears streaking her face and snot dribbling from her nose. "How can they do that! How can they do that!"

Marigold was always asking how they could do something when, invariably, they did it.

Babs took Marigold in her arms because that was all she could do and held her close and stared off into the distance, thinking of Low Tide Jenny, as Marigold sobbed.

"I'm sorry," Babs said stupidly. "I'm sorry. Maybe it'll get better. Maybe they'll reopen the roads. Maybe the tourists will come back."

"They won't."

Babs tensed. Marigold was like that: she wanted hope and then she spat it back in your face.

"This is all I can give you," said Babs.

"You hate me. All I do is cry. Why are you even still with me."

Babs pretended that the question was rhetorical and she went with a distraction.

"I saw Low Tide Jenny today."

"Why are you always talking about Low Tide Jenny? I don't want to hear about Low Tide Jenny."

"Why? Are you jealous?" Babs laughed. Good. She should be jealous. Let her feel bad. Let her be jealous of a dead woman, dead from before either of them was born, because it was absurd, so absurd that it would make her feel stupid for thinking it yet also maybe she was right to feel jealous.

"I need my husband," said Marigold miserably. Liquid snot cascaded from her nose. "Please."

"I'm going to the beach," said Babs.

"Is that what you're going to do? Go to the beach? Instead of trying to help me?"

"I'm going to the beach," said Babs again.

Babs stomped across the shoreline, kicking up sand with every step. Things washed up on the beach more and more. The usual plastic bottles and Styrofoam bins, of course, but other things too—pinkish purple blobs that Babs had to assume were some deep sea creatures roused from their usual haunts in the trench by the coming cataclysm and now throwing themselves onto the sand to die. It gave her a sick feeling in the pit of her stomach to see them and she was thankful that Marigold never came down to the shore because surely the sight of them would just incite yet another ugly crying fit, where Marigold would bawl for hours and demand that Babs tell her something good, tell her it would all be alright, tell her they would leave Santa Carcossa and move someplace nice where the world wouldn't follow. There are so many stories about falling in love, thought Babs, but they don't tell you what it's like to fall out of love. They don't talk about the long nights lying in bed, listening to the steady breathing of a stranger and wondering how it came to this. She ran through the arithmetic in her head: How many more years of this.

One day, Babs came home and Marigold was gone. Her closet was empty. She probably left for Las Brujas, she always thought that she would be safe there—the sky was reportedly still blue there for now, there was no ocean in sight, and road access was plentiful. She would have left via sector E; it was the last accessible road out of town.

Low Tide Jenny would never leave, not for good. She might vanish momentarily, retreat to whatever otherworld ghosts retreat to, but she was doomed to haunt this stretch of beach indefinitely. She might still be here after Santa Carcossa was gone, after the oil black waves rose and swamped everything, until there was nothing but dark waters under a yellow sky. She had waited on the beach for three days in a row, which was highly unusual, and Babs wondered stupidly if Jenny was waiting for her.

"Are you appearing for me," asked Babs. Jenny didn't respond. She just stared out at the ocean.

"It was blue when I was a kid," said Babs. Jenny didn't respond, thank God. There was no sound but the wind and the pounding surf and Babs felt the tension drain from her body. It was quiet. Thank God for the quiet.

Babs put her forehead to Jenny's and closed her eyes. Jenny's skin was brittle and papery-thin like the rind of a wasp nest. Babs sighed. Her hand slithered under the cups of Jenny's bikini, her fingers closing around the ghost of a breast, feeling the fossilized nipple against her palm. Her tongue probed Jenny's dry mouth, running over cracked lips and rows of perfect teeth.

Babs parted Low Tide Jenny's legs and heard a brittle crack like a rotten log bursting. She crawled between her knees and put her face on Jenny's lap and looked out at the black ocean. She felt a hand drop, feather light, against the crown of her head and rest there. They sat there together, under a yellow sky, and waited patiently for the tide to come in.

MACHINE (R)EVOLUTION

Colleen Anderson

When Archimedes arrived
    We gathered on clifftops like hungry birds
    staring into the wide cerulean sea
    awed when the screw turned water uphill

                           ἔτοια θαύματα

    the hanging gardens of Babylon thrived

                           Such wonders!

When the printing press arrived
    We peered through paned glass
    as the great screw pressed down, inked new paper
    books and pamphlets and broadsides appeared
    words traveled the land as masses began to read
                       We'll start a revolution!

When the threshing machine arrived
    We wiped sweaty brows, breathed in relief
    no longer need we thrash and flail till day's tail end
    grain as plentiful as gin and our bellies filled
    with time on our hands, we looked to the skies
                       What is out there?

When hot air balloons arrived
    We gaped as the woven basket ascended the sky
    bit lips, wrung hands, searched for impending descent
    shading eyes, we stared at Icarus lights in the ether

MACHINE (R)EVOLUTION

from heights we viewed land, imagined new vistas
>*People should not imitate gods!*

When the cotton gin arrived
>We bought calico and denim and fine woven fabrics
>profits gave airs—finely dressed people promenaded
>plantations brought slaves to heel to pluck plants
>Luddites smashed mills as jobs disappeared like freedom
>>*We will fight the cotton states!*

When the telegraph arrived
>We invaded borders while sitting at home
>commanded armies with no red stain on our hands
>found friendships and trysts spanning long distances
>>. . . . . / — .- -.-. . . . . -. . / .- —. .
>harnessed electricity to span global commerce
>>/ .- -. .-. .. . . . -. . . . .

When computers arrived
>We studied hard to learn machine dialogue
>>01010111 01101000 01101111
>considered the speed of electronic brains and devices
>>00111111
>one hundred, one thousand, million gigabytes
>><code emotion: confusion>
>people grumbled, old ways   l o s t . . .
>><ooo> *Luddites go home!*
>>*Move on, Gramps*

When the internet arrived
>We wanted . . . *everything*
><code emotion: avarice>
>The NEWEST
>>SHINIEST
>>>FASTEST
>>>SLEEKEST
>>>>*Buy now while quantities last.*
>games and memes, bulletin boards and sexxx sites
>avatars demanded our time 10 . . . 9 . . . 8 . . . 7 . . .

COLLEEN ANDERSON

Aliens! Gunslingers! A
thrilling sensaround experience!

We couldn't have it all
    <code emotion: disappointment>
    <program expression: sad face, tears>
the rich as always picked first
    <code emotion x2: envy-hate>
we brokered ourselves, our relations for more

We came to accept
    <program motion: formal bow> —error—
    <program motion: high five> —error—
    <program motion: handshake> —error—
    <program sound: sigh>
continually chased the dream of mastering all
    <program: exhaustion> —error—
    <program: self replication>

When the robots arrived
  We constructed all sizes, industrial, menial
coated in durable silicate, smooth flowing pieces
sexy Von Neumann machines, cellular automatons
    <program motion: fornication>
  <code speech: erotic vocabulary>*Oooh baby . . . yesss*
workbots to petbots that fill our spaces
  <code speech: animal vocabulary> *Purrr, rowf!*

When the AIs arrived
    01001000 01100101 01101100
  We meet Pygmalion
    01101100 01101111 00111111
  <code emotion: fear>
  <program: logic sequence>
  <program motion: random reactions>
  <code emotion: random expressions>
can no longer see the line that separates

MACHINE (R)EVOLUTION

When the spaceships arrived
    [We] gathered like rabbits in the field
            <code emotion: terror>
    our dogs, cats and birds and our wide-eyed children
            <program motion:
    docilely watching glittering spires settle, rumble earth
            hesitancy>
    leviathan mothership seen only through telescopes
            <recording>
            Do you come in peace?

When the spaceships left
    [We] had been plucked liked cotton, trembled in bays
            <code motion: observation>
    these alien rustlers laughed, pleased with the crop
            <initiate subroutine:
    their larders stocked for some light years to go
            Rosetta Stone>
    we bided our time until they entered FTL mode
            <initiate subroutine: MI6-
            SAS>

When the aliens left
    [We] counted their orbits of jetsam, castoffs
            01010011 01110101 01110010
    around a dead planet or two, asteroids
            01110110 01101001 01110110
    [We] are onboard, full of self-replicating humans
            01100001 01101100 00100001
    part machine and well equipped on this ark to the stars
            <initiate prime directive: Harmony>

When [We] arrive
    [We] will be like no other—greeting.
            — . / -.-. —- — . / .. -. /
    any species that chooses to present itself.
            —. . .- -.-. . . .-.-.-
    a mirror we will be, regroup our nanites our lives
            01000100 01101111 01101110

family, our programming, all for one, only one

00100111 01110100 00100000
01100110 01100101 01100001
01110010 00101110

Have we got a deal for you!

SKIN

Isha Karki

FROM OUTSIDE COMES the scour of frost, the trail of a lit cigarette catching at your eyes. You drag the bathroom window shut and go back to watching your face mask harden into a white crust.

A rap on the door, and there's your mother's soft voice: 'Chhori, I'm making momo for dinner tomorrow. You'll be home, right?'

You twist open the tap and massage the mask with wet hands. The motion is soothing. But this skin, it won't let you be. It's tightening even now, pinching at your chin and nose.

Speak, it commands.

The words tumble out instantly: 'Hang on, I'll be done soon.'

A flash of a memory—your mother on her knees, scraping mould sunk into the grout, your father looming behind. You shove the image away and scrub your face. When it's dry, you unscrew a glass bottle and squeeze out a few drops of night recovery oil, a birthday gift from Eddie. Its fragrance, that sweet smell of wealth, wafts around you. Everything feels clean and new.

Your nails creep up to scratch at the line where your right ear meets your neck, the skin sliding with reptilian ease. There's a hard nub of heat below your lips. When you were young, your parents took you to Biratnagar for the summer holidays, airfare for three and gifts for the sprawling family bought on credit, and you returned with a month's worth of mosquito bites. You haven't been back to Nepal in years, and still this familiar bump has appeared on your face—as if the skins are malfunctioning. Every hour you spend huddled in classrooms, galleries, darkrooms, your armpits prickle with monsoon sweat, nose peeling like you've spent hours under a scorching sun, when outside, the London sky is speckled with ice.

You look at the pot of face scrub—perhaps one more round will leach the unseasonal tan from your cheeks—but your mother is waiting.

Go outside, the skin commands. Immediately, you are at the door, palm wrapped around the knob—

'Did you ask her about her plans?' Your father's rumble cuts through all other sound.

Go outside. An immense pressure on your back. *Speak to him.* You shake your head no.

'You've been too lax with her.'

Your mother's placating murmur. That low rumble, then your mother again. A pause. The creak of footsteps disappearing down the stairs. Finally, your breath evens. You wait till you're sure no one is standing outside before you leave the bathroom.

Your bedroom door is ajar, your mother's shadow falling across the table where you work. You think about what is hidden in your wardrobe, the pouch you carry everywhere: tucked inside, the skins. Now here's your mother, standing so close to it. There is a hot beating in your ears. This house, it cherishes your mother; it's prepared to open any door for her. She's the only one who tends to it, even when her knees and spine ache from hours of drudgery at the nursing home. Yet the house never considers what else it can do to make her life easy, never thinks of heels slipping on the jut of a step, a body thudding, a crooked outline on the floor in the shape of a man. Only you think of that, and every time you do, this skin grips your throat tight.

Inside, your mother is looking with interest not at your wardrobe but at the prints scattered on the desk. You watch her reach for one, perhaps the image of a pyre or urn drawing her curiosity, but at the last moment something makes her hesitate and draw back from the fresh-cut edges, their promise of blood.

You walk to the mirror and pick up a tube of eye cream, making sure you can speak calmly. 'I have dinner with friends tomorrow. It's in the city, so I'll stay over with them.'

You dot the dark patches under your eyes, though nothing ever lightens them. You know without looking that your mother's expression has changed: a downturn of her mouth, that familiar groove on her forehead.

'Which friends?'

'You don't know them.'

'And Friday?'

'We've got an evening exhibition.' The lie sharpens your words.

Her mouth will have drooped even more. Still, you don't turn. Your fingers feel swollen against the crush of skin.

She sighs. Before she leaves, she comes to kiss you, a goodnight ritual she will never forgo. Her breath is milky with a trace of Tiger Balm, and it dredges up a flicker of the past: you're sniffling under heavy covers, cocooned in her arms, her palm smoothing your back over and over. That cigarette sting is in your eyes again. Your skin is shrinking and—

—*choking*—

—you slam the door as your mother steps out and snatch at your clothes, sloughing off the skin. Its seams tear open. You spill out, a slop of a mess. But you don't care, because the slippery brown thing is in your fist, and at last, even if for a moment, your pulpy body breathes.

***

The next evening, down rain-slick steps on a Soho side street, inside a low-ceilinged bar, you take a sip of a cocktail to give your hands something to do. The liquid is muddy, fuming its way down. Eddie got the drink for you, jostling against elbows and shoulders, the bar too crammed for him to check if you wanted a different taste on your tongue, something sharp and clean. You glance around the table, the familiar bodies leaning towards one another, you perched at the edge. You feel your face beginning to unstick. You stand with an abruptness you don't intend. 'I'll be back.'

The girls from art class—your friends—are flushed, cradling goblets of wine, stroking the rims of shot glasses filled with top-shelf tequila. They are deep in conversation. None of them look up as you leave, not even Eddie.

In the toilet, the light bares you. Lipstick is smeared on your chin, a spot of grease at the corner of your mouth. Your eyebrows sit misaligned; in this moment, their shape is so like your mother's, you feel that familiar pang.

Your mother, cheeks rosy from the kitchen heat, will be wrapping momos, popping them into the oiled base of a steamer, even now glancing at the door to check whether you might step through. She will pick up the just-cooked parcels of minced lamb and drop them into a container, blowing on her burning fingertips, humming off-key to old Hindi songs. Your father will be away, working a night shift, and the house will float with her.

There's a yearning inside of you: for that kitchen, for your mother, for the bite and burst of momos.

You should have stayed, then, comes this skin's spiteful voice. No.

You yearn for it only in your father's absence—but he's there, all the time.

Better to be here, with the flow of drink and laughter and Eddie, dear Eddie, your ticket out, ready with his credit card, impatient to whisk you away to his king-sized bed and have your tongue work him. His presence here has done it. You've been accepted into an inner circle you weren't quite part of, now good for plus-one invites and double dates, no longer the spare wheel unable to afford lavish weekends in the countryside.

When you first met Eddie, a friend of one of the girls' boyfriends, you'd paid him no mind till he asked if you wanted fresh air, offered you a smoke. That quirk of his lips, how he leaned in close to the shivery curve of your ear, zeroing in on you and only you; you'd felt the lick of fire inside. When you went back into the bar, the girls had raised their eyebrows, stroked Eddie's lapels, impressed with what they could scent burgeoning between the two of you. *Drink,* your skin had urged, and when the room grew hazy, *drink,* it said again. Later, on the curb, his jacket draped around your shoulders, a garbled text sent to your mother—you can't remember who leaned into who, whose hand held what, but the next morning, you found it: the singed spot where a cigarette tip rested for a brief moment on your lower lip.

Now, this skin—the lightest, brightest one you reserve for Eddie and your friends—is coming loose. Today, there are two mosquito bites pulsing on your chin. You glance around to make sure the cubicles are empty before you peel off your face with a slow ripping sound.

You readjust the lining, then layer it back over your eyes and mouth, swiping away the ooze. The skin is still sinking in when someone enters, pauses. You catch the woman's eyes in the mirror. The stranger's lips curl—her nostrils flare—then she disappears into the farthest stall.

Your fingers tremble as you lift the lipstick. You can't hear the woman rustling or splashing—as if she's standing by the door, inert, ears pricked to the telling sounds of you. The tube clatters into the sink. Here it is, the creeping doubt, the fear that even with Eddie's diamonds draped around your wrists and neck, his gifts of expensive perfume, they can smell the real you underneath.

Get a grip, the skin hisses.

You lean against the counter until the pounding in your ears quietens. You practice moving your mouth, fish out the lipstick, and slick on the glossy red. You dot on concealer and rub until everything appears smooth.

When you walk out, your face is fixed into a bright smile.

***

In the classroom, the heating is cranked up so high it's drying you out. The world is a black mass outside, though it isn't five yet, the nights encroaching earlier and earlier. Every time you look up from your laptop, you are startled by the ghost of your pale face reflected in the windows.

You are scrolling through images of a havan and don't notice Caroline until she's right behind you. 'How's the research coming along, dear?'

You feel a sudden urge to angle the laptop away from Caroline. But you can't do that. This laptop is borrowed, university property, and this woman is the judge of your worth. In a couple of months, Caroline will pull a number out of thin air and tell everyone whether your work is good enough—and wrapped in this bleached skin, best suited to boozy brunches and alpine breaks, you *need* to please Caroline.

Smile, comes the command, and you look up and stretch your lips.

'Hmm,' Caroline says, 'seems you haven't made much progress.'

Your face floods with heat. You've spent hours in the darkroom, attended a string of obscure exhibitions, written pointless reflective pieces. The stack of theory books next to you: Caroline could leaf through any of them, quiz you about the dense prose within, and you'd respond with confidence.

But that's not the progress Caroline's talking about. A few weeks ago, Netflix released a documentary on the modern-day practice of sati. The documentarian, descendant of a celebrated colonialist, was lauded for his commitment to social justice. You shouldn't have been surprised when Caroline said: 'Suttee is the perfect subject for your project. A regal pain. Why don't you play around with some props, create a suttee scene? We'll put in a low-income funding application to get you resources. They're generous with those.'

Your hands had shaken throughout. *Thank her,* your skin had commanded. But you hadn't gushed, hadn't said a word, afraid of what might spill out. The same day, you'd asked a question in front of the whole class and Caroline had paused and looked at you with bemusement, perhaps sensing the impostor couched in the foreign inflections of your tongue.

'Babe, you should totally do it,' Eddie had said when you told him about Caroline's idea. He'd watched the documentary too and was writing an essay on it. 'You can look over my research if you want.'

This project is the crux of your three years at university, to be presented at the student show where curators, magazine editors, private buyers, and collectors will swarm. It's meant to give you a foot in the door of an impossible industry. After this, you will all be cast out on your own. You should do as Caroline says, you know that very well—and yet, deep inside, underneath all the skins, you feel a flicker of dissent.

'Did you research the suttee goddess I suggested?' Caroline removes her glasses and peers at you. 'Only a few weeks left now.'

Sati. All those brown bodies, breasts and cunts, burning alive. To recreate that as Caroline demands—the women would completely disappear. Only their bodies would remain, charred and mute. And you know something of what it is to be a skinless thing, waiting to have words put into your mouth by someone who isn't you.

As Caroline walks away, you catch Hye Jin's eyes and note their flatness. Caroline must have spoken to the other girl already. You can't give Hye Jin your usual commiserating smile. Instead, you turn back to the laptop and close the tab of images. You ignore Caroline, ignore the squeezing of your skin, and read instead about men who burn themselves in protest and are called blazing beacons.

***

That evening at Eddie's flat, in the stolen hours between class and home, Eddie asks you the question again. You feel a heaviness in your limbs, a weight attached to their ends, dragging. 'It's just that,' he says, waiting until you look up from the buttons of your SLR, 'you've met William and Liz, and they adore you. Don't you think it's been long enough?'

William and Liz.

Eddie, dear Eddie, who calls his parents by name and won't understand that you can't ever do the same.

The first time you went to his parents' house—decked out in pearls, a chiffon blouse, a fur coat you returned after wearing only once; armed with your slickest voice, dripping private school vowels you'd borrowed from Eddie—you struggled to cut the slab of meat on your plate. You'd only just started eating beef and had discovered a surprising penchant for rare steak, its velvety bites, the juices that flooded your mouth. But the steak on the mint-green dinner plate in front of you had been too polite. Like Eddie's mum, perfectly coifed and manicured, and his dad, wool-jumpered and monosyllabic. Only their teeth, the insides of their lips, the secret glimpses you got as they ate, were stained red.

That night, you'd seen them through a crack in their bedroom door: his dad on the bed, rolling a stocking off his mum's raised foot. His mum had turned, and you'd rushed away before your eyes could meet. Early the next morning, after Eddie left for a run, you'd drifted in and out of sleep, hair sticking to your forehead with sweat, convinced that someone was dragging the duvet off your naked body, slowly licking the skin stretched across your spine.

'Babe,' Eddie says, behind you now, massaging your neck, 'it's important to me. I want to know your life completely.'

Eddie doesn't know what he asks—this impossible thing—though you tried to explain it once, the many lives you inhabit. He'd looked thoughtful, then asked, 'Is it like this for everyone?'

'Everyone who?' you'd returned, challenge flashing in your eyes, though your skin warned you not to push it. He'd stammered, not saying what he was thinking. Everyone. *Your* people.

Later, mid-fuck, he'd groaned, 'Your gorgeous skin,' like there was something about it he just couldn't take, and you'd been too astonished to say anything—just let him thrust harder, the tearing pain jolting you out of desire. You wore your palest skin with him, bleached and waxed and plucked, a sleek humanoid who knew when to open her legs, when to open her mouth, when to suck and spit. Even so, he'd asked about your childhood, the sick hot poor place you came from, ready to take notes for an assignment he was writing on the humanitarian crisis and foreign aid.

Now, he moves his hands lower and palms your nipples. *Fuck him,* the voice says, so you lean against his hardening body. 'I don't want to be your secret forever.'

The laugh is almost pushed out by the secrets damming your throat, jostling for space. You let him press you into the bed. You sink into the duvet as he hooks his fingers beneath your underwear, pulls it down, and licks the truth of you.

When your pulse finally—*yes god please*—blooms out, the thought flits through your mind: if he didn't make you shudder and clench, would you still be in this room, stroking his cock?

Just as swiftly, the answer solidifies: Eddie is your ticket out.

When he raises his head, mouth glistening, there's something in his smile, something in the way he wants to eat you all up, which reminds you of his mum, of Caroline—and every time you see it, you shut your eyes and pretend you didn't.

✳✳✳

At the dinner table later, your phone pings. *Babe, what if I came to M's wedding? Might be the perf opportunity to meet everyone? x*

You stare at the message. *Delete it,* this skin whispers. You swallow a spoonful of jaulo, the heat of it pooling in your belly. You texted your mother that you were feeling unwell, and when you got home, there was a pressure cooker full of the mash of rice, dal, and vegetables waiting for you. The clove-laced aromas of your childhood soothe you. Your father is at work, and the whole house is full of gentle warmth.

The phone pings again. *Only if you want ofc. Tarantino marathon tomorrow? x*

You swipe to delete the message and turn your phone on its face.

Your mother glances up, but only asks, 'Will you be here tomorrow night?'

'No.' The word is curt. *Please don't ask any more,* you plead silently, lies bubbling on your tongue.

'Have some more chicken,' she says, ladling out chunks. The gravy splatters on your clothes.

'For God's sake.' The words erupt, and when she gets up for a cloth, you snap, 'Leave it. I'll do it myself.'

She sits. The house grinds down, detecting the heft of your father's ghost in your words. Here it is, the thing you fear. The longer you stay here, the more like him you become.

Silence hangs in the kitchen. Both of your spoons lie untouched.

Then she begins telling you about an elderly resident who locked their carer into the laundry room and went for a stroll, a common occurrence in the care home where she's laboured for the past twenty years, wiping shit and reporting dead bodies without complaint. The sounds of her Nepali carry the warmth of the jaulo, and you're so grateful—for the softness, for the gift of words you aren't brave enough to utter outside these walls, for the sudden loosening of your skin—that you duck your head and blink back tears.

This skin, though often shroud-like, bears the weight of your mother's love, the lullabies of your youth.

****

The next morning, you're putting on your coat, winding a scarf snug around your neck when—a shadow against the door. The stamp of boots, the scratch of a key in the lock.

Fuck.

Fuck.

He's inside. At any moment, he will glance up. You want to open your mouth, gasp for air, but that would be too much noise, too much.

How could you be so careless? You carry the skins everywhere, afraid they will be found, afraid *you* will be found. You have strict rules about where and when you can change. But you overslept. You spent the night resting against your mother's arm, under a blanket, watching one of those frothy romcoms you both love, something you haven't done in a long while, and this morning, a pale sun filtered through the gaps in the curtains and you felt— light.

You thought it no great risk to change into one of your other skins here.

You are slipping, becoming reckless. Neither your mother nor your father have seen you as anything but what they believe you to be.

When you pass him—*please don't look at me*—his eyes are fixed on your face. You imagine his focus blurring as he tries to make sense of you. He might've said, *What have you smeared on your face?* or *What's that smell?* But you haven't spoken to one another in months, not really. Your mother tries every few days to smooth things over: *You know how he is, chhori.* In those words, a soft plea: please keep the peace. Just as she has always done, just as she will spend the rest of her life doing.

Which is worse, the fear of turning into your father or of climbing into the husk of your mother?

He is looking, not saying anything. The thump of your heart is loud. You keep your head down, huddled into your scarf, and stride past—*please don't*—stuffing your feet into trainers as you reach for the door.

Your skin tightens around you. *Say something.* This command, coming at the last second, is so incongruous from this almost-white skin that has always soothed your guilt, always said you need to *get out of this place,* that you are caught off-guard. You choke out a word.

'Bye.'

You clamber through the door—letting it bang shut—into a gust of wind outside, walking fast, yanking at the scarf, trying to loosen its grip around your neck.

Later, as you wait for the train, your pulse finally stops stuttering; you find yourself back in the slip of time, just before the door slammed. You think you hear it, the sound of your father's voice, giving you the answer you want but cannot bear.

SKIN

***

When you get to the multimedia art show, notebook and SLR in hand, the time window printed on your ticket is almost over, but they let you in without fuss. The exhibition explores the state of modern relationships in parts of South Asia, everything from arranged marriage, elopement, and divorce to live-ins, dowry deaths, and sati. You wander through the rooms and loop back to the performance piece, watching it in the dark. There is a lunchtime Q and A for which you've shelled out an extra fifteen quid. On the stage, you see that only the interviewer is a brown woman. The audience is a sea of pinks, whites, and beiges, seashells and blanched bones found on a cold, sandy beach. A few brown faces are dotted here and there: three older ones at the back and two girls sitting in front, whispering softly during the break.

A woman with snow-white hair and a carefully lined red mouth, her face a papery crinkle, a glittering brooch pinned to the lapel of her cream-coloured suit, turns to the girls to say, 'So how did you two get away from all this?' She makes an expansive gesture towards the exhibition. The girls glance at each other, and the woman pushes on, 'It must be hard, getting that kind of pressure from your family.'

Their answer is drowned out by the audience surging back with steaming cups, packets of crisps, and cookies crumbling in their hands.

You try to focus on the panel, to not look at those girls or that woman, but there's a drumming on the right side of your skull, the throb of mosquito bites, four or five of them, hot and tight.

Later, when Eddie asks why you're upset, you tell him about the woman. He rolls his eyes, says, 'Generation gap' and 'Just forget it, babe,' and turns back to his laptop.

You glance down at your phone: three missed calls from your mother. The flash of your father's eyes. The world blurs as you stare at the unedited photos on your laptop. Eddie's got the sati documentary on in the background to help you 'get in the mood'. A close-up shot of a woman's body engulfed in flames takes over the screen.

Your skin feels thin and taut, ready to snap.

***

'Hey, what's this?' Eddie asks.

You're engrossed in an article on political immolation, so you don't look up immediately. He's just back from a coffee run. The cafetière shattered that morning, and you spent an hour hoovering and fishing pieces of glass off the floor, slicing your palm only once. You stood for a long time at the kitchen sink letting the blood drip and pool before bandaging up.

The smell of freshly roasted coffee fills the room, and you turn to him with your left hand outstretched, anticipating its sweet bitterness.

You still when you see what he's holding. 'Where,' you say through numbing lips, 'did you get that?'

'Oh, on the floor, fell out your bag maybe,' he says, but you *know* you zipped up your bag and stashed it away like you always do. He grins. 'Is it a treat for me?'

Lingerie.

He thinks it's lingerie.

The whites of your knuckles are jutting out, the wound on your palm threatening to split. You ease your grip on your laptop and conjure up a laugh-like sound. It's brittle, like glass. 'You wish. They're body suits for slimming and shaping.' You stand and take it from him faster than he can blink. He looks at you strangely, a curl to his lip, a slight flare of his nostrils.

'Love the colour.'

You put the silken parcel, the whole truth of yourself, back inside the bag. A film of sweat dampens your clothes. His voice finds you through the walls. 'Wear it to bed, babe, bet it's dead sexy.'

You don't respond, and by the time you emerge from his room, he's busy tapping away. Your heartbeat is tripping. Eddie doesn't *know* what he found. You repeat this. Your secret is safe.

But there's something else too, under it all, deeper than flesh and bone.

How *dare* he touch you?

As the day unfurls, slow and lazy, the knotted muscles of your shoulders and neck loosen. You eat sashimi dipped in soy sauce thickened with wasabi. Placing slice after slice on your tongue, you binge-watch horror movies until they become a part of you.

Nothing happens—and though you don't want to, though the thought of it makes you sick, this bleached skin makes you fuck, drink wine, and fuck again till you are raw and worn, and finally it makes you sleep nestled into Eddie—so you start believing it.

You are safe.

***

'Babe, wake up.'

When you come to, your chest is on fire. Heat crawls into your stomach.

'We have to go.'

The room is hazy. You drag in a breath and—you're up, coughing hard. Something dry and ashy fills your mouth. Eddie's tugging your hand. There is smoke everywhere.

'Come on, please. We need to leave, right now.'

You let yourself be pulled. Eddie snatches up your phones, half-drags and half-carries you out of his apartment. Other bodies rush down the stairs. Instead of the cries of groggy children, shouts of parents, and drunken swearing, there's a deafening hush. In his arms, you float out into the cold where a soot-covered swarm stands, solemn.

There are no sirens, no trucks, no hoses. The night sky blooms into dawn, and you watch black smoke plume from Eddie's window. You step backward on the pavement, seeking Eddie's warmth, when a sharp jab into your naked foot shocks you.

Fuck.

Wetness seeps into the ground, and you think immediately of rusted needles and infected blades. You can't wait to get this *thing* off and change into another—

Panic, hot and electric, courses through your body. Your eyes are darting, searching. You need to get back up, need to get to your skins—

'Hey, hey.' Eddie is grabbing you, trapping you against his chest. There is menthol and tobacco on his breath. You don't want his arms around you, but this skin, the traitor, makes you sink in, close your eyes; the bristle of his chin resting against your head, his lips moving against your forehead as if turning up in a smile.

Then, you know.

Eddie's cigarettes. His habit of flicking them where he pleases, not checking if the life is crushed out. His habit of leaving butts on windowsills, where they can roll onto the carpet, into the bin, against the drape of curtains.

Eddie's cigarettes.

It rushes back. Your skins between his fingers. That look on his face. The flare of his nostrils.

Was it—did he—

You look down—*Eddie's the ticket*—and see, with horror clambering up your throat, the only skin you are left with.

Your father's face flashes in front of you.

Then your mother's.

She is spooning jaulo into your mouth, smoothing your hair, smiling; she is on her knees, scraping mould sunk into the grout, your father looming behind—

Eddie's the ticket, you think, shoving him away to squat and retch on the pavement—*Eddie's the ticket*—your skin tightening and shrinking until every single seam is stitched together at last.

EAT YOUR COLORS

Sonora Taylor

ANGELA ASSURED HER it'd be easy. She gave no impression of anything else on her Instagram feed, one that Eve followed with keen interest in her seemingly never-ending quest to eat better. She didn't want to diet, and she didn't want to starve. Nor did she want to spend a lot of money.

"You can give a big middle finger to the diet industry," Angela said as she held up a bowl of oatmeal dotted with the freshest blueberries Eve had ever seen. "While giving your body the big hug it needs."

Angela promoted clean eating and whole foods, a way of eating so rooted in common sense, Eve didn't understand why it was so hard for her to follow. But for every one day of eating the right thing, she'd follow it up with two or more of candy and French fries punctuating the salads and grains. She wanted to know Angela's secret—so much so that she was willing to pay for one of Angela's one-on-one's over Zoom to get on the right track.

"So how are you looking to change your relationship with food?" Angela asked. She sat on a beautiful pillow with her legs crossed. She wore flowing white capris and a matching long-sleeved t-shirt, and her blonde hair fell out of a swept bun in delicate swirls around her face.

Eve, on the other hand, sat below the bright glow of her desk lamp. She'd run a comb through her own dirty blonde hair and put on a bit of lipstick, but still felt drab pictured next to Angela on her screen.

"I just want to eat better," Eve said. "I want to stop eating so much—"

"Stop right there." Angela held out a finger towards the screen. "Your relationship with food shouldn't be about stopping or ending, it should be about adding. I don't promote minimizing. Nothing about you needs to be diminished, not even your plate."

"Not even candy or fried things?"

"If you want those, have those!" Angela laughed as she tucked a strand of hair behind her ear. Eve waited patiently for the catch. "But have them as well as healthier things. Add the colors of the rainbow to your plate, and you'll see how much better you feel even when you eat artificial stuff."

"I've tried that. I eat salads and whole grains and—"

"Do you eat your colors?"

Eve furrowed her brow. "I mean, I eat foods with color."

"Eating your colors means eating food that shares a color with every shade of the rainbow. Red, orange, yellow—"

"I know the colors of the rainbow." Eve softened her expression when she saw anger flicker across Angela's otherwise serene face. "Sorry for interrupting."

"Hey, no sense going over what you already know." Angela smiled again. She was always so happy. Eve wondered if the food she ate was why she was so cheerful. "Well, that would be my advice to you: each day, eat all the colors of the rainbow. Red apples, oranges, yellow peppers—"

"Greens, blueberries—"

"Exactly! It's so easy."

"What about indigo?"

"Let's make a deal with ourselves." Angela held her hand towards the screen. "Let's make a pact to our bodies, right here and right now, to eat our colors and bring a bright rainbow into our souls."

"Sure, okay," Eve said with a nod.

"Come on. Put your hand on the screen."

"Why?"

"Because we can't touch palms in person, silly!" Angela giggled, and Eve tried not to show her discomfort at how bubbly Angela was acting. She wanted professional advice, not silliness.

"Come on. It'll be like a virtual pinky-swear to our bodies," Angela prodded.

Fuck it, Eve thought, and placed her palm on the screen.

"Okay. Repeat after me," Angela began. "I, Eve Middleton—"

"I, Eve Middleton—"

"Love my body so, so much."

Eve hoped that Angela wasn't recording this. "Love my body so, so much."

"And I will add to its loveliness by eating my colors and helping it shine!"

"And I will add to its loveliness" —Eve held back a snort—"by eating my colors and helping it shine."

Eve felt a shudder pulse through her body, one that made her twitch and remove her hand. The sensation soon became warmth.

"That was great," Angela said with her brightest grin yet. "You're great, Eve. I know you'll feel amazing!"

Eve certainly hoped so—if she'd paid $100 to touch a laptop screen and recite inspirational words, she was going to pitch a fit.

***

Eve spent the next day grocery shopping. She tried to find food in every color, which was harder than she thought. Some were easy, like the apples and greens that she and Angela had discussed. She didn't like bell peppers, so carrots and oranges would be her best orange bet. She was glad she liked blueberries. And what exactly did count as indigo? Eve found some dark blue plums next to the purple ones and hoped for the best.

Still, Eve had to admit that the bounty of colorful produce in her cart was much more appealing than the usual frozen meals. She made herself a salad with almost every color of the rainbow, and finished off the one missing color with a snack of plums before dinner. "That wasn't too hard," Eve said to herself as she threw away the pits.

The days went on, and she made sure to eat the rainbow. Her plate looked incomplete if she didn't have at least three colors of the rainbow on it. Eve felt her mood improve and saw an extra bit of dewiness in her skin. For all her woo-woo talk and all the money she charged, Angela had helped her—Eve couldn't deny it.

Towards the end of the week, Eve noticed she was out of purple plums. She was also waiting for her paycheck to deposit. She supposed one day without every color of the rainbow wouldn't kill her. She ate her food with diligence, though a nagging feeling of guilt at not following instructions today wouldn't leave her mind.

The next morning, Eve woke up incredibly sore. She stretched her arms, then gasped. Her arms were covered in large, dark bruises. Eve whipped off her blankets, then cried out when she saw her legs were spotted as well. "What the hell!" she cried. She looked like a fricking Dalmatian.

She went through the possibilities in her head. Maybe she'd been sleepwalking. Maybe she tossed and turned too much the night before, even though she didn't recall having any nightmares. She poked at a large bruise on her forearm, one that seemed to glow and throb like a purple beacon. Maybe if I ate my arm, I'd get my purple for the day, Eve thought to herself with a smirk.

She chilled a little at the memory of missing the one color of the rainbow. She then shook her head. Missing one day of plums wouldn't cause bruising.

All the same, Eve searched her cupboards for something, anything that might be purple—to start the day fresh with a new rainbow, not because of the bruises. She saw a carton of forgotten raisins in her cupboard. Grapes were purple. Raisins had been grapes. They counted, right? Eve's heart thumped as she sprinkled the raisins on her cereal. She hoped it counted. She didn't want to slip two days in a row.

She took one bite, then another. Eve glanced at her arms. She saw with relief that they were beginning to fade. A blip—nothing more.

***

While the bruises may have been a blip, Eve found that eating her colors was difficult in other ways. She was getting bored with some variation on salad every day. The foods she did like in certain colors were starting to get tiresome. But when she thought that maybe just this one day, she didn't need her greens or didn't have to eat a bowl of pineapple chunks with organic cottage cheese, she saw Angela's face looking at her in disappointment, as if Eve were betraying her by going against the simple obligation to be kind to her body.

One day, though, the mere thought of salad made Eve nauseated. She decided to skip her greens. The ones she'd bought were starting to wilt anyway, and she was going to the store the next day. She'd have a salad then. She didn't need every color every day.

The next morning, Eve woke up barely able to breathe. She lifted her head from her pillow, then felt suction in her nostrils as a small gap formed in whatever had stuffed her up. Sticky liquid seeped over her upper lip. Eve wiped her nose and looked in disgust at a thick, slimy trail of bright green snot across her palm.

Both sides of her nose leaked. She clamped her hand across her nose and darted towards the box of Kleenex. She blew and blew, but the snot would only start to trickle again once she was finished.

What the hell! she thought. It wasn't allergy season. Eve's stomach grumbled, and her heart sank when she remembered the lack of salad the day before. Had her body gotten so used to salad that she was having some kind of allergic reaction?

She raced downstairs and searched through her fridge. The only green item in there was the remains of her wilted spinach. It had even developed a slimy sheen overnight. Eve moved to shut the door, when another torrent of snot bubbled out of her nose. She grabbed a paper towel, blew her nose, then stared at the fridge.

Eve cooked the spinach with eggs. She hoped that sauteing them and adding salt would reduce the slimy taste. The final product was only somewhat palatable, and Eve felt her stomach lurch with every bite—but she also felt her nose run less and less. She finished the eggs and spinach with one last painful swallow. Her nose stopped running.

Within the hour, Eve had vomited up her semi-rotten breakfast. But at least she'd had her greens.

***

Eve's next trip to the grocery store was a challenge in not only finding all the colors of the rainbow, but finding them in varieties to ensure she wouldn't get bored and skip a color. Though Eve didn't understand how, she gathered that the bruises and the snot were related to her missing one of the colors. She had no intention of making the same mistake again.

She left the store with cherries, apples in three different colors, lemons, pineapples, fresh and frozen greens, berries, even her dreaded bell peppers. Eve had no intention of harming her body further. Angela was onto something with eating the colors, something her body loved so much that it was reacting when it went without. Eve wondered how she ever functioned before taking on this new way of eating.

Eve went several days without issue. Even when the bile rose in her throat at the taste of bell peppers, she preferred that to the thought of deviating from the rainbow. She could do this. She smiled to herself as she sauteed frozen spinach with red and orange bell peppers to make a fat-free stir-fry. Everything was fine.

The next morning, though, Eve awoke with another stuffy nose. Her eyes widened as she sat up and felt the all-too-familiar trickle of snot begin to course down her nose. "How—" she muttered, but stopped and gasped at the sight of her arm. It was covered in red splotches, all of which began to itch. She scratched her arms as she dashed to get a tissue. Before going downstairs, though, she had a Zoom call to make. She scrambled to her phone, DMed Angela, and wrote in all caps, PLEASE TALK TO ME.

***

"Hey, beautiful!"

Angela looked as radiant as ever. She wore a silk shell-pink bathrobe, and her blonde hair was swooped into a messy bun that looked perfectly coiffed. She looked better than ever, which made Eve feel all the worse for being on camera with a runny nose and blotchy red skin.

"What's happening to me?" Eve wailed.

Angela puckered her eyebrows in what Eve thought was a trite look of sympathy. Maybe Angela was so busy being beautiful and perfect that she didn't know how to be sad. "Looks like you're having an allergic reaction," she cooed.

"I don't have any food allergies. I ate all my colors yesterday."

"Has this happened before?"

"Yes, when I haven't eaten a color. I got bruises when I skipped purple."

"Ah ah ah!" Angela waved her finger in disapproval, though with a cheeky smile on her face. "So did you skip your greens and reds yesterday?"

Eve's mouth fell at how blasé Angela was acting. "Did you know this would happen?"

"Once the body sees what it can be, it reacts pretty harshly to not getting those good foods it needs to be perfect."

Eve dropped her gaze in disappointment. Just like she'd suspected.

"But I ate all my colors yesterday. I had red and orange bell peppers with sauteed spinach for dinner."

"Ah ha, red and orange. Your body needs a different red food in order to count. Otherwise it's just peppers on peppers."

Eve furrowed her brow as she snerked back a trail of snot. "Seriously?"

"Afraid so." Angela shrugged. "I mean, you get some benefit, but it's better when you have different colors and different foods. That way you're getting the best variety!"

"I guess that makes sense." Eve began to dread her next grocery store trip. How would she find so many different foods? "But I had my greens yesterday. I had frozen spinach."

Angela clucked, and Eve felt like she'd been stabbed. "Fresh is always better than frozen," Angela said. "You don't know how old that spinach is."

"I thought frozen was actually really good for you," Eve replied.

Angela's expression grew cross, and like the time Eve interrupted her, Eve shivered a little at Angela's wrath. She felt an icy pang strike her heart, one that melted when Angela smiled once again.

"Nothing's as good as fresh," Angela said. "Stick with fresh, and you'll be A-ok!"

Eve remembered the green apples in the fridge, and sighed with relief. But she soon panicked again—she also had red apples. What red item would she eat to get rid of the rash?

"It's all worth it, I promise you," Angela said as she held up her palm. "Remember what we said: I will add to my body's loveliness . . ."

Angela waited for Eve, palm up. Eve brought up her palm, and repeated, "I will add to my body's loveliness—"

"By eating my colors and helping it shine!"

"By eating my colors and"—Eve removed her hand to cough and wipe away more snot—"and helping it shine."

****

Eve's fridge became a plethora of colors that even a Care Bear would envy. Fruits and vegetables—all fresh—poured from the shelves and beckoned to be eaten.

Eve's body behaved, but otherwise, she'd never felt worse. Every time she prepared a meal, she wondered if she'd done everything correctly. She'd go to bed afraid of waking up with some sort of malady related to whatever she'd missed—and what she missed seemed to constantly change. One morning, she awoke freezing cold. She looked at her nails and saw they were blue; a glance in the mirror showed that her lips matched.

"Blueberries are out of season!" Angela chirped when Eve called her.

"I can only eat in-season fruits?" Eve asked with a shiver.

"They're certainly best! I know you'll find something. Teas help too—though only loose leaf, never bagged! Have you tried butterfly pea blossom tea?"

Eve hadn't, and when she saw the price, she knew why. But she bought it anyway, because sipping it meant she wouldn't wake up feeling like the dead of winter.

She'd easily take blue fingers, though, over what she awoke to the following week: seeping boils that blubbered yellow pus onto her skin. "I eat something yellow every day!" Eve screamed over Zoom before Angela had a chance to say good morning. "And different things too! Lemons, carrots, bell peppers—"

"Peppers are out of season—"

"Lemons aren't!"

"Have you only been eating lemons?"

"What the hell else am I supposed to eat right now?! I could only find orange carrots at the store last week, and they were out of goldrush apples! How many of these fucking rules do I need to follow?"

Angela smiled, and for the first time, it made Eve feel dread instead of warmth.

"As many rules as your body needs to be its best," Angela said sweetly.

Eve swallowed back tears as she looked at the pus on her arms. "My body was fine before," she sniffed.

"It's better now."

"How is this better?"

"Because you're worried about it!" Angela grinned wider. "And something's only worth having if you're terrified of doing the wrong thing and losing it forever! Your despair is how I thrive, and it's exactly what I need!"

Angela clamped her mouth shut as Eve snapped her attention to the screen. "What did you say?"

"I said it's exactly what you need."

"Don't lie to me!" Every session with Angela came flooding back to Eve, with Angela's sweet smiles and glowing cheeks that only seemed to brighten while Eve poured her heart out in her quest to be healthy. All that time, Angela was feeding off of her—an appetite that grew with every new rule Angela made to keep Eve in check. Eve stared at her boils and wanted to cry.

But Eve was done crying. She glared at Angela. "Stop fucking lying to me," she said, "or I'll stop consulting with you."

Angela snorted. "I don't need your money. You know how many followers I have?"

"I'll tell them what a liar you are and what you're doing to me. You'll lose followers so fucking fast—"

Angela's face showed a flash of fear before she settled back into a sweet smile. It was enough for Eve. Finally, Perfect Angela had a weakness.

"What would you tell them?" Angela sneered. "That you can't follow a simple path to wellness? That you don't want to be your very best?"

"I just want this bullshit to stop!"

"And I want something from you: a testimonial."

"What?" Eve couldn't believe the nerve of this woman.

"A live testimonial to my followers and yours, talking about how great my consultations have been. Who knows—maybe doing a good thing for someone else will help you out, and make your body more receptive to less strict of a regiment. Maybe it'll stop rebelling against you."

Eve felt one of her boils throb. She had to admit, the offer was enticing. "Will it stop completely?" Eve asked.

"You should never stop being good to your body," Angela said, her serene smile glued in place.

Eve should've known that Angela wouldn't let her off so easily—not while she was thriving on whatever power she had from Eve and likely countless others' despair at wanting to attain Angela's perfection. The only way to break free was to break Angela. Eve sniffed again as she stared at the boils on her arms. They were disgusting.

Eve stared a moment longer in thought. They were just what she needed.

"Okay," she said to Angela. "You're on."

***

"Hi everyone! I'm Eve Middleton."

Eve looked better than she had in days. She'd eaten all her colors, followed all of Angela's rules, and been rewarded with clear, glowing skin and shiny hair. Eve did her makeup and put on a glittery top. She'd asked Angela if she could do her testimonial close to midnight East Coast time, so she could reach West Coast viewers after they'd had their evening meal. "Sure," Angela had agreed. "Especially on a Friday, people will be up late and coming home from evenings out."

"And feeling like crap," Eve added. "They'll want to know how to feel better."

"Yes!" Angela's eyes lit up, and Eve imagined her thinking of all the late-night regrets she could feed upon. "You'll be thinking like me in no time! Maybe I'll make you a representative."

Hold that thought. Eve simply smiled in reply.

Now, Eve was live and making her debut as a testimonial to Angela's help. Angela had been promoting it all week, and Eve had hundreds of new followers ready to watch her live. "A couple months ago, I reached out to Angela and asked for a health consultation. She promised me assistance focused on wellness and feeling good—no restrictive dieting, no starvation, no thinly-veiled eating disorders, just listening to what my body wanted and giving it what it wants. She gave me a simple instruction: eat your colors. Every color of the rainbow on your plate, every day."

Eve saw the clock on her laptop switch to midnight. She tucked her hand under her chin to show her arm. "Easy, right?"

A comment came to her almost immediately: Is that a bruise?

Bruises slowly bloomed on Eve's arms. She smiled wider. It was exactly what she wanted. "Yes, it is a bruise," Eve said. "It's purple, because I didn't eat anything purple yesterday."

The bruises grew and turned shades of gray and indigo too. Her lips and fingernails began to turn blue. "In fact, I didn't eat any of my colors today," Eve said. "I ate burgers, fries, and pizza."

Pizza has tomatoes, one commenter said, behind a sea of shocked emoji faces and concerned question marks.

"Ah, but pizza has tomato sauce!" Eve chuckled, and a burst of green snot came from her nose. "And only fresh tomatoes count!"

Eve had hoped for boils as her lack of yellow began to make itself known, but instead, her skin began to turn a sickly jaundiced shade. The exclamation marks and wow faces told her the transformation was having its effect.

"Angela wants to make sure you follow her rules to be the best you can be," Eve continued. "Once you shake her digital hand, she'll be in complete control. She'll hold your hand and keep you on a regiment of color, and if the rules change—" Eve held up her hands, which were now fully yellow and slowly becoming covered in crusty orange scabs—"she'll let you know!"

WHAT ARE YOU DOING? Angela wrote in a private message. Eve picked up her phone, then used the opportunity to check Angela's follower count. It was down. #TerrifyingAngelaTestimonial was trending. Eve's viewership was going up, and Angela couldn't stop her because Angela couldn't feed off of anger—only despair. And Eve didn't feel despair, not anymore. She marveled at her colorful body, which was almost every color of the rainbow.

A salty, iron taste on her tongue told her she was almost there. Eve smiled sweetly. "So if you want to be like me," Eve said, "then talk to Angela. Because thanks to her, I've added to my body's loveliness—"

She waved her fingers, showing off the orange scabs and yellow, bruised skin with blue fingertips.

"By eating my colors—"

She wiped snot from her nose, and saw red streaked within the green. Her nose began to bleed, as did her eyes. But it was when Eve grinned that the full effect was there for all to see. Her mouth, gums, and teeth were stained with red, blood flowing over every crevice as it coated her lips and tongue.

"And helping my body shine!"

PARADISE

Sloane Leong

ALWAYS NOW, the world sits in a halo of green. Kolea takes off her respirator, knuckles at the tiny leaves growing from her eyelids, fuzzing the edges of her vision into a hazy emerald tunnel. It is late afternoon, the sun high but softened by a generous foam of clouds. Daylight refracts through her tears. Kolea blinks, clearing the moisture from her itching, viney lashes as she takes in the stretch of ocean before her. She tries not to scratch anymore. It only makes it worse.

It's not that bad compared to the rest of her hair: on her head, it's thickened into vines so heavy, she has to cut them or else her neck is forced to arch back. If she falls asleep under the sun, the tendrils will rise towards the light and it will take a whole day before she can push them back into place. Her body hair thickened too, the follicles forking out like hungry roots, threatening to block her holes. She has to trim them or it's impossible to piss or shit. Her vined, rooty hair bleeds when she pares it back now.

It's strange growing something from your body that knows how to hurt when it didn't before. The first time she'd taken her hunting knife to the thatch between her legs, Kolea had jumped right in to hack away the hair-vines then screeched and passed out from the pain as multiple stalks gushed arterial watery red fountains.

Another lesson from her dear sister. Fucking bitch.

Sand sprays sharply across Kolea's spine, sea salt catching at her thighs and belly. Ghost crabs bubble up around her feet as the tide slides in to lick at her soles. Their eye stalks bulge out and sparkle like beads, their claws brushing at her skin warningly. One is grumpy enough to pinch her pinky toe but she bears the sting and it withdraws, shuddering itself back beneath the sand.

Her face feels worse than their little pinches, anyway. It itches hotly from where the swim mask and respirator have been chafing against her heat-rashed skin. She pulls on a smaller, lighter pair of swim goggles, leaving the respirator on a tide-softened rock, and wades into the ocean, the only place she can breathe safely without a mask to filter the air. The pollen catches in the sea spray here, grows heavy in the humidity baking off the summer sea and sinks.

But that, of course, only preserved her from the land and air. The sea would make its own judgment of her.

Diving into a cresting wave, she cuts through the water like a blade, arms scooping the salt water hard until it's almost like a solid pulling her into the ocean's depths. As a little kid, she'd raced her sister Nakana out into the deep. As a teen, she'd sat in crowded lineups waiting for her turn to take off, watching herds of haoles patched with rot congregate in floaties out on the waves, turning the water oily with sunscreen.

Now, the very idea of swimming with another person—already a risky endeavor solo—seems like a greedy fantasy. Deranged. Kolea hasn't seen a tube of sunscreen that hasn't expired or piled up in the landfill. She hasn't seen anything imported that isn't sun-faded and coated in pollen.

Just like her sister wanted.

Once past the white of the sandbar, Kolea gulps air and then floats belly down, focusing on the seafloor. She could harvest a few uni and some limu to eat without upsetting the ecosystem. Through the tidal tremor, life swarms and darts in primordial play. Fish and crabs of every stripe and spot skitter to and fro on invisible undertows. Urchins and sponges crown the corals in black and red. Turtles nip at strands of sweetgrass.

Twenty years ago, the reefs had been a killing field, bleached of all life by heat and artificial chemicals. Sea turtles floated listlessly in the waves, tumors clotting their vision, immobilized with growths. Foreign algae curdled on the acid shores. Fishing lines and nets tangled up dolphins and sharks while the rest choked on all manner of plastics. Myriad amphipods boiled to death, starving whale after whale. To say nothing of the land, the air.

Now the color of it all is so bright, it becomes violent to her eyes, Medusal in its piercing, motional beauty. As Kolea watches the life drift and dart beneath her, she grudgingly gives her sister credit. All the honua had needed was a helping hand and she had given it. And now it has healed itself. Escaping from the grave humanity's greed had dug for it.

It had made itself free.

***

weke
1. nvt. to open a crack, as a door; to free.

***

It'd be easy for Kolea to say she knew what was going to happen all those years ago. Sometimes, when she meets another survivor on the island, it slips out; there's some power there in pretending to have known, to have seen the signs. And with a little rewriting of history, she can self-flagellate at the same time.

But the truth was, her sister Nakana had never stood out to her. Not in any meaningful way.

Constant community service and volunteer work, Straight As, advanced placement classes, a Hawaiian language immersion princess—Nakana was a cheery, likable girl, and pretty. Pleasantly innocuous. On track to go into environmental sciences because of her love of plants and animals. A try-hard kiss-ass, all told.

Nothing like Kolea, who'd been held back and then placed in schools where security roamed the campus with batons and mace at hand and teachers napped at their desks while the students scratched graffiti into the wooden desktops. Kolea didn't have the loamy rich skin her sister had, the perfect long Hawaiian hair; she'd inherited her father's Germanic looks and was pale with thin, straight hair, tall and bony. Going into Hawaiian immersion felt like a farce. Besides, she was never one for community; she got into scraps when she should've smiled, cursed when she should've sang. While her sister made her way up the STEM path, Kolea resigned herself to the destiny of most island kids: hotel work.

But of course, fate had more in store for Nakana, as it always did. Why, Kolea couldn't say. It should have been her to wake the islands up, if it had to be anyone. She hated people as much as she knew the trees did, the animals, the boiling ocean. Why hadn't that hate made a bridge between her and the islands? Why had it been *Nakana* of all people?

Kolea's last memory of normalcy was working with her sister at the Grand Orchid Resort, taking all manner of tourists out on kayak tours. Fangless, passive invaders. It was almost an insult when Kolea learned a tourist was the catalyst to it all: Beacon. The woman-worm that had burrowed in Nakana's ear.

✳✳✳

Kolea's first impression of Beacon—the humble moniker the woman had assumed once she became leader of the Seekers Of Universal Language, or SOUL—was that she was simply the wealthy hippie-type with a nerdy, yoga flair. She was well-tanned and mottled in freckles, with long, weightless blonde hair. Maybe forty or so. Typical enough tourist fare. She probably intended to go on a transcendental meditation retreat upcountry or maybe try and set up some essential oils apothecary in the strip mall.

"Aloha, 'o Nakana ko'u inoa. I'm Nakana and this is my older sister Kolea," Nakana said, her chipper white smile gleaming against her warm skin. The group of tourists blinked back expectantly, their smiles limp from mimosas, their skin oily-white with noxious sunscreen. Hotel management insisted all the employees introduce themselves in Hawaiian to honor the local culture, but it always made Kolea nauseous to speak it to people who clearly only appreciated the exotic performance of the words without any interest in the culture or people that spoke it. "We'll be your guides today. We've got waters and lunch in the cooler and our own environmentally-friendly sunscreen for you. If you have trash, please make sure to give it to me and don't toss it in the water."

"Of course! I so appreciate your care for our dear Mother Nature. I am Beacon," the woman said, delivered with the same tone one had when giving someone a gift they're sure to appreciate. The self-satisfied knowingness forced Kolea's mouth into a tight line. The rest of the tourists, a significantly younger group of nine and mostly white, all introduced themselves with the name name: Seeker. It took everything in Kolea to keep a sneer off her face as they repeated their name to them. Seeker, Seeker, Seeker, Seek her, Seek her, Seek her, Sicker, Sicker Sicker.

117

After running the group through safety precautions and the route they'd be kayaking, Kolea loaded them up into two-man kayaks and they paddled out. She took a solo kayak as lead while Beacon shared her kayak with Nakana. A sea turtle with a tumorous eye watched them as they moved past the sandbar.

"Just paddle regularly, Beacon," Nakana said kindly as Beacon continued paddling haphazardly as if she were trying to steer. "I'm steering for us so you don't have to worry about keeping us on course."

"Ah, of course, sorry about that. I'm not used to letting someone else take the lead. A fault of mine I'm trying to meditate more frequently on."

"No worries," Nakana chirped. Kolea slowed down until she was parallel to Beacon and rearranged her grip and posture while Nakana waited; it was a common enough correction with new kayakers.

"We'll handle paddling," Kolea said, trying to keep a pleasant smile on her face as she tied the nose of Nakana's kayak to her stern. "Just take it easy, okay?"

"You're so kind. All of your people, really. Even your language has a sort of . . . gentleness, about it," Beacon said with a maternal fondness. "It's like music."

" . . . Thanks." Kolea tried to unclench her jaw as she paddled hard, trying to expend her shitty mood by pulling Nakana and Beacon's kayak along.

"So, where did you fly in from?" Nakana asked, matching Kolea's paddling rhythm with ease.

"We've just arrived from a retreat in Brazil. Lovely community deep in the Amazon, not unlike here."

"That sounds amazing! I've never been to Brazil, but I've always dreamt of joining the conservation efforts there. Any highlights?" Nakana asked with practiced sincerity. It was a voice she used on their parents all the time when she needed something, sugared in a smile. Kolea made a concerted effort to dig her paddle in faster. The sooner she got them to the snorkeling cove, the sooner she could get everyone in the water and be alone.

"Oh, plenty," Beacon said. "It's truly a spiritually abundant place. We stayed quite a ways out from any major cities or villages. Very private, enmeshed with the natural environment. That's what we Seekers prefer, you see. To commune with nature, it's important to detach yourself from the artificiality of society."

"Yeah. I feel like that, too," Nakana said with a reverent quietness. "If I could stay out on the water or in the forest forever and out of my head, I would. So did you just, um, meditate in nature?"

Kolea restrained herself from scoffing. Her sister could be so corny.

"Something like that," Beacon said, turning in her seat to face Nakana. "Have you ever heard of the giant leaf frog? They call it the Kambo there. I would say that was the highlight of our retreat. It's an amphibian that produces a toxin that decouples the self," she stopped paddling to lace her fingers in front of her, then parted them, "from the ego. It's very freeing. Soul cleansing."

"Oh, kind of like, what's it called . . . ayahuasca?"

"Mm-hmm, you've got it. A few months ago, we also partook in an ayahuasca ceremony. Incredibly profound experience, if you ever get the chance."

"Sounds intense."

"Indeed. The shamans call it 'plant teacher' because of its ability to tell you exactly what you need to know. It allows you to access a super conscious state and receive visions of the energetic world. It's part of our practice to connect with nature through itself. To hear what it needs and its wisdom by taking it within."

"Yea, totally," Nakana said, voice brimming with interest. Kolea rolled her eyes. "Don't know about plants but we got kava, which is supposed to make you feel funny. We have a few animals, too. No one really, like, gets high off them, though. Too dangerous."

"Oh?"

***

weke
n. Certain species of the Mullidae, surmullets or goatfish. Both red and light-colored weke were popular as offerings to the gods to turn away curses.

***

A shadow shimmers silver-green in Kolea's periphery. She whips her head up for a breath and spots the jagged fin of a dolphin—a pod—circling. A warning. She had stayed too long. The swim back is always easier than it is out because she knows her destination and when she hits the shore, she holds her breath until she's pulled the respirator out of her backpack and onto her face. Salt and sand chafe under the rubber of the mask's tight seal.

A helicopter propels itself across the perfect blue of the sky. They'd been making flyovers more often in the last few weeks—or maybe months, it was hard to gauge time anymore—spiraling around the island, pausing above certain points. Looking for something, maybe. Not survivors, that was for sure. In her darkest moods, Kolea assumed they were weighing whether they should bomb the place. That was what she would do, if she wasn't trapped here. What good was this island if it swallowed everyone that set foot on it?

It takes her an hour to hike back to her tent. When she arrives, she zips it up, then runs the air purifier, siphoning the pollen out through a duct tape-sealed hole through the canvas. After fifteen minutes, she tugs off her mask and flops flat against the canvas floor. She snacks on a mango then settles in to read. In her years scavenging and surviving, she'd only found a half-burned Hawaiian dictionary and the torn-out middle of some nameless airport thriller. She chooses the dictionary more nights than not, reads in an undertone until the sun grows low and the sky flushes orange.

Māla; garden. Malau; decomposed. In the safety of isolation, it feels comfortable to indulge in her heritage; her parents would've been thrilled to see her taking an interest in her mother's native language. Or, more likely, they would have compared her pronunciation and proficiency with Nakana's. It was stupid to think anything she did would escape the orbit of her sister's competence.

"Hello?"

The shaky greeting sends Kolea jerking upright, scrambling for her mask and spear. It's far enough away that the voice echoes in the canopy, but it's clear they've spotted her tent.

A survivor. And a foolish one at that.

The ones that hadn't escaped on the container and cruise ships had quickly been subsumed. Her family and friends, her schoolmates, her neighbors: all of them gone. But there were still a small handful of survivors who managed to eke out an existence like Kolea, cautious and smart enough to stay isolated and keep their lungs protected. Crazy or stubborn enough to try and live in this paradisiacal hell. For Kolea, every day alive and untransformed was a satisfying 'fuck you' to her sister. Over the years, she and the other survivors managed to stay away from each other, leaving signs and visible boundaries so they wouldn't congregate too closely and push the limits of their environment. A single human in the forest was tolerable as long as they didn't burn or trample the flora. But two in close proximity? The trees would start emitting warning chemicals, riling their faunal counterparts.

"Anyone home?" The stranger calls out, obviously counting on her absence and being able to rob her blind. Kolea peeks through the narrow mesh flap window, sees a scruffy haole with no mask and a hunting rifle poised toward the ground in front of her tent. There were still guns around, but she doubted that he'd found ammunition to arm it. If he did, the bullets would be over a decade or so old.

He walks toward the tent with his gun at his side, focused on stepping soft like it's the *sound* that would wake the trees, the animals. A useless endeavor; the land could feel them just like Kolea could feel a static shock, could smell waste in the air. Their very presence was an irritation.

The wind shimmers the trees. Pollen falls slowly, filling the air like static.

Kolea unzips the tent door slowly and the man stops cold, snapping his rifle up to her head. She steps out into the twilight, empty hands up. Her machete isn't far. Her spear is an arm's length away.

"It's not safe to be here. You're too close."

"I need food. Supplies." He looks her up and down, licks his lips. Seeing him closer, without mesh to obstruct her view, Kolea observes the actual state of him: his eyes are bloodshot, lids puffy. His hair and skin have been mostly scraped away, leaving viscous, gritty scabs in their wake, weeping with infection. He'd tried to cut away all the flora his body was producing, effectively cutting away himself. He was nothing but a walking wound now.

Kolea swallowed, throat tense. "You need to leave."

A pause, considering. Then a smile, facial scars pinching around his mouth. "You're a . . . girl. Been looking for a girl. Local girl."

Kolea's stomach tightens, fills with ice. Clearly, he was already pollen-crazed. That meant dangerous, unpredictable.

"Hah . . . I—" The man holds a hand to his mouth and hacks into it. His nose leaks a mix of chlorophyll and blood, a braid of green and red. "This damn air!" He takes a deep breath to try to clear his throat, but it only forces another cough from his chest.

"You're sick," Kolea says calmly, hand out in front of her, palms down. "You need to find a respirator and get your wounds treated. Do you have a respirator?"

"I'm fine. I just . . . I lost it. My mask. But I'm fine." He opens his mouth to say something else, but all that emerges is another wet hack. He tries again, manages to rasp, "Come with me. It's . . . what it wants."

It.

The trees. The animals.

Kolea wonders if it was truly in the soil, microbial organisms all exuding some psychic desire for them to die, driving them all to violence and suicide with every pulse of their tiny protozoan hearts.

The survivor levels the rifle at her. "Come here. Hands up."

A guttural grunting echoes from behind the man, catching in the koa trees. Something skitters in the underbrush. Chittering, hissing, an angry cacophony. It builds in the air like a breeze wracking up to a gale. Boars pass behind the trees like bristling shadows, the pale glint of their tusks a warning. Kolea eases back a step toward her spear.

"D-don't move!"

"They'll charge us," she whispers, panic infusing a sharpness into her words. "I need to protect myself. And you . . . you need to fucking go. Now."

"No. No, I need . . . I need . . . " The survivor ambles forward, each step slightly off-kilter. The pollen was getting to him now, she could see it in the glaze over his pupils. The muzzle of the rifle droops from her head to her chest, down to her feet. He was going to pass out but he was still advancing on her. Kolea moves backward with each of his closing steps.

A boar squeals and growls to her left, emerging from the trees. Three more boars follow it, their long, coarse hair bridled and high. Mongoose seethe around their split hooves, darting toward the man's feet and Kolea's, hissing like windblown reeds.

The survivor lurches forward, gaze fogged, unseeing. Kolea lunges to the side. A boar howls.

The spear tip pierces his throat before he even realizes she's got it. Blood spouts from the exit wound then razors across a koa tree as he staggers and falls. He gargles half-formed words then goes silent. Kolea shivers, holding stock-still, throwing hand still extended. Please, she thinks, leave me alone. She repeats the thought in her head, hoping it's conveying through her scent or her heartbeat, however they communicate.

The angry snuffling quiets. The mongoose chatter but melt back into the brush. Kolea collapses onto the gore-darkened soil, the leaves gemmed with blood. A new vine curls from her tear duct, studded with a single bead of salt.

***

pahulu
1. nvs. Nightmare (named for a chief of evil spirits on Lā-na‘i who was killed by Ka-ulu-lā‘au; his spirit enchanted certain fish, especially weke. If a weke head is eaten near bedtime, nightmares are said to result.

***

Price is no object, Beacon had told them, legs hanging off the side of the kayak and circling contentedly in the water. Under her feet, the fish darted away at the agitation. *Transcendence is beyond valuation.*

So, as the rest of the group of Seekers snorkeled in the cove, Kolea named a ridiculous number as a joke, expecting a laugh in reply. But Beacon only nodded and agreed with a casual tone that told Kolea she should have asked for double, maybe triple.

Kolea should have said no. Nakana should have never offered her spear at all, never even told the haole about the weke. But they had rent to pay, family to care for, and a future to try and build. Nakana's future, at least.

"You have to watch out for your sister, Kolea," her mother had said. "Don't you want to see her succeed?"

'She'll succeed without me just fine.'

"That's not true. She looks up to you. You affect her."

"I don't know what you're talking about."

123

"And you affect *us*. Your papa and I need to . . . focus on getting her out of here, into the colleges she's working so hard to get in."

And what about me? Kolea had wanted to say. Maybe she wasn't as accomplished as Nakana, but didn't she deserve their efforts? A means to escape this dead-end island? But the answer was clearly no. They could only afford to rescue one child and Kolea had already proved too risky of a venture. But maybe with this weke money, she could put some away, pull herself out of the shack they were living in. Make a future with her own two hands.

"It's easy money, sis! Less risky than weed," Nakana had said as she rinsed off the kayaks. She was too confident for someone who'd only dealt a few times and only as a go-between for her boyfriend.

Kolea snorted. But she was right and besides, worst case scenario, Nakana would get in trouble with their parents right along with her; a rare treat.

Beacon told them to bring enough weke for each of her followers at their rental in Paia. The fish were sleek and whiskered silver-white with neon yellow stripes. Kolea had never eaten them before, but they were plentiful enough; at least Nakana hadn't told them that manini and ʻaloʻiloʻi could produce the same toxic effects. They were tiny and impossibly quick, difficult to spear.

It took them two days to catch enough for the nine Seekers. When they finally arrived at the SOUL house, a yurt-style bamboo rental hidden away in a cluster of kukui nut and avocado trees, they were stopped by four of Beacon's followers as they exited the car.

"She asked us to bring these," Kolea said, deadpan.

"We need to confirm it with her first," one of the followers said. "If you could just wait here."

"Sure!" Nakana adjusted her grip on the fish cooler, her smile unperturbed.

"We have to protect the energy of our sanctuary here," another follower said quietly, as if offering a secret. "Surely you understand."

After a few minutes, one of the Seekers returned with permission to enter and they were escorted to the backyard. Beacon sat beneath a Balinese gazebo, legs crossed in a meditative pose on a worn cushion. Her eyes were closed, not a ripple in the pond of her face. Other Seekers were scattered around the yard, spread out on the grass under the shadow of swaying palms or napping in hammocks. Pakalolo was rich in the air. Kolea hadn't noticed then, but there were more Seekers than she'd seen at the tour, more hippie transplants they'd hooked up with.

"There's a lot of you," Nakana said, glancing around the premises with interest.

"Indeed there is," Beacon said, not opening her eyes. "Sit with me?"

The sisters paused then hauled the cooler of fish over to the gazebo, leaving it on the grass before joining Beacon on the warm wooden platform.

"We've been studying the Language all weekend while we waited for you. We've heard so much in such a little time, but now we can truly open ourselves up to it. You can make your entire body an ear if you try." Beacon dragged her hand along a curling fern brushing at her thigh. "I knew it wouldn't be long for you to find them," Beacon said, gently tapping her temple knowingly.

Nakana gestured with her chin at the cooler. "This is dangerous, you know. People get really sick from these toxins. Why take the risk?"

"Anything worth doing is risky." A smile spread across the woman's face, an encapsulated serenity that Kolea found immediately irritating. "I've been in contact with a local *kahuna* here for many months now. He's shared such fascinating things about your belief system. It's interesting how the more ancient, elemental tribes of humanity knew how important it was to listen to nature and its creatures."

Kolea breathed heavily through her nose. "Hawaiian spirituality is different for everyone, miss."

Nakana gave her a scolding look that said she needed to reign in her rudeness, at least until they were paid.

"Yes, of course, of course. It's just so simple to prioritize that connection first and yet, most of humanity doesn't. There's an almost embryonic spiritual clarity in native religions and their animal and environmental gods."

Kolea needed to leave before she got into a fight, but every word that left Beacon's mouth began to itch like a sumac rash. Why was it that haoles always insisted that, with a brief conversation, they could ascertain the depths of any topic they deigned to give their attention? Embryonic spiritual clarity, her ass. Hawaiians were polytheistic, monotheistic, and animists at once; all of their 'gods' were simply spiritual energy from pō poured into various shapes. That was why all their thousands of gods were referred to as ke kini akua with the singular indefinite marker, ke, not the indefinite plural marker, nā. The thousands were separate at the same time they were one.

But there was no way Kolea would gift this understanding to the woman. She could continue seeing the world from her blinkered, self-satisfied point of view.

A breeze rustled the leaves in the palm and mango trees around them. Beacon closed her eyes, held up a hand to catch the passing current. Kolea looked at Nakana, who seemed unperturbed. Curious, even.

When Beacon opened her eyes, she smiled as if awoken from a sweet dream. "There it was," she said. "Are you listening?"

After a curt goodbye, Kolea drove Nakana up the 37 toward home while the sunset bled rainbows behind them. She'd ranted her frustrations for a full twenty minutes before she noticed Nakana's silence.

"Kans, are you even listening to me?"

"Huh? Sorry, yeah, she was full of shit," Nakana said, forehead pressed against the grimy truck window. "I was just thinking . . ."

"About?"

A pause, fateful, pregnant with all the destruction Kolea wouldn't know until weeks later. " . . . listening."

***

pahulu
2. nvs. Exhausted, worn-out, of over-farmed soil; to let the land rest and lie fallow.

***

Kolea wakes to a dimming in her legs. Not a numbness, that sleepy prickling nerve-crawl; a dimming, as if the perception of her limbs is fading into nothing, into absence. She reaches down to her knees, her calves, tries to squeeze some life into them. No sensation. Jerking up, she slaps on the solar-powered lantern and hangs it over her legs.

126

Long, skinny white roots have taken the place of her toes, popped from the soles of her feet in thick skeins. They trail across the canvas floor and out the tent, through a small unzipped gap. Cursing, she tugs her lifeless ankles toward her to pull the roots back in, but finds resistance. Scooting forward, numb legs a dead weight at her side, she opens the tent with a zippered hiss and shoves the lantern out into the black night.

The tendrils have rooted deeply into the soil just outside of the tent. Deep enough that they've displaced a small crater of soil around the hole they've formed. Shock keeps her still, forces her mind to search for sensation where her feet should be. Instead, her perception moves her past her toes and deep into the ground, a psychic taproot her mind can't help but anchor itself to and follow. And in the depths, she feels something. An activity at the tips of her perception like frothing clouds of flies humming and twitching, infinite wingbeats battering at her mind for attention, for her to *hear*.

Kolea . . .

Kolea's stomach goes cold and hollow, the tingling surge before her body urges her to vomit. If she didn't uproot these now, her legs would be permanently paralyzed. By the next day, her entire body would give up movement and slowly slough away into nothingness.

No, not nothingness.

Into soil. The language of all flesh.

Kolea?

Can you hear me?

No, no, no. Kolea dropped the lantern and scrambled for her machete. She arranged her feet as close together as the roots would allow and brought the blade to where the roots started, at the top of where her toes had been. Her breath scuttled in her chest, her grip sweaty and shaking.

Are you listening?

She could do this. She could do this because this wasn't her arm or her feet or her legs. She wouldn't feel a damn thing.

Kolea?

She drew her hand high, sweat trickling from her palm down her inner wrist.

Please. Come to me.

Ear-rending screams carried up into canopies, echoing among the birds and bats and bugs, clotting the air with agony. With each choking howl, each stuttered chop, the voice calling Kolea—the voice that couldn't be—began to quiet.

***

ulu.ā.hewa
1. nvs. Mania, delusion, craziness; deranged; somewhat crazy, sometimes believed due to possession by a spirit.

***

It had been bitterly fun for Kolea to watch the falling spiral of her sister. Nakana had begun to hang out with Beacon and her growing entourage of haole tourists, going so far as to miss classes, come home late, and then, eventually staying away from home for days at a time. It had been tolerable until their parents began blaming Kolea for being a bad influence on Nakana because she was older and the family fuckup. What other rationale was there for her sister's corruption? It was delicious watching her butt up against their authority for the first time. For once, Kolea had almost felt a kinship with her sister.

Then, once they'd finally sat down and spoken to Nakana, they'd realized she was simply following her own pursuits, a path that had nothing to do with getting into college or planning for her career, and no matter how their parents pleaded or threatened, she gave them that high-beam smile in place of assent. And they had shied back, at a loss. Short of keeping her under lock and key, they had no way to stop her. Besides, what Nakana wanted, she got. Why would that change now?

"You're really into this whole hippie stuff, huh?" Kolea asked after the blowout with their parents, bitterness edging her voice. Leaning on the doorframe, she watched her sister change from a bathing suit into dry clothes. Her back was darkly tanned and flecked with deeper freckles and a criss-cross paleness where the straps of her bikini had blocked out a pattern.

"I guess you could call it that," Nakana said, neither offended nor pleased as she stripped down.

Kolea snorted. "So you really buy all of that SOUL shit? Even you said it was bull."

128

"No. I'm much more interested in them as a group. They're so sure of themselves, you know? And loyal to Beacon. There's so much you could do with people like that." Nakana turned as she pulled a blue t-shirt over her head, flashing the band of her belly quickly, but not quick enough.

"Kans! What the hell is that?"

"Hmm?"

"Your stomach . . ."

"Nothing, just a sunburn. I'm peeling," she said with a chuckle, half-moon smile in place, placid. She smoothed her t-shirt down and grabbed her mini backpack, walking past Kolea. "I'll be back tomorrow night."

Kolea should have stopped her. Should have looked again. Should have trusted in what she thought she saw. But it couldn't have been real, right? Because what she'd seen had been red like a sunburn, shiny like blistered skin, but the shape of it . . .

She'd seen flowers. Flowers on her sister's belly. Fleshy red petals blistering around her belly button.

But she didn't stop her. Didn't look.

Days later, a scent wafted in from the backyard through their bedroom window. An edged putridity. Following her nose, Kolea found the source; behind the old unused shed, in an ivy-covered plastic drum, a horde of headless goat fish floated dead. Needle-like ribs and spines littered the ground around it. On a rock, a paring knife and a spoon sat, stained with rust.

Beacon was turning Nakana into an addict.

If there was anything worse than Nakana being the perfect poster child, it was her being a druggie. Because what would happen? Her parents would start doting on her, send her to rehab, start spoiling her as she advanced through the program—another little success to lord over Kolea.

Furious, she drove to Beacon's rental where her sister surely was, fingers burning around the driving wheel. Idiots, fucking idiots, all of them. She'd chew out Beacon and her freak followers for seducing a teenager into their cult and then she'd drag Nakana away kicking and screaming if she had to. It had been fun at first, but now Nakana's little rebel scheme was pissing her off.

But when she arrived, it was to darkness. Curtains were drawn tight and no light bloomed in the windows or under the rim of doorways. Kolea skulked around the property, looking for an unlocked door or window, but found no entry. What she did find was a gap in a curtain, into a living room. No light except candles to cast them in orange contours. The SOULs were all kneeling on the floor, heads tilted up, palms cupped as if they might catch a rare indoor rain. Some held an object in their hands, a mound of some sort. Others were eating from what they held.

And at the center of them all, stood Nakana, bare as the day she was born, arms extended slightly to her sides. This shocked Kolea for a moment, the intimacy of it jarring her twofold—she hadn't seen her sister naked since she was a toddler, and now she was a woman among adults. A sexual being, Kolea's mind supplied. Her nakedness, the darkness of the room, kept Kolea from noticing what was truly different. But, finally, with a straining eye, she saw it.

Shiny red fruit dangled from under her sister's breasts like perfect opaque blisters. A large one hung from her belly and smaller ones necklaced her pubis. Fruit, small as figs and large as pomegranates, sprouted from thick vines which in turn sprouted from . . . *her*. Kolea knuckled her eyes, her mind refusing to process what her eyes were telling her. Around Nakana, more supplicants knee-walked toward her and plucked the smaller fruit from her body, bowing their heads repeatedly in thanks. Dark moisture shone from the broken stalks, deep as blood.

Kolea clamped a hand over her mouth, a knot of disgust tangling acidic in her belly. It had to be a costume. Make-up. Some fucked up performance or ritual. But it looked so real; the vines smoothing neatly into Nakana's chest, green to brown, into the soft folds of her belly. Kolea's eyes watered from refusing to blink and her mouth had gone gravelly and dry. She watched as Nakana lifted a heavy fruit from her body and brought it slowly overhead. The fleshy stalk connected to her belly pulled tight, tugging the flesh until it wrinkled over her abdominal muscles before snapping. Nakana didn't flinch. The fruit was tender enough to rip in half, which she did with a little laborious twist. It popped apart, pulp fibers hanging between the two halves.

And in the air, glistening in the candlelight, pollen danced like fireflies.

PARADISE

***

ulu.ā.hewa
2. nvi. Overgrowth; to grow wild and lush; bushy.

***

Kolea drags her belly across the broken asphalt now, down on all fours. Sweat pools inside her respirator, fogging her lens. The entirety of her feet are bursting with fresh roots; pale white and searching, stretching for purchase. Thinner roots fur her body under her clothes, pulling painfully against the ground. The road is better to move on even with all the debris and shrapnel from combusted cars, fires started by people in the throes of infection. It's safer here, too. At least, she thought it would be. With the soil walled off by asphalt, the roots seem to sense there's nothing for them to dig into, no place to anchor. But still, her body pulses with new growth, angry roots shooting out from her forehead, her belly, seeking and grasping at the rubble around her.

Rebar scrapes under her gut, glass shards jam into her elbows as she crawls on. The skeletal remains of buildings loom over her, burned cars tar-black and half-melted funneling wind through their empty windows. Nakana's followers had wandered into every small and large structure on the island and released the spores they'd been gestating like suicide bombers. The hotels, reservoirs, hospitals, the airport, the cruise port, even the supermarkets.

Groaning, Kolea crawls around a corner of detritus and stops.

Red.

The air is thick with pollen. Pollen from one of Nakana's people. It's been awhile since she's found one. Most were burned in panic or dragged away to hospitals. But some survived, like this one, contaminating the air, making anyone who breathed them in agonizingly ill if they fought it or lulling them down into the soil where they were meant to be.

"Damn it. Fuck!" Of course when she needed refuge the most, one of these red, rotting corpses makes an appearance. Kolea feels for the machete strapped to her back then crawls forward. She finds them—it, *it*, they're not human anymore—anchored to a spot between a mound of ash and concrete rubble. What were arms and legs are all roots now, thick as cables, stabbing into the ground

131

below. From head to chest, they are flayed open, as if someone peeled them perfectly from the top of the skull down to their belly button, undressing flesh from muscle. And from within the cage of broken ribs and withered skin: flowers.

A whole bouquet of healthy blooms with pink petals thick as a finger, bigger than Kolea's entire upper body. Where a head should be, a pollen-dense stamen waves in the wind, an obscene crimson, bleeding its seed into the air, collecting in the crevices of her respirator. Kolea snorts at the sight then cackles, her eyes pricking hot with each unwilling laugh.

Of course. Of course, there was no stopping it. There was no end in sight. What Nakana wanted, she got.

What was the point in fighting?

Mucus muffles Kolea's airway as she begins to cry, the heat from her sobbing choking her. Fuck it. Fuck Nakana. She rips off her respirator with a ragged scream, pulls the machete from her back. Cuts her hands on shattered asphalt as she hauls herself up onto her feet then falls. No feet, not anymore, just a cluster of roots around exposed tibia and fibula, the seams of new vines beginning to fissure up her calves. Screaming, enraged, she drags herself forward and begins hacking at the base roots of the human flower, saliva flying, her voice raw and breaking with every screech. Blood floods from the cut roots and pools around her arms, her chest. Pollen clots in her nostrils, turns into a paste in her mouth, but she doesn't stop chopping, not until the stalk begins to bend under the weight of its bloom.

Kolea.

The vine crunches, the human stalk snapping and keeling over.

It's all right now.

"Shut up! I fucking hate you!" Kolea sobs, coughing through the pollen, hacking away at the plant with fury. Maybe it was all right now. But this was how it was meant to be. Maybe it was better for everyone, everything. But she was done living in her sister's wants, in her dreams.

There is no you, Kolea.

The machete falls from Kolea's hand, grip too blood-slick to keep hold of it. Tears drip into the paste of floral blood and pollen. Her legs spasm and begin to tingle. The roots have found somewhere to descend, between the rubble, following the path of draining blood for purchase on stone and silt.

Come with me.

Rooting tendrils weave through the red coagulate, taking on the contours of a face, eyes and nose, lips moving in time with the voice Kolea hears in her head.

This is where we belong.

"No." Kolea tries to smear the tendrils away but they only reform, the rough outlines of her sister's face in blood and blossom. Her legs are limp now, fully numb. Her arms follow and then her neck, leaving her prone on the blood-wrecked ground. "I don't want this . . . this future . . . this world . . . I don't want you! Let me go, Nakana, please . . . "

Someone was always going to choose how it ended.

Nakana's voice is loud as a shout in Kolea's ear, louder than the beat of her stuttering heart, than the rasping breaths. She tries to open her mouth to scream, to curse her sister, anything. But now she is completely paralyzed, the tingling spread fully throughout her every cell.

I just made sure it was me.

Kolea's body is forfeit now, unraveling into red roots, squirming back into the soil. Her arm, bent limp by her head, bristles with vines, snaking past rubble to the ground below. Tears collect in her root-throttled eyes, faceting the world with her hate, her fear, and regret until the last thing she can see is the emerald glow of an empty world.

Perfect, silent and green.

THERE IS NO EASY WAY TOWARDS EARTH

jonah wu

1.

CAR BROKE DOWN. Too much dust in the engine, I dunno. Wheels kept kicking up land all the way through California & eventually the car sputtered and died. No cell service. I walked in circles for what felt like an hour before I saw another car down the road. I waved them down & they stopped, rolling down the window. An older white man, maybe 50s. Asked for the nearest mechanic and if he could give me a ride.

"Ain't one for miles," he said, "and I ain't driving that direction." The sky was darkening. Okay, then the nearest town? I asked. His face darkened as much. "Los Suelos, but I ain't taking you there. No way." I begged him, please, I've been driving for almost 3 days straight, I just need somewhere to lay my head down and rest. He narrowed his eyes. "You're not from around here, are you?" His gaze raked me clean, flesh stripped from bone. I pulled my cap lower over my eyes—very inconspicuous, Terrence. "Just passing through," is what I told him. I dunno, maybe I looked pathetic, dog-tired, or simply contemptible, b/c he sighed, reached over, and pushed open the passenger seat door for me.

As he drove, he kept asking me questions—what I was doing out here all by myself, where was I going. Thought I was still in college & I didn't correct him. Yeah, I do astrophysics, the science of giants moving across the sky, I told him, even tho that's an old dream, a very old dream. He wasn't sold on anything I said, but it didn't matter. "We're here," he suddenly announced. Here? I looked around, & around was some ramshackle town that god himself had forgotten. You know, the type of place that feels, even when inhabited by humans, like a watering hole for ghosts. "Thanks," I told the driver, & he sped off. Never got his name.

Lucky for me: there's a tiny motel on the edge of town. Giant metal tomato out front, for some reason. I'm the only visitor tonight. Room smells stale and sheets look suspicious. Whatever. I can handle all that, but I plugged my phone into the wall and turns out there's no cell service anywhere in this place. Motel has no wifi, either. Truly some middle-of-nowhere shit. Cross that off my bucket list. But like every motel there's a pen & pad on the bedside table, and I don't know what it was, maybe the exhaustion from the road, maybe everything that's happened in the past few weeks, but I sat down and started writing. It's like this blank page was calling. Is that how writers feel? I'm writing and the words keep going. God, I'm tired. I can't wait to get back on the road & drive.

2.

Fuck, I should've listened to the guy who drove me here. It's impossible to get out. There's no cell service, no internet, hell, no telephones. No one has any useful info. It's like I'm stuck in the pocket dimension of some bad sci-fi show. While I was out searching for a mechanic, anyone who knew anything about cars, some locals started chatting me up and roped me into a night of drinking. They took me to this dive bar and just started pouring me drinks like they'd always known me. Said they're part of some special church here. Crazy motherfuckers. Couldn't even figure out half of what they were telling me, why did I stay the whole night? Just smiled & nodded. I must've been really lonely.

Don't remember how I got back to the motel; woke up with a blaring hangover, couldn't even see straight. I was still blinking off the remnants of last night's dream, where I sat in the center of the earth, watching its iron core spin. Reminded me of being trapped at the bottom of a jar—that old folktale A-gong used to tell me. How did it go again? Anyway, tonight I'm gonna try to find some more info & go to bed early. I hope this place is as remote as it seems. Maybe they won't be able to find me.

3.

God, my head hurts. How have I already been here a week? Time slips like water here. My brain's messed up. Keep having visions: tiny tyke me, pointing up at the stars, naming every constellation, A-gong grinning down at me with pride. *I'll go far,* I promise him. And when I snap out of it, it's like I'm moving thru mud. I spend my days looking for telephone books, maps, anything that'll help, & then inevitably the church people will find me, take me drinking, & I'll lose entire nights to my dreams.

You know, last night I was almost certain that A-gong was standing over me while I laid in bed. He's already dead, so I knew it was a dream. But the motel room around me was so realistic that it felt like I was dreaming with my eyes open. He never said anything, just stared with two black, empty eyes. If he was alive, he wouldn't like me. He never wanted a grandson after all.

I ran out of all my money already. I've gotta get a goddamn job.

4.

Some of the church folks got me a gig at the slaughterhouse, called Schaefer Meats. Looks like they aren't so bad, huh. I'm not a sick fuck so I'm not excited about the prospect of killing cows or anything, but money's money.

Paperwork was simple & quick. Hiring manager barely asked any questions. "As long as you're ready to work," he said, "that's all we're looking for. Speak English?" He said it so casually, that was the worst kind of knife. I'm speaking it to you right now, I smart-mouthed back. "Good," he said, I guess missing the sarcasm. "Driver's license?" And now my blood ran cold. I pulled it from my wallet and slid over the table. I'm gonna be found out, my heart kept thumping, I'm gonna be found out, I'm gonna be found.

He looked for a long while at my ID & then back at me. "Terrence Chen?"

Yes, I said. Trying to sound as *me* as possible, yes, that is me, the man known as Terrence Chen, who has existed for all of his 28 years on earth, from the first day out of the womb up until the day we sink beneath the dirt. Except the womb was not my mother's, but my own. Like in sci-fi: the mother and the son are the same person. The mother gave birth to himself, the mother cracked open her skull and out of her cranial pussy burst the fully-formed body of a man. And now I was trying to prove this was true with a fake ID.

I was boiling in the depths of hell, trapped at the bottom of a jar with the creepy-crawlies all over me, sweat pouring out of my skin—but the guy didn't even notice. He slid the ID back to me and smiled. "Welcome to the Schaefer Meats team, Terrence. Tomorrow's your first day, so let's go and get you acquainted with the rest of the guys, huh?"

He led me to the breakroom. Whatever conversation going on instantly died, the air stilled & cleared, leaving 20 or 30 pairs of eyes on me. Trying to assess me. See what I was worth. A lot of different skin tones in the room, black and brown and white, but no other Asian guys around but me. Looks like I was the first one.

The hiring manager broke the silence. "Everyone, this here's Terrence. Terrence, everyone. He's starting with us tomorrow, so let's show him the Schaefer Meats hospitality, yeah?" No one seemed particularly moved to show me any hospitality, save for one of them who stepped forward with an outstretched hand. "Hey, I'm Nate," he introduced himself. "I'll be your supervisor on the floor." He seemed friendly enough, so I shook his hand. The other guys still said nothing. Fine by me.

"Well, that should be it for now," the hiring manager said, turning back to me. "Any questions?"

"Yeah," I said. "Where's the bathroom?"

He gave me the directions & I went by myself. There was a women's bathroom, of course, but it looked small from the outside. The men's bathroom, by comparison, was vast—a seemingly endless line of grimy urinals against one wall, several stalls against the other. Bustling with bodies. The men chatted to each other while peeing, exposing themselves to each other like it was nothing. No privacy, anywhere. I panicked and ducked into a stall. How long could I do this for? It was my first time in a men's bathroom, it always felt forbidden & unreachable, and now that I was actually here, I was terrified.

How long before they find me out? How long until I expose everything?

5.

It's nasty work, this. Of course it is, Terrence, what did you expect—but now I know why the cows are "special." Nate got me set up with the bolt gun. A captive-bolt pistol, he called it. "Nice and easy," he said. "You wanna send them off quick and painless." I held the gun steady in my hand until the first came down the line towards me. *Thank you,* it said politely before closing its eyes and resting its large forehead against the muzzle of the gun.

"What's the matter?" Nate asked when I stood there doing nothing.

I looked at him. He was serious. "It just . . . it just . . . "

"Oh, that." He shook his head. "Forgot you aren't from around here." He tried to smile kindly at me, but the light turned every curve of his lips sinister. "Don't worry about it. Just makes our job easier, don't you think?"

When I got back to the motel I threw up for the first time in years.

6.

A-gong visited me again last night. He said, I see you've changed your skin. He held a knife against my throat and said, Last time I was here, you were loved, & small enough to fit in both my hands. But I see that my daughter, your mother, has performed the alchemical trick of turning blood into poison. Do you know how gu is made? A black magic practitioner will capture all manner of toxic creatures at the bottom of a jar: snakes, scorpions, toads, spiders, centipedes. In that concentrated hell they will fight to the death until one alone has absorbed all of his enemies' venom, and their rage and resentment too; that tortured spirit is what we call gu. Gu is animated darkness, it cannot survive for long in the world of the living. And I am sorry to say, my grandson, but you have consumed too much of the venom. You have already destroyed too much.

The Belowdowners at work have taken a liking to me, I think, b/c I'm one of the few outsiders who'll listen to them. Not that they won't try to convert me. They talk a lot about some guy named Hibiscus, how he's saved them from the rot of life, how I should attend one of his sermons soon. Sounds good and fine, I told them, but I'm a bit done with churches right now. I'll still go drinking with them when the time comes, though.

Before my lunch ended, Nate cornered me in the breakroom. Seems like the church folks aren't popular outside of their little group, and Nate thinks the Belowdowners are bad news. "You seem like a good kid. Don't get too mixed up with them."

I nodded and told him I'd be careful, but I wanted to say, I'm not sure if I'm the one you should be warning about danger, Nate. I'm already full of venom.

7.

You think too much, someone on the killing floor told me. *You identify too much with the cow.* It's considered a weakness. Might be written up in my performance report. But I can't help it. When the animals look me in the eye, I feel like I can see the soul of them. The inner being. I got the hang of the bolt gun so they said, We're gonna move you on up, & now I work on skinning because I have careful, small hands that can get around all the curves of a cow. Now I'm splitting the carcasses open, relieving them of their body, slipping the skin off. Like it's a magic trick.

It's so hot in there but I don't want to pee at work, so I don't drink water until I get back to the motel. It's starting to mess with my head, I think. Dehydration makes me sway on the work floor and I've come close to slicing my own fingers off. If it's the town, the cows, the thirst . . . I don't want to fall asleep anymore. The slaughterhouse keeps coming back to revisit me at night.

Like this: I have a dream of my mother's hands. She's rubbing lotion on them the way she always does, in that dainty manner, dragging the sludge across her palms with her fingers. But now it's not lotion, it's blood, it's cow blood and she's reaching into the deep belly of it and pulling out its flesh until only the skin is left. Then she turns the bolt gun on me. *Disappointment,* she seethes. Cracks my skull open, drives the iron deep into my brain until it's touched the very core of me. *Thank you, thank you . . .* The cows are marching down towards me in a single file. Bleeding, oozing, etc. All moaning, *Thank you, thank you.*

8.

It's 4am & I have to get up in 3 hrs for work tomorrow but I can't fall asleep. I can't remember anything these days. My memory's like rotten meat. The blood on my hands, I don't know if it's from today, yesterday, or from 3 months ago. The only thing I can remember is that I have to leave. To where? From where did I come? Or maybe Los Suelos is the beginning and the end . . .

How did I even end up here? When I think back on the trajectory of my life, it doesn't make any sense. When I was younger I wanted to be an astrophysicist, like my grandfather. We used to stay up together talking about the stars until my mom would come home & scold him for keeping me up too late. But then he died, & those dreams died with him. & then I had to run away from her . . . I loved my car. Driving was the only thing that made me feel free. So when I think of my car right now, out in the hills, abandoned, collecting dirt, rusting away, I get a little sad. In a thousand years the earth will swallow it whole, and it'll just be another part of the landscape.

I'm trying to remember what the car used to look like . . .

9.

I got sick. It was only a cold, but when I came into work coughing someone barred me from the door and told me I had to stay home until I got better. When I got back, I checked my stash of cash & only had $89.45, so there goes that. Can't get to the doctor. Can't leave town at all, even if I wanted to.

10.

Woke up hot & screaming. I feel like a phantom visited me again in my sleep, but I can't remember. I ended up on the floor, slept several good hours there. Being close to the ground helps.

The fever's worse. Headache so bad it's like a bolt driven into my brain. I went out for hot food and meds, stumbling the whole way. Whatever few people in the street cleared the way for me. I'm a walking disease, I'm spreading rot. I walked, heard several thumps behind me. It was oddly rhythmic. Like if I listened too long, I'd get hypnotized. I looked behind me.

Birds around me, falling out of trees, dead.

11.

Mother poisoned me it wasn't my fault
Where was I supposed to go
Los Suelos is the beginning and the end of everything

12.

Not supposed to stay at the motel anymore. I took the pen & pad with me b/c somehow writing helps, writing helps to calm the fever. Like uncorking the firebomb and letting the heat out.

I started eating the dirt. It settles my stomach, and I'm so hungry for it that I suck all the dirt that gets stuck under my fingernails from digging. I remember the church people talking about it. But is it a cure? Closer to earth, closer to earth . . .

13.

I'm walking into the hills right now. I feel sudden clarity, like the fever is fueling a singular purpose. I'm going back to my car where I'll be free. Poor empty metal skeleton. I used to have dreams and aspirations, just like everyone else . . . Now all that's left for me is rot.

The animals are here. The scorpions the snakes the toads the centipedes the spiders. They smell the venom in me and they follow, trailing my footfalls. The venom is named *sorrow* and I'm sorry, mom, I'm sorry, A-gong, I'm sorry every cow who pressed its furry pate against my palm and asked for death . . .

The earth is calling. When I reach the peak of the hills, I will get on my knees and start digging with my hands. The dirt will spill over my fingers like so much cool water. And when the hole I dig is just wide and just tall enough for my body to fit, I will lay down in it to watch the night sky pass. I still remember the name of every constellation, and I will speak Orion, Perseus, Cassiopeia, loud enough for my grandfather to hear.

NOTES ON THE FORUM OF THE SIMULACRA

Cadwell Turnbull

MEMBERS OF THE Forum of the Simulacra believe that the world has been copied many times by an entity of unknown origin for an unknown purpose. (*Note: A god, a computer, a cosmic force?*) They call this entity the Simulacrum and its collection of worlds the Simulacra. The Simulacrum doesn't just copy the world, it adjusts it, adds things to the world, deletes other things. But its most terrifying power is its ability to alter meaning: to change what people care about or find interesting or the very relationships people have to things, to other people, to themselves.

CrayonsAreChanging (8.29.2018.8:57PM): I have a sister now. Just walked out of a room that wasn't there before. She's nice, I guess.

LuckYNo15 (4.30.2017.12:04AM): No one likes Caramel deLites? How the fuck does no one like Caramel deLites? Apparently people aren't buying them so they're discontinuing? What the fuck? (*Note: Caramel deLites were awful. Almost as bad as Thin Mints. This is likely just group preferences masquerading as the Mandela Effect.*)

JUDAHS4 (6.6.2018.2.09AM): Pretty sure Montana had a population of over a million. Now it's 20,768. Weird. Also Hawai'i is its own country now.

It's impossible to tell if this is truly a mass delusion or a belief system inventing its own mythology. Oldest posts on the site appear to be no different than recent ones.

NOTES ON THE FORUM OF THE SIMULACRA

TheLostSheepKing (4.20.2007.6:06PM): The house I grew up in now belongs to a very polite old couple. They said they've been living there for 37 years. I'm only 21, returning for summer break. They invited me in and showed me pictures of their time in the house. Asked me if I was sure. I was until I saw the pictures. Anyone else experienced something like this?

Neverender (4.20.2007.6:08PM): I have. My childhood home is now a meadow. The town's name has changed.

Colleen (same time): I woke up this morning in a different house. Parents are the same but the dog is different. Her name is Snowball. She sits on the floor and stares at me and I don't like it.

Twenty-seven posts on the names of cities changing, all in the first day. By the following day, over a hundred posts about missing people or people with changed personalities or people whose roles have changed. Teachers becoming neighbors. Mothers becoming aunts. One incident of a husband of several years disappearing and turning up as the mailman. Speed of posts was very alarming, and the genuine horror of them.

What's strange is that there's no origin post coining the term "Simulacrum." The concept exists without a referent, rules for the entity sprouting up like mushrooms, simultaneous. The earliest reference occurs over six years after the launch of the site.

TRutHsEeKR88 (10.04.2013.12:09AM): I'm pretty sure the Simulacrum has been altering the site. I tried to go back through old posts and it gave me a nosebleed. Anyone else getting nosebleeds?

To date there have been no responses to this post, though other members have described headaches, bouts of nausea, fainting spells. Always around perceived edits to reality.

Interestingly, only a few people without "edit experiences" have posted on the site. Their responses are what you might expect.

Simmons3 (7.23.2012.3:47PM): Are you guys for real?

Shinobi299 (9.11.2014.8:18AM): You people are nuts.

NguyenOcean (3.32.2016.7:09PM): This shit is really messing with my head. Please tell me you all are playing some elaborate joke?

Members of the forum respond to these inquiries with contempt.

"Another sheep has stumbled their way onto the forum."

"Fuck off, sheeple."

Or philosophical musings:

CumulusTen (2.14.2014.11:22PM): "Is it possible that the Simulacrum sends people here every once in a while to mock us? How do we know that what we know isn't also to mock us? What if we wake up tomorrow and forget everything ?"

It does feel genuinely eerie that more people don't visit the site, but perhaps this is my own obsession speaking. Most people probably dismiss the site entirely, and why wouldn't they? There are only a handful of active users at any given time. Private conversations with members have proved fruitless; everyone is fully committed to the ruse or they truly believe what they are saying. (*Perhaps convince someone to meet in person?*)

I've been researching the site for months(*?*) and still have not gotten any closer to understanding why it exists. With each day I gain less clarity, having forgotten why I started this research in the first place. I write these reports and journals and notes and leave them all over my apartment with no idea why I am writing them or who I might want to read them. Each note begins the same but morphs as I continue, until the thing before me fills me with horror. These notes are all punctuated by the same symbol: a circle with arms, a serpent around an apple, an all-seeing eye? I never remember drawing the symbol, and have difficulty describing it. When I sleep, I see it in my dreams. A door opens in front of me, and through it I can see another world, a cityscape with a massive tower, the symbol carved into its front. And a young woman whose features shift like clay-mation putty. Her hand is outstretched to mine, but when I try to grab hold of her and step through, everything turns white, and the scene resets. This other world is always the same and I can feel a sense of longing every time I see it. After several attempts, the woman says, I keep losing track of you, and her voice is so painfully familiar that despair fills me to bursting and I wake up screaming.

(*Please save yourself, my love.*)

Some of the members of the forum believe that the true world still exists, unaltered by the Simulacrum. Most members, however, believe the true world is forever lost.

They return to places that have been altered like orphans.

Neverender (6.32.2020.5:09AM): I visit the field often. I look at those flowers and I imagine that they are the people of my hometown, swaying with the wind like dancers at a celebration that will never end.

The ones who believe in the untouched world also believe in other worlds beyond a veil no one can see, but are accessible through the ritual of performing unique actions: holding one's breath for a minute and thirty seconds, jumping from a great height, eating cake on the fourth of July. They believe these mechanisms of travel are gifted to them by the Simulacrum itself, both demon and god in their strange mythology.

Here is the earliest instance I could find regarding the subject of traveling between worlds, transcribed in its entirety:

FlowersJustFlowers (11.22.2013.11:58PM): It is it is my fault she is gone and it is all my fault

Neverender (11.23.2013.12:27AM): I'm so sorry you've lost someone. It never gets easier, but please don't blame yourself. The Simulacrum is the only one to blame.

FlowersJustFlowers (11.23.2013.12:34AM): You don't understand I came from another world I did Terrible Things to stay here and now this world keeps shifting around me likes and I did this she is gone and it is all my fault

Neverender (11.23.2013.12:36AM): What are you talking about?

TheLostSheepKing (11.23.2013.12:40AM): Which part don't you understand?

Neverender (11.23.2013.12:41AM): Sorry, I was confused for a second. It's late here.

JstPssngThrgh001 (11.23.2013.12:45AM): You said you came from another world FlowersJustFlowers. I'm curious about your mode of travel. Do you mind sharing?

FlowersJustFlowers (11.23.2013.12:50AM): Blinks every fifth and 7 in an alternating pattern.

TheLostSheepKing (11.23.2013.12:52AM): Oh god. That's hellish.

JstPssngThrgh001 (11.23.2013.1:03AM): That is unusual. Reminds me of the musical meter. If it's true, the repetition suggests design.

TheLostSheepKing (11.23.2013.1:07AM): Or a cruel sense of humor. That's a terrible time signature.

BENthoven__420__69 (11.23.2013.1:25AM): I mean, it's more that it's not really a meter unto itself, as 5/7 would be indistinguishable from 5/8, which would be much easier to read. Alternating bars of 5/8 and 7/8 would make sense, but that's not something that I think many people would immediately think of if presented with a pattern of five then seven. A bar of 5/7 could make sense in the context of another time signature conceivably, but denominators that are odd numbers are vanishingly rare. A septuplet is a septuplet by virtue of the fact that seven of them fit in whatever musical space you assign them, but if you want them to be the base rhythmic unit a bar is measured in their function as a septuplet immediately vanishes; 7/7 is just 7/8, and 5/7 is just 5/8 (or 5/4 or 5/2, depending on whether you're using eighth notes or quarter notes or half notes in the notation). No, I think we can safely rule out "time signature" as an explanation.

TheLostSheepKing (11.23.2013.1:17AM): Awesome. Thanks for the explanation. Totally needed all that.

Cartographer218 (11.23.2013.2:30AM): Yesterday I was walking down the street at midday when a young woman passed me. I thought I recognized her so I turned around. When I did, she was farther than I thought she should be, like the sidewalk had expanded between us. I considered calling out but thought it would be strange; I didn't know her by name even if I knew her. But she also stopped, and then she turned to face me in much the same way I had moments before. We watched each other as the crowd moved between us. She said, Mother? and rushed up to me. I tried to turn away, but she had me by the arm. She said, Listen, we have to leave this world. It's dangerous. I shook my head. She sounded insane. She said, Mother, your scent keeps vanishing and I keep losing track of you. I began to tremble. I don't know why. She asked me if I recognized her. I told her to please let me go. She looked around frantically. People were staring at us. She started again, her voice lower. She said, This world is unstable. I can get us out, but you need to come with me now. I asked her if she was from the forum. It didn't seem like a stupid question at the time. The woman began to cry. She called me mother again, but did not finish her statement; the sun came out from behind a building behind us and when it hit her eyes the irises changed from dark brown to a startling green. It had to be a trick of the light, but her skin brightened too, from copper to pale white, the tears drying on her cheeks. My head started to hurt and I felt faint. The strange young woman looked around again, but this time she seemed lost. She turned to me and asked me if I knew where the Copley T-stop was. I smiled and pointed the way.

(*I am sorry. I need to lie down again.*)

BLOOD CALUMNY

Joe Koch

KEUIN DIDN'T WANT to share a room with their mother. In the tiny house after the divorce, she said they didn't have a choice. Telling this to Bastien while lighting a cigarette to appear casual, because their hands and mouth need something to do in the huge chasm between speaking and waiting to be judged, need anything other than Bastien's hurt silence, Bastien's head turning away; Kevin insists it's nothing personal. "It's not you, it's me. I can't be with anyone. Not like this."

Alone again, because it's what they asked for—now isn't it? Kevin crushes what's left of their cigarette, dumps the contents of the ashtray in the outdoor bin, and washes their hands longer than they really need to. Puts the ashtray in the nightstand drawer with the remnants of a pack of camels, a bad brand and a bad habit from college that Kevin gave up years ago.

Well, mostly gave up. Kevin's not a saint.

They're not responsible for what it does though, either, because it's not their choice, it never has been, and if Bastien or anyone else could understand—but they can't. The blood, the tears, the murders— bnand now that Kevin's older, the heat, the rage, the unpredictable eruptions that never came like clockwork and come now hard with increasing frequency and capricious vengeance against the host. The parasite people call a blessing.

It's not like Kevin hasn't tried to have it taken out.

Planned Parenthood in nineteen eighty-seven, University Women's Center in nineteen ninety-two, Ladies First Fem-Care in ninety-nine, Planned Parenthood again in zero-one, Sweet Valley

Whole Woman's Health in twenty-ten, and on and on for nearly fifty years, a litany of providers saying *dear* and *hon* and *Miss Kevin,* reciting a litany of excuses with clucking tongues. It doesn't matter if Kevin's a big, hairy guy waving money in their faces and begging them to get the monster out. The minute Kevin hits an exam table, the clucking starts.

Left to take matters into their own hands, Kevin closes the tobacco drawer in the nightstand. Modeled on an apothecary cabinet with eight stacked compartments, it hides a hatch holding errata shipped across the country after their father died. Masculine objects recall life before the onset: coins, pocket knives, a rusted harmonica, marbles, an old watch. Kevin decides on a military folding knife with a three and a half inch blade. Opens the knife and places it next to their phone charger in easy reach.

In the tiny house, after the divorce, sharing a room with mom because the girls were older, the girls deserved privacy, Kevin's arguments dismissed as selfish. Kevin can't sleep. Not with their mother fighting off blankets like an invisible assailant. The house asleep, the world asleep, their mother unconscious, Kevin cornered in the extra bed between the thrashing woman and the bedroom door. Her sleeping body kicks and flails. Face flops over in Kevin's direction, pouring sweat. A smile crawls onto her slack lips. Mouth emits a pleasured moan. There's a smell of rotten musk; something meaty and slippery releases itself from tangled legs and sheets. Wet noises slop out, and a limping shadow skulks away, wandering the walls and ceiling in the darkness. Kevin freezes, stares, tracks its progress. Lumbering like a giant slug, thick and moist, it blends into the rustling curtains and merges with tossed blankets. It unfurls in recessed corners where the moonlight can't reach. Dangles for an hour above Kevin's toy chest; sways like an extra appendage from the ceiling lamp. Swims through pools of shadow poured between furniture and floor. Finally prowling to the foot of their mother's bed, turning in circles like an angry cat, it wiggles beneath the disordered covers and squeezes back into its hiding place with a loud pop.

In the morning, Kevin's mother tries to hide the stain. *Don't be scared. I'm going through the change. Someday you'll understand.*

Sometimes in the suppurating nighttime shadows, it gets lost.

Meandering senile, perched atop a tall dresser next to their mother's handbag, working its two thick, prehensile loops around to imitate the shape. Thudding on the floor and lying immobile for hours as if drunk. Kevin can't hide in the bathroom or stay awake all night watching the wandering lump of shiny musculature with its trailing webs of fat. Sooner or later, Kevin has to sleep.

One night they wake up in the dark. Their mother snores. Stuffed animals guard the L-shaped perimeter of Kevin's cramped bed. Kevin reaches for the safety of a favorite plush elephant, its floppy ears deformed by moonlight. The soft, furry body presses against Kevin's chest, but the trunk is slick, wet, and smelly. Kevin doesn't remember dropping the toy in the toilet or having an accident.

When they understand what their senses are saying, it's too late to throw the thing against the wall and escape its embrace.

If Kevin tried to explain the invasion to Bastien, imagine the derision. *You're not telling me you really believe that, are you? All kids have bad dreams.* Yes, Kevin would have to confirm. That is exactly what I believe. And then Kevin would have to talk about the murders.

Because it's never been enough for the parasite to co-opt a habitat inside Kevin's body, first snip, snip, snipping away at the natural epithelial barrier, then ballooning inward with murderous suction, and last looping its flexible appended egg sacs through painful ligatures, stringing bubble-soft proliferations within the cradle of Kevin's bones. Kevin's mother exhausted as a host, the parasite throbbing with new life. Kevin clotted with abdominal gristle as it spits irregular blood. Wandering still, it comes back sated with strange blood; black, brown, elastic, and stringy; smelling of foreign anatomies; pitted with liverish clumps. What it kills, Kevin never questions. It moves like a thief. Kevin catches it with the knife.

Marks on the nightstand, the mattress, the hardwood floor: failed impalements. Kevin feels it fighting dormancy as they age, yet still it weighs heavy, holding on inside them between erratic manic travels and explosive gore. Gone for days, maybe a whole week now, and god knows Bastien can't be allowed to stay over, can't be the next witness or victim; Kevin waits alone, armed as the sun goes down, pretending to sleep. A shadow in the dark, a lump in the sheets. All the reasons Kevin never lets a lover spend the night.

It rears. Kevin strikes.

Try explaining the knife to Bastien, the cries of the thing strong and unruly after a bloody jaunt. Insistent on its territorial claim to Kevin, it wrestles with smooth muscle and fallopian fists though stabbed and blubbering. If it squealed madly, Kevin might have the guts to kill it. Instead, pinned on the nightstand, slickly twisting, globs of empathic fat flinging, it weeps. Coagulates of mourning, choruses of outrage for the loud injustices against those who bear it, the parasite pleads for the oneness of mercy.

Did she know?

Kevin wonders, and doubt destroys resolve. Litanies of maybe, of anti-abraxas, of Hecate burning. Earthly trinities work their binding legacy upon Kevin's unquiet rebellion, begging acceptance. The subtle ache and absence. The horror cloying, wet, and warm. The spongy egg sacs sticking to Kevin's wrist, parasite climbing their arm, ripping open as it pulls free of the severing blade. Escapes the knife with its fundus spliced.

It sticks, and Kevin can't resist. Piercing like a mole, it spreads where Kevin is tender, working them apart. It lingers with maternal affinity. That in which Kevin gestated now gestates angrily inside them.

Kevin coughs up a clot of blonde hair in the kitchen sink. They know better than to risk the bathroom where the mirror reflects a true crime line up of lost lives. A dead-naming phlebotomist. A cop minimizing a threat. Store clerks saying ma'am. Strangers telling them to smile. Vengeance perpetrated against ignorant offenders, inconsistent visions shared by the parasite in its homing state, dreaming as Kevin vomits guilt like a reluctant, unborn twin.

Worst are the unknown trolls, the faces Kevin can't recognize, for unlike the foreign thing that hunts and comes back to nest in their body, Kevin can't read thoughts. They've cancelled all their social accounts. They plug their ears when gossip starts. Kevin can't carry the burden of the parasite's reprisals. They curse the media for broadcasting the personal opinions of the rich and famous, for encouraging discourse as if embedded bias was up for debate. Every keyword blocked, news seeps through.

Kevin agrees with the parasite that hatred is not negotiable.

The sight of the beloved icon's face bloated in strangulation, hair swathed around the neck and laced over the eyes like a perverse wedding veil, her swollen tongue popping through the long, blonde gauze, its red tip turning grey; the outcry of fans in grief and shock; it's too much for Kevin to bear.

Nine-one-one to report a crime. Alone in the dark, the shadow lump listening inside, oh god, it knows, please hurry; Kevin waits for a call back. A sarcastic operator, another transferred call. After midnight, with instructions to stay home, they wait for the detective to follow up. Hours later, a ringtone Kevin hardly recognizes. A deep, weary monotone.

So your uterus wanders—
Not mine. Hers. My mother.
Okay, so your mother's uterus wanders around killing people.
Yes.
But it lives inside you.
Yes.
And it's happened before. The killing.
Well, yes.
And you didn't do anything to stop it?
You don't understand. I—
We have a witness that places you in your home on the night in question at ten. How did you cross the Atlantic so fast?
I told you, it's not me—
Oh right, right. So your little friend did it.
If you insist on calling it that.
Sorry, your mother's little friend. Did it sprout little wings?
I—I just want it to stop.
Let me give you a bit of advice. My wife is about your age and she—
Kevin fumbles and hangs up.

The creature stirs. Morning's half-light quiets its rumblings, but there's no doubt the tenor of Kevin's restless night has renewed the prospective hit list. *Half the local police force*, Kevin frets, trying their best not to wish ill on the patronizing bastards, trying not to fuel the fire with vengeful thoughts. Perhaps the parasite wants nothing more than respect, like an old person sent out to pasture. It's old, at least twice as old as Kevin, and who knows how old it was before it made its way into their mother's mind, body, life.

Did she know?

Kevin hunts for clues in her curse: *Someday you'll understand.*

In response, the restless, kindred organ stretches its misplaced muscles, releasing a fast, unexpected river of blood that shoots down Kevin's leg. Pooled in their shoe, streaked on pants and bedding, splattered on the floor all the way to the bathroom in lavish drops. A bristling sensation of needles feeds on their skin. If Kevin questions how much their mother loved them, they dismiss the obvious answer in a heated decision during clean-up.

Quick, on the phone, before they lose their nerve: "I've been thinking it over. What you said about moving forward."

Bastien, wary as hell: "What happened last night? The fucking police called."

"The thing is this. I think you're right. It's time I quit running away from commitment."

"You do? Why now?"

Kevin, biting their lip. If there were any other way—but Kevin's done their time serving the unwanted inheritance. Bastien is young enough to handle the legacy, young enough to fight off public calumny, a generation younger than Kevin and reared on social justice. Bastien doesn't have murderous thoughts like Kevin, and if they find out no one can kill it—

Kevin says, "Do you want to come over and spend the night?"

LEMMINGS

Kirstyn McDermott

YOU LIKELY KNOW the game by now, or at least know of it. Can picture the little dudes, with their shock of green hair and blue . . . overalls? Onesies? Athleisure wear? Who can tell from a handful of pixels? Marching in lockstep as lemmings do, right over the edge of a cliff, or into a bubbling green tank of acid, or mangled by one of the gear machines. Just a handful of pixels, though, and not a one of them ever turning red. It was a big deal, back in its day—sales and rankings and countless obsessive hours eaten up chasing the quickest time, the highest percentage, level after addictive goddamn level. But if you've played the game, it's been on an emulator, right? Appreciating the retro graphics and simplistic mechanics, shaking your head over the clunky controls and wondering how people sat still for shit like this for so long, wondering that even as it winds you in and whispers its second-hand nostalgia right into your cortex—if nostalgia can be the right word for a time you never knew. Because if you did know it, if you weren't just alive but old enough to play the game on your Commodore 64 or fledgling PC or, hell, the original Amiga version, then you're here on another mission. You're reading this for answers, or clues at the very least. You're shopping for reasons, but we're fresh out of those. (See also: toilet paper, hand sanitiser, unsullied dreams.) We don't know why. We only know what. And we knew it first.

***

Finally. Jinx screenshots the end-of-level infodump before carefully transcribing the next level code into her notebook, just in case. She's lost screenshots before and, besides, there's something about having all the level codes written down in her own hand that feels comforting. That feels real. Listed down the page in chunky blue capitals, it looks like Egyptian hieroglyphs or notes a Russian spy might keep. Of course, what would be even better is if she could just put a pin in her progress each session, but the game dates back from before genius programmers thought up the whole "save game" concept. Whatever. *Lemmings* is worth it, the best of the bunch of archaic video games that Tyler hooked them into back when lockdown looked like only lasting till the end of term. Three months later and Jinx has ditched them all—*Lode Runner*, *Prince of Persia*, *Archon*, a dozen others she can't even remember now— and is patiently eking out her fave at the rate of no more than one new level a day. It's a dead game, frozen in silicone, and once she's played it through, she's played it forever.

Sitting on its charger, her phone sounds the bleat of a fainting goat, the novelty alert weeks past its best-by but Jinx can't summon the effort to change it. The message is from Cazz, peppered with multiple emojis: several astonished faces, three different gravestones, and a purple cat. There's always a purple cat.

seen it yet???

Jinx thumbs a response. *seen what???*

omg!! the SUICIDE its evrywhr!!

She doesn't even have time to open TikTok before her bedroom door swings wide and there's her dad, hand outstretched, face caught somewhere between furious and terrified. Jinx remembers that look from those last days with her mum, driving home from hospice each night, her dad clutching the steering wheel so tight she expected to see indentations in the vinyl cover when he finally let go.

"Phone," he says. "Now."

Jinx rolls her eyes, trying for casual. Her stomach isn't having it, is already churning up a fresh batch of anxiety. "What, I can't even talk to my friends now?"

"That's not . . . please, the phone."

She locks it before surrendering. Her dad switches the device off, shoves it into the back pocket of his jeans. When he sits down on the bed, it's right near the edge, as far from her as he can manage to keep, and the mattress sags dramatically. He wobbles, rights himself. Jinx wants to laugh, but worries she might not stop.

"It's not a punishment, Janelle." He's staring at the ground between his feet, like the manky grey carpet holds infinitely more interest than his daughter's face ever could. "Your school texted me. There's something going around the socials right now, so best if you stay off them for a bit, yeah? Just till it's cleaned up."

Jinx shrugs, whatever, no big deal, like her phone isn't a lifeline of any kind. "A virus?"

"Just a video. Some sick f—person who thinks it's funny to scare kids."

"I've probably seen worse."

He does look at her then. She wishes he hadn't. It's worse than the mum-is-dying face, somehow, even though Jinx doesn't really know how to decode it with any precision. Like Jinx killed his puppy, is how she might describe it to Cazz, or maybe like Jinx is the puppy.

"You haven't been out today, right?" Her dad stands, absently reaches round to pat the phone still in his pocket. "Why don't you go for a walk, kiddo? Get some fresh air."

Fresh air wasn't something they used to worry about much, till lockdown. Now it's all *go outside* this, *get your exercise* that, sixty minutes, five kays, blah blah blah. No one she actually knows lives within five kays; she hasn't seen her friends outside of a screen since forever. Sometimes she catches herself wondering if they still exist, if they aren't just data on a server somewhere, blipping into life at her beck and call.

What if all we ever were is data, she asked Cazz a couple of weeks back. *Would we even know any different?*

The girl on the screen stared at her through a pinkish orange fringe, uneven home-colour job that didn't really take but, hey, that's what filters are for. *Keep it together, girl. Don't matrix-out on me.*

"Janelle?" Her dad snaps two fingers in front of her face. "Exercise?"

Jinx scowls. "Okay if I get dressed first?" She grabs the hem of her pyjama top, makes a show of being about to yank it over her head. Her dad flinches and flees the room, leaving the door pointedly ajar behind him. She waits until she hears him messing about in the kitchen before retrieving her old phone from where she's stashed it between the mattress and base. The thing is stone-cold dead and doesn't have a working SIM, but she finds an old cable and plugs it in beneath the desk. By the time she gets back, it'll be charged and ready to suck down some Wi-Fi.

Jinx smiles as she pulls on her shoes and grabs a clean mask. Like she wouldn't keep a spare.

***

In real life, lemmings are a monumental disappointment. Small arctic hamsters, or some distant cousin, brown and tailless with a penchant for extreme cliff-diving if their population gets out of control, or so you'll no doubt have heard. It's not even the weirdest notion to have attached itself to them. Lemmings spontaneously generating within storms and falling from the sky like fat, furry hailstones. Lemmings harbouring a rage so cataclysmic they eventually explode, strewing pelts and body parts all over the landscape for naïve naturalists to stumble over. But lemmings as suicide squad, blindly following one another to their collective doom—that's the story that stuck, thanks mostly to Disney. An intrepid group of documentarians on the payroll of an altogether different rodent, trudging through the arctic wilderness to capture on film the fabled mass migration of lemmings, cameras unflinching as the animals tumbled from a cliff to splash into the choppy, frigid waters of the ocean below. The filmmakers even nabbed an Academy Award. But it's all a goddamned lie. Alberta, to start with, not the Arctic circle. Inuit kids contracted to bring in the lemmings, the bounty a few pennies a piece. A giant turntable swinging those same confused creatures around again and again, that old animation background trick rejigged for close focus. And then the grand finale: herding the lemmings towards the edge, over the edge, little claws no doubt scrabbling for any kind of purchase as they realised the fatality of their error. The desperation of their fall. The terror of their end. It was never suicide; we want you to see that. It was nothing less than mass murder.

***

The bin at the edge of the park is overflowing. Takeaway coffee cups mostly, and some disposable masks, their thin, white elastic twisted yet intact. Jinx remembers the short clip someone shared a couple of weeks ago: those clumps of used masks on beaches, in riverbeds, clinging to grassy verges; death-traps tangled around the legs of sea birds and other critters, one even found in the belly of a dead turtle. *Be responsible*, the voiceover pleaded, *tear off the elastic before you throw your mask away!* Such a simple request, the work of less than a second, less than a thought, and yet.

For a brief, hope-thin moment back there it looked like things might be starting to change. People bringing their own coffee cups to cafes, their own bags to supermarkets. Single-use plastics on the way out, recycling on the rise. Maybe, just maybe there was a corner being turned, however slowly, however reluctantly—or smugly, depending on the type of zero-waste lifestyle you could afford to lead.

But now, one panicked whiff of pandemic, and it's all gone to shit.

Single use *everything* and all anyone's talking about is COVID, infection rates, death counts, and how soon a vaccine might be produced. No one's looking more than two steps in front of them anymore.

Jinx remembers the climate protests last year, marching elbow to elbow with Cazz as they brandished their hand-lettered *THERE IS NO PLANET B* sign—complete with a wonky blue and green ball that only looked like Earth if you squinted generously enough— yelling for change, yelling for action, yelling because it made them feel strong and fierce and seen for once in their lives. And for what? For fucking *what?*

She kicks the bin. A coffee cup at the top of the pile teeters and falls to the grass below. She kicks the bin again, harder this time, feeling the metal reverberate beneath the sole of her booted foot. And again.

"What the hell do you think you're doing?"

The man is standing a couple of metres away, fists braced on his hips. He's about her dad's age, maybe older, and is wearing his blue disposable mask beneath his nose. In his hand is a takeaway coffee cup.

"What do you think *you're* doing?" Jinx shouts back.

His eyes narrow and he points to the rubbish that's tumbled from the bin. "Pick all that up, you little brat."

Jinx feels flushed, like when she's embarrassed, only this time she's really not. This time, the heat floods from a dark and livid well deep inside her, floods molten through her limbs until her hands are shaking and her teeth clench tight enough to crack. She wrenches off her own mask and marches up to the man.

"You pick it up," she yells at him. "It's your mess, you fucking pick it up. All of it. It's not my job to clean up after you, you . . . *arsehole!*"

Alarmed, the man steps back a pace, muttering something that Jinx can't quite catch, although the words *crazy* and *bitch* manage to make it through the triple-ply. She swallows, all too aware now of the other people in the park, all of them staring straight at her. Nearby, a mother holds her little boy close to her legs, pushing the kid behind her like Jinx might be about to rush them next. Almost all the adults are wearing masks and it's unnerving how she can only see their eyes—or not, because so many of them have sunglasses on as well. It's like they're robots, or aliens. It's like that old movie that Tyler made them watch about the creepy pods that hatched things that looked just like you except they weren't, and Jinx wonders if the park people aren't all about to point at her and scream.

Her heart beats hard in her chest and Jinx just can't anymore. She sucks in a deep breath and yells at the man one last time, a wordless guttural roar that means everything and nothing and hollows her to a spent and brittle husk.

Then she runs.

***

There is the tiniest fraction of truth in the lemming-suicide myth, a seed from which the tales grew tall. They take things to extremes, those little rodents. Tundra-bound in winter, digging through the snow for buried grasses and moss, excavating a subterranean metropolis of tunnels and burrows and generally living the hardest of hardscrabble lives. Come spring, though, they're off to the high country to hang out among the trees and heath-patched plains, catch some rays and pretty much fuck so damn prolifically that every three or four years they reach critical mass, population wise.

Too many lemmings, not enough food, not enough space, not enough of anything except more lemmings, and so off they go. Wave after furry wave they migrate, very nearly all of them dying along the way. Starvation, thirst, hypothermia, exhaustion and yeah, getting your throat torn open by your buddy over the last blade of cottongrass, or because he just doesn't like your face. You'd get tetchy too, resources stretched so slim and no promised land in sight. But enough of them survive, the species skimming extinction's edge but nevertheless managing to keep their grip, and the whole vicious cycle begins again. It'd be easier, you'd think, to simply keep things under control. To manage your shit with a little more finesse year to year and so avoid the very real risk you'll end up a forgotten, decomposing carcass on the road to nowhere in particular. But they're only lemmings. They can't see that far ahead.

***

Her old phone is almost fully charged by the time Jinx has nuked herself a cup of instant noodles—because her dad won't let her slink back to her room without taking something to eat with her and the microwave is quicker than arguing. Sitting on her bed, she slurps wet carbs into her mouth with a fork while she waits out the interminable updates, signing in to the most vital apps, putting her notifications on silent. The vid has already been pulled from TikTok but who cares when it's been copied and uploaded to any number of places since. Her friends have been passing new links around like swap cards; nothing online ever dies.

Jinx puts in her earbuds, glances up to make sure her door is closed. Taps play.

It starts with sky blue, a wisp of clouds, then pans swiftly down to a boy who looks maybe a year or two older than her. Dark, shaggy hair and a smile that wobbles at the edges. Angry rash of acne along his jawbone but still cute, in a sort of K-Pop way, if K-Pop boys could ever give up their filters. Wherever he is, it's windy and behind him, around him, are the tops of tall buildings. He's high, wherever he is. He's really high.

We are the virus, he says. The wind snips the edges of his words. *And we are also the cure.*

Another smile that stretches a beat too long, that looks scared and certain and about as wrong as a smile can look and—

—he jumps. No, falls. No, *lets* himself fall. Backwards and over and down and it's so fast it can't be real, must be staged, some clever trick and the boy is going to leap up from the bottom of the frame any second and yell, *fooled you suckers!*

Except the camera was so steady, leaning forward over the edge to track the descent as its subject flailed and grew smaller and—stopped. It wasn't a selfie. Someone was holding that phone, up on the rooftop with the boy, knowing what he was planning to do the whole time. Probably the same person who uploaded the vid in the first place.

Jinx's cheeks are hot.

She taps replay. Because there's something . . . right at the end . . . there: when the boy lands (dies), you can't see it clearly through the burst of pixels that's been put in over the top. A minor explosion of blue, green and white, like a tiny cartoon firework . . . *replay*: that sound, another digital manipulation edited in post, and she knows that sound.

She *knows* it. Jinx replays the last few seconds. And again.

It's from the game. The noise a lemming makes when it falls too far to land safely, that weird computerised *squish* that sounds remarkably akin to something very soft hitting something very, very hard. The explosion is from the game as well—the primitive pixel spray of lemming meeting ground. Someone took it all and edited it into this vid. To obscure the worst? To be funny? What kind of sick fuck thinks it's cool to make a joke of this?

Jinx replays the vid, again and again until her stomach threatens to send back the noodles, express service, no signature required.

"Okay," she whispers. "Enough now."

There are dozens of alerts and notifications all over her apps, messages from Cazz and Tyler and a bunch of group chats with randoms from school who've tagged her in the general frenetic buzz of *OMG* and *WTF* and *have you seen?*

A fresh DM pops up from Cazz who must've noticed she's back online.

whats up with all this shit??

yeah, Jinx messages back, *its fucked. that poor kid*

which one??

which what?

Over the next hour or so they find eight more. Different kids, different cities and times of day, but otherwise a terrible familiarity to them all. *We are the virus. And we are also the cure.* The same pixelated explosion as they hit the pavement, the grass, the water, the body already sprawled broken on the ground. The same squishy sound effect that seems less and less ridiculous the more Jinx hears it. *We are the virus. And we are also the cure.* Another handful by the time her dad knocks on the door to say that dinner is ready and Jinx shoves the phone under her pillow in case he comes in and confiscates it as well.

She eats as much of the home-delivered green curry as she can manage, which isn't much at all, and mumbles something about not feeling well when her dad notices.

He throws her a sharp glance, reaches out to touch her face. "Fever?"

Jinx flinches. "Jesus, it's not COVID, okay? I'm just not hungry."

He lets her go back to her room. Where she curls up beneath her doona and searches and taps and swipes until she can barely keep her eyes open. Until all she can see when she closes them is that fucking pixelated explosion. There are so many, mostly kids around her age give or take a couple of years but a couple of people who looked like they were in their twenties maybe. It's trending on Twitter and Facebook too. It's trending everywhere. Jinx keeps searching.

We are the virus. And we are also the cure.

Replay.

***

The lemmings in the game, they're organised. *Organisable* at least. Climbing, building, digging, bashing, floating—together they command a skill set that will see the whole tribe through the deadly array of obstacles and safely home. Most of them, anyway. Most of the time. Not the blockers, who plant themselves with arms outstretched, foot tapping in refusal as they shake their heads back and forth. *No. You shall not pass. There be dragons . . . or acid, or lava or a fall from which you won't recover. Turn back, stay safe.* And the other lemmings do, and they are. You'd think, wouldn't you, that the blockers would get to go home too? Once their job is done and all their buddies are successfully warned away, they could simply *unblock* and bring up the rear. But once a blocker, forever a blocker, holding the line until the clock runs down to zero. Unless you get bored of waiting and make them a bomber instead—the other specialist who won't ever see a warm burrow again. 5-4-3-2-1: POP! Five tiny white pixels be all that's left of those dudes. Blasting a necessary access point can be the only way through sometimes and they take up the mantle so readily. Hunkered down, hands on head as they shudder and shake, beeping out a tinny *Oh no!* just before they explode. It's cute, if you don't think too hard about it. But if you do think about it—all those stoic little blockers and bombers sacrificing themselves to warn the others, to forge an escape route they can never, ever take—then you might see things differently. They're *brave*, those lemmings. The bravest collection of pixels to ever grace a screen.

***

At 6:18 a.m. the multi-storey parking lot at the shopping centre is all but deserted. A handful of cars on the ground floor, spaced out and shadowed in thin dawn light, and it's one of the creepiest things Jinx has seen. Post-apocalyptic. The stairwell smells bad, rancid with stale piss. She pulls the collar of her shirt over her nose as she hauls herself up the several flights to the roof. It's hard work on so little sleep.

Out here the air is clear, crisp with the chill of early winter, and Jinx sucks it deep into her lungs. She's never paid attention to the view before: the surrounding suburbs unfolding around her, the roads eerily empty of commuter traffic. A few people are out running or walking their dogs but they all look so small and distant, like they're not really part of the world. Or like Jinx isn't.

"Hey!"

The girl is sitting against the wall of the car park, tucked into the corner opposite the stairwell. She pushes herself to her feet as Jinx approaches, tucks her curly brown hair behind her ears. Her t-shirt is bright pink with a unicorn across the chest. Its mane and tail are painted with rainbow glitter.

"Hey," Jinx echoes, offering a timid wave.

The girl looks her up and down, eyes narrowed. "We are the virus?"

Jinx pauses. "Oh, right. And we are also the cure."

The girl with the unicorn shirt nods. "I was wondering if anyone else would think of this place."

"Yeah." Jinx looks over the edge of the railing to the entrance below. Empty bitumen, a clear line of sight. "It's pretty high."

"High enough anyway. A few good seconds, right?"

Jinx leans back, rubs her upper arms.

The girl is holding out her iPhone. It looks like a new model. Expensive, encased in bling. "Have you done this before? Filmed, I mean? Obviously."

Jinx shakes her head.

"Okay, no probs. I'm signed in to everything you'll need." She spends a few minutes walking Jinx through. How to record and save, how to find the sound file and filter, how to edit, how to upload and tag and share, and even though Jinx knows almost all of it already, she lets the girl tell her, lets her tell her twice even. "Got it?

"Got it."

"You sure? There won't be a second take."

"I got it." Gently, Jinx takes the phone from the girl's outstretched hand. "Do you think . . . do you think this will work? Do you think it will make any difference?"

The girl shrugs and climbs up onto the railing. "At least we're doing something. And a few less people in the world can't be a bad thing, you know." She swings a leg over the top, spreads her arms wide. "You feel it, right? The connection? Being a part of something bigger than just yourself? Maybe if more people felt like that we wouldn't be here."

"Maybe," Jinx whispers. She steps up to the railing, phone ready.

"Hey." The girl grabs Jinx by the wrist, her dilated pupils as flat as drops of oil on a garage floor. "You're not going to flake, are you? I've heard that's happened. You know, like, people not filming, dropping the phone. Or not posting after."

"I got you," Jinx says. "Promise."

And she does. Keeping the girl centre frame as she speaks her final lines, following her descent all the way down. It's so fast, Jinx's hands only start to shake as she's editing the clip, making sure the little burst of pixels cover the girl's legs, the broken way they twist on the bitumen, and also the halo that glistens and seeps from beneath her head.

Once the video is posted, Jinx sinks to the ground. She switches off the screen and leans the phone against the concrete wall. She never asked the girl what she should do with it, after. Never even asked the girl her name. Jinx closes her eyes. Her hands aren't shaking anymore and maybe she can feel it, a million fragile filaments stretching out from her fingertips and into the world, snaking and sparking their way through the air, through Wi-Fi and Bluetooth and data driven on currents of 5G, seeking connection and, finding it, calling them all to arms. Calling them all home.

The hinges on the stairwell door screech and Jinx looks over as a boy in a grey beanie steps onto the roof. He sees her and raises a hand, more in salute than a wave, then starts towards where she's sitting.

Jinx pulls her phone from her pocket. She can't really describe it, the calmness spreading through her body. It's not that she isn't scared, but still. It's like there's a very thin, very strong cord anchored in her sternum, guiding her forward. Gently. Firmly. She's never been more sure of anything.

Holding the phone up to her face, she presses record. "Dad? I love you, okay? You're not . . . this isn't your fault." The boy in the beanie is close now. "Don't watch, okay? Please don't watch." She stops recording, texts it to her dad.

The boy has stopped a couple of metres away. "Um, hi."

Jinx straightens, swipes at an errant tear. The cord in her chest tightens and tugs. Taking a deep breath, she holds the boy's gaze. His eyes are green, bright as bottle-glass and just as hard. Jinx holds out her phone.

"We are the virus."

****

And we are also the cure. And we are also the cure. And we are also the cure. And we are also the cure. And we are also the cure. And we are also the cure. And we are also the cure. And we are also the cure. And we are also the cure. And we are also the cure. And we are also the cure. And we are also the cure. And we are also the cure. And we are also the cure. And we are also the cure. And we are also the cure. And we are also the cure. And we are also the

cure. And we are also the cure. And we are also the cure. And we
are also the cure. And we are also the cure. And we are also the
cure. And we are also the cure. And we are also the cure. And we
are also the cure. And we are also the cure. And we are also the
cure. And we are also the cure. And we are also the cure. And we
are also the cure. And we are also the cure. And we are also the
cure.
    And
    we
    are
    also
    the
       cure.

WATER GOES, SAND REMAINS

Jolie Toomajan

1

THE MONASTERY OF VARAG *was built in 653 in honor of Saint Hripsime, she of the ripped tongue, the plucked eyes, and the carved body. The Monastery suffered her same fate— ransacked, dismantled, insides pulled out. Countries formed just to raid this one building. It brought the Mongols, then the Persians, then a minor Turkish prince; each kingdom waiting a few hundred years for its chance to run away with jewel- encrusted cups, to have a tabernacle of their very own. The treasures eventually lost their luster and became an easy prize, so a hundred years or so ago, the Ottoman pashas strangled the bishop at the altar instead. The monastery was then converted into a printing house and school; right before I was born, the teachers and students were slaughtered, right on schedule, right on cue. They will destroy it this time, too.*

What I am saying is, this story is old.

***

Kharpert, Manazkert, Keghi, and Ahlat—gone. Adamakert emptied of us, bodies left to rot in the sun or bloat in the drinking wells. My father left Van weeks ago to evacuate his mother from Arjesh and never came back. This is how you lost people now. No news, no condolences, no burials. One day they were just gone from your vision, and some you barely noticed.

When I could not sleep for thinking about it, I played a game with our names, tried to lead them somewhere good.

Mariam. Short form: Maro-with-a-soft-*a*, but still the idea of bones, of cores, of being cracked and devoured.

Lusine. Mother Mama Mayr Moon—only visible at night and only partially.

Lili. A flower. Of God. Of the night. Either way, a thing to be crushed.

I dreamed of my father with flies in his eyes. In the mornings, I turned Mayr's empty demitasse upside down and studied the dregs. I saw only devils.

***

Men gathered at our house in the middle of the night. Because I was 15 and because I was a girl, I was invisible to them, but I remember their faces, their black waxed moustaches, their noses dipping over the rims of cups while they drank. They filled the rooms, spilled into the yard, crouched on top of our table, planning the defense down to a hair.

Mayr would be tending the wounded; any other option would be perverse. Before he disappeared, my father owned the pharmacy, and Mayr learned everything he could possibly teach her. Then she learned everything he could not. The Garden's women would see her instead of the hospital doctors to stitch wounds and set bones, clean and treat a variety of infections, treat infertility and pregnancy, and cure poisonings—accidental or otherwise.

When they told Mayr she would be cooking and sewing clothes and not treating the wounded, she nodded and offered a tray of tart coffees to the crowd of men. She walked past me like I didn't exist.

***

Mayr's figure stole across the lawn. When she reached the path leading to the lakeshore, Mrs. Vahanian stepped out of the tree line and took her hand. They disappeared a few feet into the path, the deep night closing behind them like a door. After a moment, the other mothers—Mrs. Krikorian, Mrs. Sarkesian, Mrs. Boyajian—followed in procession. I inched towards Lili Vahanian, who stooped in her mother's early spinach, leaning over our shared garden wall. The rope of her black braid hung over her shoulder, and she traced her middle finger and thumb over her clavicles like she wanted to wear herself away. In Old City, something burned.

"Why are they going to the lake in the middle of the night?" I whispered. Lili shrugged.

"Do you think this is about the assignments?" I continued.

"Nobody wants to cook and sew, maybe they are trying to figure a way out of it. Especially your mother."

A sloshing cut through the blackness and Lili flinched. Her forearm jumped under my hand, and I gripped tighter. Rhythmic splashing vibrated in the air, a large sound—much larger than any noise our mothers could have made—and violating, probing. Sound that entered and filled you.

I angled nearer to Lili, who curved herself the other way, towards the lake, straining to hear more. She smelled of forget-me-nots and burned flour, and I could feel the warmth of her body through my shirt. Gunshots cracked in Old City. Lili's name shot from my mouth, a warning. I dropped her wrist and ran back inside.

2

St. Grigor made his home at the Monastery of Nareg overlooking the town of Tondrak. There he burned with the glory of God, convulsing in ecstasy in the hallways. A list of miseries emerged from him, written and rewritten as Grigor tore his shirts and threw himself to the floor, shamed with the rush of blood and the knowledge of his own distance. Grigor screamed for God to notice him, and because God was too busy dealing with Grigor, the town of Tondrak advanced past them both.

The Tondrak peasants met in the hot springs that poured from the mountain at the center of the island and washed their sins into steam. They cupped calefacient water to their lips and pressed those same lips against each other. Men and women, the poor and the lords, the most and the least, each should be held as holy as the next, they said. They stormed through the city, still streaming water from their bodies, leaking vapor, mad with equity. They dismantled the castles brick by brick and then dismantled the lords. They retreated to the hot springs, built a new town around the pools, and lived there in accord with nature. Everyone being as Gods.

Buried deep in the monastery, Grigor raged and raged and God tried and tried, but Grigor could not see God in himself. Word of the Tondrakians reached Grigor and he had them rounded up for heresy and drowned in the springs.

***

Lili and I heard it start and we all saw the shots, but each of us remembers a different part, and that is how we keep the memory whole without losing our minds. I remember that they slit Siran's throat first, so her brother and uncle knew she was lost before the soldiers shot them, too. Her blood was darker than I expected, and she continued to scream until they sawed into her windpipe. Lili remembers the sound coming from Sosi, inhuman in its suffering, alternating between wailing and a high-pitched, senseless *ah*. Mayr remembers the way the air hung thick and tinged with iron, the way that the blood pooled, and the carrion crows circled over the abandoned bodies the first day.

The next day, the soldiers sawed boughs from the whitebeam trees lining the business district and impaled three bodies at the boundary, as if we had not seen the shots. When they sent a patrol into The Garden, ten of our men dragged them deep into the neighborhood. We didn't see the shots that time, but we all felt them.

***

Our mothers had been changing, but we did not know into what. We did not know from what, either.

Lili and I swayed together like stalks of wheat in the frame of the door, omitted, as Mrs. Vahanian, Mrs. Krikorian, and Mayr huddled over the kitchen counter. Their hands were marbled with raw pinks and looked burned but moist, mucosal, covered in a spreading new skin. They cleaned piles upon piles of live tarek fish that wiggled before the first slice. Intent on their task, the bones piled up.

170

3

The Lim island Monastery is surrounded by an ache of blue water. This was one of the homes of St. Gregory the Illuminator, the great converter, he who overwrites, and so it was only fitting that each time the monastery was raided, he ordered it rebuilt with the same stones—obstinate, immortal stones. Silent priests plucked them from the rubble and reshaped them, chipped away at hardened mud, and refitted them.

The stones, however, grew angry at their treatment and invited dissatisfied souls to nest in their crevices. They folded themselves into the cracks like slips of perfume paper, and the stones and the souls complained in tandem. At night, the priests woke to screaming in their ears and found their mouths filled with sediment. After a few hundred years, no conversation could be had in the building for the wailing and the raw, butcher-shop smell of blood in the mortar.

***

The night air crawled between my shirt and back as I leaned over the balcony railing, staring into the blackness that shrouded the lake. The neighborhoods blacked out at night, leaving us only with moonlight that begets a level of secrecy, stillness, the way it presses and the way it takes. Shouting and laughing in the absolute dark is familiar but wrong, like having the softest of velvets shoved in your mouth. So the neighborhoods were silent, too, and nobody went out after dark. Except, of course, for Mayr.

A lurching thump followed by a scrape echoed down the lane. A soldier tripped out of the darkness and sprawled to the ground in front of Lili's house. Four ragged slits split the back of his uniform coat and he abandoned his rifle in the grass. Dragging himself to his feet, he staggered past our house, to the lakepath, and then fell to his knees and crawled away.

I heard Mayr whistle, the same birdlike shrills she whistled while cooking, and I threw myself into the shadows. She emerged from the darkness and followed the soldier towards the lakepath, bobbing cheerfully as she walked. I gasped. Mayr stopped but didn't look back. She followed him down the path and was gone.

4

We carved Madnavank straight into the side of a mountain and named it after the holy finger bone of John the Baptist housed there. Underneath the monastery, a series of vascular caves led to oratories and cells filled with grain. These rooms provided houses for mice and hope for snakes. But deep inside the structure, the cemetery waited.

Given the limited space, bodies were interred together and mingled, crowding those caves with aphotic ghosts. Most of the ghosts only appeared as howling faces, the smell of vinegar, or disembodied screams. Commonplace, mundane. The headless corpse of John the Baptist who floated through the rooms—his body crawling with locusts, dripping with honey, sounding a company of bells—was a different matter altogether. His presence was too large to be ignored, the bells too loud, and the message, that some deaths didn't leave remnants but instead created something entirely new, too terrifying.

***

I threw myself through the kitchen door and slammed into Mayr's back, knocking her into the counter. A jar full of still-writhing squid tentacles rolled out of her hands and across the floor. The stump of the body wriggled in pain on the cutting board, its black marble eyes rolling in fleshy sockets. I cupped my nose and looked between her and the torture before I ran across the deck and vomited into the foxtail lilies. I slapped at the flowers and stood up, dusted in yellow.

In response, my mother cursed my name.

***

The soldiers moved artillery to the boundary between The Garden and Old City and fired at the buildings one by one until we fled. The Garden dissolved under the onslaught, and I hadn't seen Lili since. Her house, empty and desolate, hulked above me. I dusted the window with my palm. Legs stuck out from behind the kitchen wall, naked and blood smeared, ending in swollen and mangled feet. Otherwise, the place was abandoned, the furniture gone, and every photo missing from the wall.

WATER GOES, SAND STAYS

A laugh hit me from behind and I whirled, looking towards the lake. Inky streaks emerged from the path, first striated and then spreading like branches. A wriggle of black water streamed along the ground to each house in The Garden, even the toppled. The trickle inching towards my house stopped a moment as if considering me, before pouring up the steps and through our back door. I vaulted over the garden wall and followed.

Our door now hung from a single pin, the frame splintered into porcupine quills. The black water slid to the edge of the room, soaking into the crack between the wall and the floor. The animal smell of dung and dander and oily fur hung thick in the air. I caught the vaguest hint of Mayr's perfume, vetiver and sumac.

A hand materialized over the scraps and floated down the railing, followed by a torso sprouting from wrapped wool pants. The soldier pawed at his eyes, flicking the sleep to the floor. When he finally saw me, he yelled, "Hey!" and slapped the wall three times. He plucked ribbon from one of my mother's dresses and stepped through the debris, rolling bottles away with his bare toes. The sounds of waking came from upstairs.

"Here, little birdy," he said. I staggered towards the kitchen as a murky trickle emerged from the waist of his pants, crawling up his stomach and chest. He brushed himself, scattering droplets, but the water circled his neck and reached into his mouth. He spat a curl of seaweed onto the floor, and when he lifted his head, rivulets bled from his nose and flowed up to his eyes. The unmistakable briny smell of the lake filled the house and I fled into the abandoned street, half-crawling through the neighborhood to escape, and in each of the destroyed houses, I heard gagging and soldiers crying "No, please," in miniscule, wet voices.

5

The Cathedral of the Holy Cross sits on Akhtamar island, which was named for a princess who fell in love with a peasant we never bothered to name. The princess, however, was Tamar the longing, Tamar of the bookfair, Tamar who would die if he didn't stop dragging the pad of his finger over the ridge of her first knuckle and teasing it across the web of her thumb. Tamar the burning, the scorching, the searing. Tamar the beggar. Tamar the boatless.

Tamar the siren. Swim across the lake, it is just the lake, chilly in the night, but just the lake. Tamar of the signal, of the sigil. Tamar of the torch, flame-handed Tamar.

But also Tamar the detectable, the conspicuous. Tamar patria potestas. Tamar the thoroughly disciplined. Tamar of the bruised jaw and the fat mouth. Tamar the helpless, as her father tumbled her signal lantern into the water. Tamar the listener. Tamar who cannot hear splashes without screaming. Tamar who cannot hear her own name without screaming.

She transformed into Tamar the grieving, Tamar the responsible. Tamar, owner of the boy's corpse washed on the shore, eyes eaten by fish and ears pitted with rot. Tamar the tormented, as every night the corpse screamed her name. The voice rang from the corner of the room, then the dressing table, and finally rolled, shrieking, into the royal velvet cover embroidered with crinkling gold threads.

***

I stumbled to the lake to escape the colony hum of fighting, and it took no time for me to crash into five soldiers walking the shore, leaving me scrambling to hide in a crook at the lake edge packed with tall grasses. There might be worse things than to die on my own land, under the enormous sky reflected in the still lake, but there would be better things, too. If they caught me, I would be another nameless corpse, part of the sum but not the expression.

As I cringed in the grasses, strands of seaweed shot from the lake without disturbing the surface and whipped towards the soldiers so quickly, they broke my senses, my exactness, the surety of my own stillness relative to the rotation of the world. I stopped knowing anything.

When I slammed into another body in the dark, a scream rattled in my throat. Hands pinned my arms and shook me until my head rolled.

"Stop! Maro, Maro, Mariam!" Mayr yelled.

I heard the wild firing of rifles, wrenched myself from her grip, and turned back to the lake. A hulking shape rose from the water under the soldiers.

"Don't look. Don't look." She twisted my shoulders, but I would not budge, and I did not listen. I looked. I looked and thought of tree boughs, of coffee cups.

***

The lake surface lay as flat and still as glass. Mayr's hands, the same raw pink as red snapper, fluttered at her chest. At the lake edge, she dipped her hands under the water, wincing from the salt, and emerged with a tendril of rotted brown seaweed, which she stuffed into her mouth. Muddy slime leaked from the corners of her lips. She vomited the seaweed back into the lake.

"What was that?" I asked.

"It is a thing that lives in the lake," she answered with the same disinterested tone that one uses to say *Those are my shoes* or *The door is open.*

"What are you?"

She wrapped her hands around my wrists and dragged me back to the ground. Another patrol crossed the beach heading for The Garden, another whip of seaweed, another snap. Mayr again plucked a frond of lake fern, ate it, and vomited it back into the salt. She took a slit-bellied fish from her bag and placed it in the water, beckoning for me to join her at the lake edge.

"I'm your mother," she said.

***

There was once a thief who walked straight up to Lmbat Monastery, full of confidence, and unhooked the great stone door. As he loaded it onto a canvas to drag it away, he let his fingers play over the bas relief, skipping over curves and bumps with delighted shivers. Though the locals were not known as fighters, he prepared to meet resistance on the way back to his boat; however, the island villagers did nothing, said nothing as he absconded. They merely lined the cliffside overlooking the beach and stared down at the thief with liquid black eyes.

That night, the thief set the door on a flat stony patch near his boat and set up camp, intending to leave in the morning. He drank a little drink and smoked a little smoke and charred a little lamb while he thought of his great plunder and his own cleverness. The thief dropped into a happy sleep, but he dreamed of his eyes and nostrils stuffed with wriggling red cochineals, and

175

when he woke from his nightmare, he found the monastery door on his back, pressing him into the ground. Struggle as he might, he could not escape. The carved ridges rubbed against his skin, tearing him open with filigree. Glass-sharp pebbles split his fingernails. When he heard the first rib snap, he wished for death. It took three days.

On the fourth day, the villagers followed the great track he made through the dirt with his tarp, peeled the door from his body—which they left to be eaten by the cochineals—and returned to the city. Linen cloth soaked the blood from the larger swaths; a broom took care of any bone fragments; and the priest was given the honor of cleaning, with a tiny brush, the rivulets of gore stuck in the curves of the carved figures. The villagers hung the door back on the church and the dead stay asleep, illuminated.

THE MULES

Jennifer Jeanne McArdle

JORDAN HAD BEEN riding mules since she was a small child. She knew to trust their intelligence, especially Yule, whose wide ears twitched towards her as he breathed in deeply enough for her to feel his ribs expand under her legs. The AFR infected areas had their own unique beauty, she remembered as she followed the trail of sun rays that had found their way through cracks in the thick canopy of waxy, spiral leaves hanging over her. A puffy white spore landed on Yule's nose. He sneezed.

"Bless you," she whispered as she pet his dappled gray fur, and urged him forward. She always liked foxes, so she tried not to look at the corpses of a few cubs, their skeletons and bits of wet orange fur intertwined with the spiral green leaves. The plants that had been growing here before the infection were dead or dying, their leaves having dropped off and their stems wilted due to lack of sunlight and the AFR sapping all the available water and nutrients from the soil. AFR forests were always especially quiet; corpses of song birds were strewn about, and the legs, wings or bits of other insect parts floating through the air, dirtying her goggles. The leaves of the AFR softened any noise, like fresh snowfall.

Yule, her handsome and strong mule who had been born on Christmas seven years ago, reached a sure-footed trot, avoiding tangling his hooves in the AFR vines or corpses. Jordan was sure they weren't far from the source of the AFR infection now and hoped to uproot it and destroy it before nightfall.

Her mind began to wander. When Jordan was in high school, she had been taught by an English teacher who wore floral prints on unenhanced fabric, used a handheld mobile phone, spoke with a vocal fry, and therefore seemed truly old fashioned. She had once assigned them a bunch of old, historic feminist essays. As a teenager, Jordan wasn't sure how she felt about feminism and often wondered if it applied to *her*.

She had read one essay a couple of times, turning a few of the sentences over and over again in her head. The writer described how her society assumed a biological destiny for women, trapped by their monthly cycles, and the physical and emotional burden of pregnancy and breastfeeding. Society determined that just because women could carry children, they must.

Jordan had realized then that although she could not give birth or breastfeed, she too was trapped by biological destiny.

Yule stopped when they reached a thick green curtain of AFR vines. He pawed at the ground. Jordan pulled an apple from her pack and offered it to Yule. He had always been such a brave creature; many other mules got spooked the first time they were brought into AFR infected areas, and some never got over that fear.

Alien Fungal Root spores had first been brought to Earth from the Jupiter moon where they had been identified as a potential cure for the growing human infertility rates. However, the lab where the spores were being housed was attacked by anti-science terrorist groups, and the spores were released into the wild.

Jordan got down from the animal and pulled her machete from its holster in Yule's saddle. She put large headphones over her own ears and then put ear plugs into Yule's ears. She began hacking at the green curtain, wincing as the AFR vines emitted a piercing whine each time they were cut apart. The leaves here were especially thick; the area of this infection was far from the major cities, so no one had noticed it for some time.

AFR wasn't able to reproduce on its own; rather it infected the reproductive cells of animals as a means to reproduce itself, but the process killed the host fairly quickly. The initial infection that began an AFR colony only succeeded if a spore was able to enter an open wound and if the animal's immune system was already weakened. Then the fungus needed hospitable soil, where it could plant itself and grow a network of roots outward.

Now that Jordan finished hacking through the curtain, she saw the deep magenta flower at the center of every AFR network. It pulsed; puffy white spores burst onto her face. These spores, emitted in the proximity of an established AFR root network, became more potent. They only needed to be breathed in; the gametes of animals were then infected and transformed. The spiral leaves grew from inside the creature until they too could reach the ground, sending their own roots towards the main network, strengthening it.

She could swear that the AFR colonies were conscious to some degree and that this one had just spit at her. She returned the gesture and walked back to Yule. Jordan had no fear of the spores. While most infertile people made eggs or sperm that were of a poor quality or something about their reproductive organs was ill-formed, Jordan had been born without any reproductive organs and was incapable of producing any reproductive cells. Most mules, due to mismatched chromosomes, were also incapable of producing reproductive cells, making them the best pack animals for travel into an AFR infected area.

Jordan found a red flare in her pack and walked away from Yule towards an open spot in the canopy. The flower continued to pulse, and Jordan had to wipe her goggles a few times as she set up the flare. She stepped back and watched it burst into the air and explode. The AFR disrupted most electronic devices, and the spores and other debris often jammed delicate mechanical contraptions. The one red flare was a signal to other Professional AFR Uprooters on her team that she had found the major root.

Now she had two hours to pull the root from the ground, poison it, burn it, and douse all the AFR leaves she came across in flammable chemicals. Other Uprooters would start dowsing their own sections of the infected area.

She needed Yule again for this part. She took thick ropes from Yule's pack and began wrapping them around the flower. It continued to spit spores at her, continued to pulse, and screamed when she dug metal hooks into the base of the flower. At each end of the rope were metal clasps that attached to the harness around her waist and to Yule's saddle. She attached each end and patted Yule's rump. She sneezed a couple of times and Yule shook his head.

Jordan had been a new Uprooter apprentice and twenty years old when she saw Yule being born; his mother was a large draft horse. His gangly body had looked so small next to hers. Jordan's grandparents owned a farm. Her parents had separated her from her brothers and sister when she was ten and sent her to live on that farm where she could learn to care for animals firsthand.

Because she was born without a biological sex, and she was related to someone who trained mules for AFR Uprooters, it was assumed since she'd been a small child that she would one day become an Uprooter. Before Yule had been born, Jordan was a little bitter that no one even entertained the idea that her future would be any different, that she might want a different profession.

But Yule, sweet Yule, was a curious, precocious creature. He seemed to know when she was sad and nuzzled her shoulder. He was courageous and treated each mission as a new adventure, as though each AFR infected area they traveled through wasn't something diseased, cast off, or blandly repetitive, but a magical otherworldly experience, transporting them across space to a moon in some far off corner of the solar system. She tried to explain this feeling to one of her brothers.

"I mean, maybe he's just confident because you're confident." Her brother told her. "He's just an animal, and he's not quite as impressive as a horse. Although, I guess Uprooters are something like modern day knights or samurai? Instead of demons, you exorcise aliens."

Jordan stepped away from Yule and began walking forward, pulling the rope taut. Yule took her cue and began pulling as well; his back legs bending low as he strained. He brayed deep and loud, and his breath could be heard puffing from his flared nostrils. Drool dripped from his lips. She pulled with him, but of course, her power was nothing compared to that of a mule weighing over a thousand pounds. But she knew Yule; she knew that seeing her pull with him was the best motivation. Sweat dripped down her forehead, and her heart pounded in her chest. This was a stubborn root, but she and Yule were more stubborn. A horse might have given up, and donkey would have lacked the power, but the mule, this marvel of human genetic engineering before humans even knew exactly what genetics were, would pull and pull until the task was completed.

Finally she heard and felt the flower rip from the ground. They tugged together for a few more moments to drag the main root from its hole so that Jordan could cut it open and burn the core. Jordan stopped pulling, dropped fully to her knees and sucked air into her lungs. She began coughing; some spores had been caught in her throat. She felt hot breath on her cheek and reached up to pet Yule's nose.

"You are a good boy," she whispered into his ear as she used his body to get back on her feet. Sometimes thinking about mules made Jordan believe in some kind of god or supernatural force. What luck to humans that this animal existed or all life might have died out due to the AFR infection.

"Man made the mule," her grandfather reminded her often. "They're unnatural and sterile. There'd be no mules without man." *Still*, she thought. *What luck that this experiment worked. Man didn't make life.*

She made her way over to the uprooted flower. With her machete, she sliced open the thickest part of the root, which was now exposed. The core was a neon pink liquid. Tiny bits of the bones of whatever animal had been infected by the spore bobbed on the surface. She opened a flask of poison and dumped it into the core.

After she had moved to her grandparents' home, she hardly ever saw her siblings or her parents. Her older sister and brother were already married with small children. The rest of her family wasn't wealthy or well-educated, but their fertility had somewhat elevated their place in society while many others struggled to conceive.

Her nieces and nephews wrote her emails or called her sometimes. Next month, she was supposed to visit her niece's kindergarten class to talk about her job as an AFR Uprooter. Most Uprooters weren't like her, completely sexless. Some people and animals had a natural immunity to the AFR spores. Still, it was a dangerous occupation for them as sometimes that natural immunity broke down and the AFR succeeded in infecting them. Prolonged exposure to the spores and the chemicals used to kill them also sometimes caused diseases and cancers.

During the long, quiet nights on the roads in between cities or infected areas, Jordan wondered what she would be if AFR never came to Earth. Would people have mocked her oddly shaped body and childlike features?

"You're my hero," her niece had told her after she agreed to come to her class.

She doused the flower and the core in flammable chemicals and lit a match. The growth burst into flames. She adjusted her breathing mask over her face as the foul-smelling smoke began to rise and fill this area of the AFR forest. She put a mask over Yule's nose and climbed up to sit in his saddle. Then, she tossed balloons filled with flammables as they rode out of the AFR infected area until they finally cleared the orange sticks that marked the perimeter of the infection. When she reached her team's truck, a couple of miles away from the infected area, she shared dinner with her teammates.

Now that the core of the infection had been destroyed and the signal the AFR emitted that messed with electronics was weakened, jets could fly over the area and drop bombs, incinerating the AFR forest. Fire trucks zoomed past them towards the infected area to keep the fire from spreading.

At the truck, they were sprayed with disinfectant to kill any errant spores. Still, some spores would escape, and eventually new AFR infections would grow.

***

Years later, when the bank and government employees came to close down Jordan's ranch and reclaim the land, Jordan watched as each mule was led out back and shot. Then the men loaded their bodies onto trucks; each *thud* as their bodies landed on top of the other animals felt like being stabbed in the heart. She heard a few of them would be stuffed and preserved, others would be chopped up for meat and frozen. In the future, when real meat would become rarer and rarer, someone might pay for the novelty of eating mule, even if it wouldn't taste very good.

Jordan and Yule had spent a couple of decades on Uprooter teams around the world. They had climbed glaciers to find infections that had started in herds of wild reindeer. Another time, they had got lost in a sandstorm for days until they both met at a tower of alien green, its core at the center of a watering hole in an oasis. They had scaled canyons covered in twisted vines, ripped an infection from what had been the nest of a falcon on a cliff-side tree. They trudged knee-deep in infected swamps, still filled with a species of hungry mosquitoes that were naturally immune to AFR.

Jordan had tried, when she could, to collect samples of the dead animals and plants. The AFR infections had finished off a number of flora and fauna just barely hanging on to existence, and for a while, most people believed the planet was doomed. But eventually, the Uprooters had succeeded in saving the planet; AFR infections seemed to be completely eliminated.

"Were you a part of the team that got that infection a few miles outside Chicago?" a woman in a bank employee uniform asked her, maybe to distract her from watching the ongoing animal massacre.

"Yes."

"Er. Thank you. The house where I grew up wasn't too far from that infection. You stopped it before it reached us."

"A couple of the animals in that pile were on that mission, too." Jordan continued to watch the culling. The woman watched for a few seconds before turning away and leaving Jordan's side.

After the Uprooting teams had been disbanded, Jordan used some of her savings to buy acres of empty prairie land. She had built the Hybrid Heroes Ranch and Museum for Yule and the other retired mules. The mules had spent their days running over rolling hills, kicking up dust over the short grasses and little flowers.

Jordan had obsessed over the presentation at the museum, which featured rooms on the history of AFR, pictures of infected areas, and old tools and outfits Uprooters had used. One room had even listed the names of Uprooters and mules who had passed.

Jordan watched as some of the government men now raided her museum for any artifacts they felt were worth saving for other, better museums before they demolished the building.

After Jordan had first opened Hybrid Heroes, people had come from all over the world to see the mules, to pet them, to ride them, or to see the artifacts. They had donated money and other supplies. Her nieces and nephews had brought friends and then their own children to see her on the ranch. Her family, except for her, remained extraordinarily fertile. They spent a lot of time bragging about how scientists were studying their genes to help the human race.

Jordan had spent her days caring for the animals and cleaning and rearranging the museum rooms, telling and retelling her stories to any visitors who would listen. But, as the years passed, fewer visitors came and less donations were received. People remembered that the planet was running out of resources. They had less time for art, or music, or history.

"What exactly do the mules do now?" more and more people had begun to ask her when they visited. Jordan always felt taken aback by the question no matter how often she heard it. Hadn't they already done enough?

"Would you let me take him for one last ride?" Jordan asked the government men on her ranch about Yule before they could shoot him. They eyed human and beast suspiciously as they both stood on thin, wobbly legs. "This is my own mule, which I rode into the alien forests for years. I trained him since he was born. I should be the one to shoot him." Perhaps some latent guilt about the way retired AFR Uprooters had been poorly treated and cast aside caused them to relent to her request.

At one point during her their career, Jordan and Yule had been well-known and won awards for their skill and dedication in stamping out the infection. They were all over social media, in memes, and had appeared a few times on television or on magazine covers. Jordan got letters from children all over the world, and a toy horse company even asked Yule and some of the other mules to model for a collectors' series.

"I'm sorry it had to turn out this way," a young government employee named Wagner told her as she prepared for her ride. "I always get depressed when we have to kill lots of animals like this. With the way things are going, people can't bring themselves to spend money on animals not producing anything."

Most commercial farming had been phased out years prior due to its effect on the environment. Millions of cows, and chickens, and pigs had been slaughtered at once, and the meat was distributed or frozen in special freezers that would keep it unspoiled for decades.

Jordan had been forced to use her savings to keep the ranch alive these past few years. She had written letters to other retired Uprooters. Only a few sent her money. Many of them had already passed from diseases likely caused by exposure to the spores or the chemicals used to kill them.

"I've got nothing to send you. We can't even get donations to save the sick human Uprooters," one of her old teammates had told her.

"He's really handsome for a mule," Wagner told her as his hand hovered a few inches from Yule's nose. "Is he the biggest one on the ranch?"

"He was."

Jordan had been riding Yule months ago when she fainted for the first time. At the hospital, the doctors told her she was sick and wasn't going to get any better. She contacted her brothers and sister and told them that she needed their help, but they told her they had no money to spare. They were angry that she used all of her savings on the mules. What about her nieces and nephews? Didn't she want to leave them something for the future?

"Do you need help packing any of your stuff? You won't be able to come back to it tomorrow. They're gonna demolish your house first thing in the morning." Wagner told her as she brushed Yule's mane for the final time.

Jordan had been given just a few more months to live. She had wanted to spend them on the ranch and not in a state-run facility the government had designated to care for her. As the days passed, caring for the mules had become more difficult until it was impossible. The money, except her small pension, was gone.

Jordan went inside to get her lunch from the kitchen and carried it out in a cooler. She tied up the saddle on Yule's back and struggled to mount him. Wagner finally helped her up.

"Are you sure you can do this, Sir? Ma'am?"

"Ma'am is fine." Her breath made a cloud in the cold air. She gripped the reigns in one trembling hand and shaded her eyes from the sun with the other. "I'll be back in a few hours, I think."

"Don't take too long," one of the other government men told her. "We're only on shift until 5pm. Then you'll need to get your own ride to the nursing home."

"Do you want to tell us where you're going? We could pick you up?" Wagner asked her.

She didn't bother answering, but urged Yule forward. They slowly made their way to the edge of a pond a couple of miles from the ranch. Some people complained the water here contained too much algae to be pretty, but some fish and frogs and waterfowl still managed to live in the pond; it was nothing like the quiet AFR areas.

Jordan managed to get herself down from Yule. From the cooler, she removed two apples, giving one to the mule and biting into the other. She hugged Yule and praised him. He nibbled her shoulder and whined.

Her hands trembled as she removed the pistol from Yule's saddle. Yule was forty years old now; he only had a few years, or perhaps just a few months left in him. Or did he? Some mules lived past fifty. She thought about chasing him into the woods and leaving him there, but he'd probably starve to death or loneliness would kill him. If she hadn't been sick, maybe she would have had the energy to find someone to take care of him for the last few years of his life.

She raised the pistol to his forehead. He grunted and pointed his ears towards her. Did he trust her completely and not know what was coming, or had he simply accepted his fate? She and her Uprooter teammates had often debated how smart or aware these animals were. Whatever was true about their intelligence, Yule had been her best friend, perhaps her only real friend. She breathed in deeply.

She pulled the trigger. The contents of his head erupted, some splattering her face and arms. His large body immediately crumpled. Her ears ringing from the gunshot, she mustered what strength she had left to slowly push him a couple of feet into a grave she had dug a couple of weeks prior. She covered him with dirt until her energy was completely drained.

She rested for some time until she could stand again. Then she found the cooler. Under the apples was a small block of ice. She took it out and held it up to the sun. Encased in the ice were a few AFR spores that she had managed to save and freeze years ago.

She put the block of ice directly under a bright ray of sun and stepped back. It was just a few spores; the chances of them actually reaching a vulnerable host and starting an AFR infection were quite low. If the infection was successful, she likely wouldn't live to see it. Still, she liked to think that there was some chance in the universe that people like her and animals like Yule might be needed again.

As she scrubbed the mess from her body and clothes at the edge of the pond, the ice melted, and a soft breeze carried the few white spores on the wind.

STAGE FIVE CLINGER

Nikki R. Leigh

ITELL THE HAND to pull up the voice memo app on Nadine's phone. She's sleeping. The Temple has walloped her internally so that she's out for longer than last time. I've only just begun my story, and there's still at least ten of us to go, all new additions from the past year.

We're careful not to make too much noise—no errant moans or gasps from our many mouths. Our lips are tightly pulled together, as if glued and zipped and sewn just for good measure. We know that our stories must be heard clearly. Spoken with no interruption.

We don't want to be stuck to her much longer.

The Hand and Arm work together to bring the phone closer to where I am: the Hip. The Hand pushes record, and I open my mouth, stretch my lips and wet my tongue. I speak.

I'm going to start this story at the end of the first night. The beginning of the end, really. The first time I felt simultaneously in control and out of it. Bear with me, it's a windy road, but love—and obsession—usually is. I can admit that now. Can still see it, that first night, circular, replaying. Live it. Try to sleep and can't, so I live it again. Welcome to my thoughts, it's all I have left anyway. Let's go.

***

Three Weeks Ago

I'm paralyzed by her.

My face was stuffed somewhere in the crevice of Nadine's shoulder blades. I'm careful not to pull away, for fear of waking her with that unflattering sound and feeling of naked flesh unsticking itself from other naked flesh.

Since I couldn't move and my mind was far from sleep, I let it wander and take adventures, hoping to burn off the excess energy. The buzz of the night. The vibration still humming through my veins. I needed to let it fizz out so I could get some semblance of sleep before work tomorrow.

I yawned, smelling her again as I do. I couldn't help but feel a rumble of excitement, accomplishment, and a bit of anxiety swirl together when I caught that hint of her sex on my face.

It was my first time—with another woman at least—and I never thought that I'd feel so much like a toddler again, my legs wobbly beneath me as I try to navigate new terrain.

I thought about that gaze she sent my way, across tables at the bar, the local lesbian watering hole, from what I had gathered in my Yelp research. Apparently *the* spot for new and old queers. A drink or ten to build up the courage, a feast—of both women and really good sliders if you could stomach the grease.

I'd stared, mouth open, beef spilling out of my mouth when I made eye contact with her. Felt heat flush to my cheeks and my groin and a guttural, audible groan escaped my lips.

"No, no, that one's trouble," Addie said. "I've heard that half the San Francisco girls have been her prey. Do you know how many queer people San Francisco has?"

"Shut up, Addie," I said.

"Why not that one, over there? She's cute and looks safe. You can probably figure this shit out with her and she wouldn't eat your head off in the process."

I looked over to where Addie was not so inconspicuously pointing. A sweet looking girl in a button up shirt and a cute nose-piercing waved in my direction. I waved back, letting my fingers dance like blades of grass in the wind.

She was pretty, and like Addie had said, probably safe. Not that I knew the first thing about dating girls. And that was my problem, because my ignorant ass seemed to be drawn to the most dangerous girl in the room.

"No, stop it, Suzie. I'm telling you, don't even bother. You know how many hearts she's broken? It'll be whatever that astronomically high number is plus one once she's done with you," Addie said.

I watched the girl lick the excess alcohol from her lips, the honey-colored drink on the rocks making her look goddamn untouchable.

"The heart wants what the heart wants, Addie."

"The heart doesn't want that. Trust me. The loins might, but the heart doesn't."

"Please stop telling me how to gay. It's my gay or the highgay."

"How are we friends?" Addie sighed dramatically.

"I'm going to the bathroom. Want me to bring back a drink?"

She smiled. "Ah yes, that's why we're friends. Margarita please. A double, if I'm going to have to watch you make ogley-eyes at her all night."

I smacked Addie's shoulder and headed to the bathroom, which had a line of dancing queers that nearly reached the bar. Yet another unforeseen drawback of dating at the local lezzie bar: ridiculously long waits for the restroom.

I really did have so much to learn.

I tapped my foot impatiently on the sticky ground of the bar floor. My eyes darted around the room, falling on the array of missing posters behind the bar. At least a dozen faces, all young women, were tacked up on the wall along with the number for the local LGBTQ+ Community Center. I remember thinking that was odd—you'd think I'd have heard of a group of young women who'd recently disappeared before that moment.

I tried to note their faces, but they were blurring together from the alcohol buzzing through my veins. I turned my attention to the rest of the room. All around me, women were coupling up, eyes glazed over from alcohol, discarded plates forgotten beside them. There were new dishes each night, served hot, after all. The soft glow of string lights hanging from the wooden rafters made it all seem so idyllic. So normal. Maybe one day I'd find my peace here, but for now, I was overstimulated and stressed from its newness.

The line shuffled forward. With too much time spent waiting to release my bladder, I found my mind drifting to how I got to this spot. This oversexed bar with these overhorny people, in over my horny head. I didn't even know I *was* horny for other women a week ago.

Hardy-har, right? The thirty-year-old who finally figured things out after forced and failed relationships and a near giving up on love. How could I not have realized? Not have known?

I could probably overanalyze my sexual orientation-based misgivings until the cows come home, but I'll just settle on this: I didn't know, until I did. Just kind of struck my mind like a flick to the forehead one night, lying in bed with too much anxiety swirling in my brain. It struck me, it settled, and since then, the rest of me just fell into place.

And then I was there. In the bar. Apparently with a taste for the most off-limits girl in this humid, loud place.

The line shifted again.

A voice in my ear caused me to almost piss my pants.

"Hive mind urination, am I right?" I jumped a bit more than I would have liked in front of the girl I'd been making lovestruck eyes at not five minutes earlier. Addie's warning echoed in my mind. I ignored it.

"You've surely got a better pick-up line than that?" I fired back, hoping to sound as cool as I wished I was.

She laughed, the sound like a rainbow arcing over the loud music in the bar. Ugh, even my intrusive thoughts are gay.

"Who says I was trying to pick you up?"

"Everyone does, you just can't hear it over this abysmally loud bass drop."

"You're right, my mistake. In that case, do you have plans later?"

And that was all she wrote. My naïve, fresh-lesbian soul felt like it had mated. Within the hour, I had left the bar with Nadine and was making my way up the steps of her apartment complex and into her bedroom and clothes were off and we were having sex and I was becoming whole. My whole world was vibrating and sending out ripples of color. I tried to let my instincts take over, remembered what felt good for me, see if it felt good for her.

I didn't tell her it was my first time. I didn't want to scare her off. But somehow, she knew, I learned, panting naked and slippery with sweat later that night.

"Pretty good for the first go at it," Nadine had said. "You going to stay the night? I've been told I snore."

I was still feeling whammied by the realization that I was exposed and revealed to be the complete newbie I was.

"I . . . I can stay," I stuttered out.

"Just don't get too attached or anything. We can spoon, but I'm not really looking for anything serious."

I couldn't think of a response that wouldn't make me sound any less like the loser that I was, so I settled on latching onto her back, draping an arm over her midsection, and trying to sleep.

She didn't say another word, and my mind was racing. I don't think I slept a wink that night, nor any of the nights since. I sighed. *See? We've been here before.*

I started the night over in my mind again.

***

That's how we met, so I'll tell you how we ended. I'm not sure I can continue tonight though. The sun is starting to come up and wheezing out these words has taken more out of me than I thought it would.

We're all in agreement, the Hand and Arm, and I, the Hip. We shut the phone off, place it back where it was as Nadine begins to stir.

Crisis averted. I know our mouths will seal when she awakens. Disappear when she regains control, and we'll revert to our place in the trunk, forgotten as she goes about her day. As I let myself fall back into her, I almost shout with what little energy I have left. I can feel her hunger, her need to consume. Maybe she'll go out again and gather another one of us. Her knee is looking rather bare these days.

***

It's a few nights later now. She's asleep again, and her bed is finally empty. She had a girl over the last two evenings, and I can only hope she's strong enough to fight the lure Nadine exudes. We couldn't, and we're paying that price.

The Temple, Arm, Hand and I work at it again, setting up the phone so I can tell the rest of my story. It'll be their turn soon, if this works out, and I know they're excited to use a voice they'd lost months ago.

Alright, the rest of my story. I started with the beginning of my end, so allow me a bit of meandering now so I can explain how I turned into nothing but a puckered mouth that only breathes when she's asleep.

191

***

One Week Ago

I found her at that bar again. A solid seven days had passed since we had sex for the first time, and my *first* kind of first, and I hadn't stopped thinking about her since. The morning after my inaugural trip down under, I made her coffee, eggs, awkwardly fixed my hair and pressed my clothes under my palms as she sauntered to the table. She had this look of pain in her eyes, like she could see what was happening and wanted nothing to do with it.

"Thanks . . . what's your name again?" At least she was honest.

"Suzie." My cheeks flushed.

"Suzie, right. Look, don't take this personally, but this isn't going to be a thing. Unless, you know, you're okay with just the sex."

I looked at her longingly.

"I'm not opposed to the sex, you know. You were pretty good. I'm just not looking for commitment. You've got that look like you're ready to lay down roots here in my apartment. Like you skipped stages one and two and hopped right into stage three. Don't. You wanted a good, easy first time, right?"

I think this is the most I've heard her speak since we've met. I stayed silent.

"So, you got it. Easy, no strings attached."

"Okay," I finally said. "Okay."

"Alright, glad that's sorted," Nadine said through a smile.

I excused myself, went straight to work in last night's clothes, reeking of alcohol.

"Sorted" she had said. I couldn't help but feel used. I spent the next few days thinking about just how used I had felt until all of a sudden that feeling of being yesterday's garbage finally got taken out to the dumpster and I seemed to forget my torment.

I found her at that bar. We went back to her apartment. We had sex.

We did it again the next night, too. I craved the way my hands seemed to find holds everywhere in her body, like I was climbing a rock wall and she was the path. It felt like I was slipping into her, becoming her when she reached her peak; we'd climb Everest together, flesh and flesh.

Each time she finished it was an orchestra of moans and screams. It sounded like she was everywhere at once, and for a second, I wondered if she had an extra mouth hidden somewhere.

I lay nestled into her back again, thinking about her dimples, her laugh, and how much of a woman she was. And that was really something to me. She was a *woman* and I was a *woman* and I couldn't get over the fact that we had been together in that way, after spending a whole life not realizing just how amazing it could be.

The next day at work, Addie pressed for information, teased me for falling in deep. Said she could see it written all over my face like I'd fallen asleep first at a party and someone had scribbled "this bitch is in love" in Sharpie across my forehead.

But she was right. I couldn't believe it. A week and a half, and my heart was hammered, drunk with Nadine.

I texted her that night. "Can I take you out?"

"Drinks?"

I tried to be bold, texted: "Dinner???"

There was a long pause of blinking ellipses on the screen as she typed. "No strings remember?"

I breathed, chose my words carefully so I could get what I wanted: "No strings, just burgers."

Another long pause, but she agreed to meet me at the restaurant next to my favorite park where I planned to win her over under the stars.

We met, we ate, I paid, and made some excuse about walking the food off. She didn't protest, claiming to need the fresh air herself.

We walked, moonlight illuminating the way. I tried to grab her hand, but she shoved it in her pocket. I tried to kiss her, but she turned her cheek.

I longed for her touch, and she seemed to want to be anywhere but with me, her phone buzzing occasionally in her pocket. She stopped walking, turned to face me.

"Please don't ask me to be your girlfriend."

I sputtered, feeling called out and ashamed. She turned down the thing I wanted and I hadn't even asked her.

"Look, Suzie, you seem real nice and all. You're going to make some girl really happy. But that girl isn't me. I promise you that."

"But how do you know?"

She sighed. "I see this all the time. The first girl you sleep with, that one that basically reorients the rest of your life, it makes you fall in deep. You can't help it. I try not to make a habit of sleeping with the newly gay, but you were so forward in that line to the bathroom I didn't think you were."

"Can't you just pretend I'm not?"

"That's beside the point. It doesn't matter what I want, it's what you *think* you want."

I was trying not to cry.

"I'm not worth it," Nadine continued. "Do you know why my phone keeps ringing? It's my on-again, off-again girlfriend asking if I got my free dinner from the Stage Five Clinger."

"Ouch," I said, wincing internally more than I let on, trying to mask the utter raw pain.

"This girl, she's my puppeteer. When you and I sleep together, she's the one I wish it was. You fall, and no matter what, I can't stop you. I'll eat you alive. And I'll smile the whole time."

I could see what she was doing, being needlessly cruel. It was working.

"I get it," I said. "You can stop."

"I'm sorry."

"Can we still . . . you know?"

She laughed. "You do have those talented fingers. Just a fuck?"

I nodded my head, weighed down by the lump in my throat. "Just a fuck."

And we did.

I lied to myself as much as I lied to her. For another week I tried. Just the physical. Grunts late into the night. I wouldn't stay over, but rather gather my clothes and shuffle off for long night drives wishing I wasn't doing exactly what I was doing.

I kept having sex, because it was the only way I could be with her. It was humiliating, but exhilarating.

I'd stare into her eyes and imagine a lifetime of doing so, and she'd stare back, challenging me. She had all the power, and she knew it. From her coy smiles, I could tell that she liked it. Thrived off it, even as she protested against it. It was a dance she danced often, and she had mastered every step. Every house I imagined us owning together, every kid I imagined cradled in our arms was another card in her voraciously selfish deck.

She was winning every night, but at least they were nights with her.

I was falling in deep. Trying not to let her know. But somewhere within the confines of her hardened shell, her body knew. And it was absorbing me.

Talented fingers and all.

***

Nadine rolls over, and I shout at the Temple. Scream at it with my mouth and tongue flapping at her hip to slam a concussive force into her skull and stop her. I'm almost done with this story.

If Nadine learns that we've grown, this whole thing is over and we're back to being trapped.

If she figures out that we've opened like slits across her body at night, that as we remember more about who we are, that we become mouths and speak, we're done. We've learnt about each other each night and want to tell the world about Nadine, the many-mouthed beast.

We can't lose. We have nothing left of ourselves.

The Temple does her job. Nadine is out again. The Hand and Arm reposition the phone by me at her Hip.

My story. The rest of my story.

***

Last week

Deeper, harder, faster; I fell. And the night that it happened, that I lost nearly all of myself, I was full of regret.

I remember that first time I saw Nadine, at the bar when Addie told me to choose a different girl, that nice-looking girl. Someone easy and kind and who wouldn't eat me for breakfast. I chose to be a meal, though, I just didn't realize how literal it would be.

I was in her bed when every colossal shit from the past month hit the fan at warp speed. I found myself doing something I had promised myself I wouldn't do.

I was crying into Nadine's back, clinging to her tight.

"I'm sorry," I sobbed, ashamed that I couldn't help the attachment I felt.

"Oh, Suzie. I didn't want this for you."

"It's not like you didn't warn me."

"Yeah, about that—"

"I just can't help it. You're so great and everything."

"I'm really not."

"You are, and I don't think I'll ever find anyone like you."

"Please don't say that," she said, and for the first time I heard fear in her voice.

"What's wrong? Why are you so resistant to this?"

Nadine's body tensed, and in that moment, I felt a shift within her. She started to sweat, and my arms wrapped around her body had become soaked with her. I knew that if I didn't act fast, this might be the last time I saw Nadine, and I didn't want to lose her. I started to rub her skin with my clammy hands. She told me not to stop. From my position, behind her goosebump-covered frame, I tried to work my way into her, ready to pull her apart with my teeth and lick her wounds with my salted tongue.

She climaxes, fast, and when she does, all of her mouths open.

I stare at the gaping slits. They're close to everywhere: a pair of full-bodied lips on her shoulder, a cleft-lip at her temple, a pinched mouth on her forearm and a toothy mouth on her hand. Mouths, teeth, tongues, everywhere on her exposed skin.

I don't even have time to think about how I never noticed them. Later, once I was assimilated and started seeing it happen to someone else, I realized it's because when you're face-deep in someone, you're not really paying attention to much else. Especially not in *that* moment, when the stars align and the climax triggers.

But here I am, fully aware in her moment of glory and I can see them all, the dozen mouths, all groaning at once, making up a monstrous scream of ecstasy that tumbles from every pair of lips Nadine has.

Then, for the first time in our short-lived relationship or whatever this was, she turned to me, her voice—*voices?*—hoarse and offered the magical words of reciprocation.

"Your turn," she husked.

I scrambled away from her naked body, her mouths gasping at air, moaning in an off-tempo and out-of-key way that sounded like a whole graveyard of encroaching ghouls.

She grabbed my hand.

STAGE FIVE CLINGER

"Let me teach you. You just place your hand here, and I'll do the rest."

I hated that I was so turned on by her still, with the mouths on her body aching for air, aching to scream again. She was finally giving back, and I just wanted it so badly that I didn't even notice when my fingertips started sinking into her skin, through it, as if her very pores were inviting me in.

"Stage Five," she said, when I finally realized I was wrist deep in her hip, my flesh fused to hers.

She reared her head back, and all her mouths smiled.

"Now *cling.*"

And with that, I was lost. I could do nothing to pull away, my body sinking inch by inch, folding and melting into her own. I funneled into her bones, her flesh, her blood, and became as much her as anything else.

I felt myself disperse into her, stuck on everything inside, my entire existence squashed into hers. Sucking and squeezing and breaking and realigning filling every gap in her already crowded body.

I finally had what I wanted, attached at the hip. I wondered if Addie would miss me. I'd been kind of a shitty friend for the last few weeks.

I hoped she'd feed my cat.

***

So that's how I became the Hip. Not all that different than the Arm and the Hand, though the Temple's story is a bit more treacherous, I'm told.

Fell too deep, and now we're stuck. Forever falling, nothing but flesh around us to cushion the blow.

The Hand taps the phone to end the recording. My story is over. It took us a while to figure out how to navigate Nadine's body while she was sleeping. But when we did, we reached for the phone. We hit record. We spoke.

Tomorrow, a new story. Until then, our lips seal together, we recede, and we wait.

THE DAY WHEN THE LAST WAR IS OVER

Sergey Gerasimov

IT'S THE DAY when the last war is over, and skeletons of swallows are already starting to return. They don't have beaks, and their white, hard-boiled eyes fly three inches ahead of their semi-transparent faces, or sometimes on their side.

Skeletons of babies start whimpering in the cradles, and a small skeleton of a doggy digs itself out of the ashes. It tries to find its collar, but fails and disintegrates melancholically into mush and bones. Then everything is quiet for a long time.

A man's skeleton in an orange gas-mask comes out onto the porch. He stares at the skeletons of chickens digging the radioactive ashes and listens to the pensive cawing of crow skeletons on the lampposts. He stands, doing nothing, because everything has already been done. He is just watching, just listening, just feeling for the last time.

In the house he has left, a girl's skeleton gets up from her bed. She looks around. Nothing has changed much in the room. The windows are not broken; the wallpaper is not scorched by fire. The only sign of the war that has passed are skeletons of fish swimming in the fish tank. No bomb has fallen close enough to really destroy things, to turn people into something charred, flat, and flaky, to make them stick to walls like wet leaves, but the radiation has eaten up everything made of flesh. It is so quiet in the room. The air smells of something poisonous, like diesel smoke.

The skeleton of a girl picks up her phone, but it doesn't work. She flips the light switch, but there is no power. She presses the power button of her laptop, and it hums, coming to life. She is surprised to see that the internet is still working. It works in patches, as if it is not the real internet, but the skeleton of it. Probably it can live without people like a chunk of prickly pear cactus chopped off from its roots.

She almost jumps when she sees the message on the screen. Her bones rattle. A shoulder blade falls down on the floor. But she doesn't care about the shoulder blade. Anyway, there is not much time left for her. Minutes or hours, at most.

"hi," someone writes.

"Hi!" the white, smeared in soot, bones of her fingers type. "Who you are?"

Her English is far from perfect. She lived and died in the country where no one speaks English. No one reads, writes, or hears English. There used to be a lot of signs written in English, though, like 'Sex Shop' or 'Second Hand'—sometimes it was 'Cekond hend', but the difference was too subtle to be noticed. Her life-long dream, her secret obsession was always to speak to someone who knew real English. It looks like her dream may come true now.

"hows it going?" a stranger writes to her, "r u alive? i am from us. no one is alive around here. i saw you are online and was curious. peace."

Peace. What a strange word. For many years, the war had been warming up its engine, standing motionless on the rails, like a monstrous diesel locomotive, and that sound vibrated both in the air and in everyone's heart. Then gazillions of bombs fell, gazillions of missiles were launched. Sprawling burdocks of nuclear explosions shot up, blinding the sun, making the sun beautiful but not really important, like a first lady among many presidents. And then peace came at last. An absolute peace that will last forever.

The bones of her fingers hit the keys.

"Hi! Not alive, no one alive anymore, and you? How are you doing? If you agree write with me, it will nice. peace."

A new message appears on the screen.

"nice to hear from you. i'm doin good for a skeleton . . . still have 8 fingers that can type. we can practice some informal English if u want. Joe"

"Want I?" she types. "Practice English is my dream. Never had chance in my life."

She's been studying English since she was six, even though her schoolteacher could not tell "how" from "now". After ten years of study, all her friends could say was, "My name is this and that." But she's always been more hard-working and persistent than the others.

She was ten when an American delegation visited her school. Being the best student in English, she had to say something to them. She was so proud then, so excited. She said, "Hello, my name is Lyn." They smiled widely, and she went on about her hobbies, inspired, "I like read books. I like wash TV-set." She saw in their eyes that there was something really wrong about it and had a sick feeling in her stomach. She corrected herself, hurriedly, "I like to saw a TV-set." "I'm ten," she added. "I'm high. I have big green ears. Beautiful green ears." She meant eyes, of course.

New lines pop up on the screen.

"i like biking," the skeleton of a stranger writes, "and also music, sometimes i am djing at small parties. i love to travel. i also like to read and draw and of course just chill with some good people. i try to be adventurous when i can. i enjoy being outside and some partying. what do you do for fun? are you a calm or crazy girl? peace."

When the skeleton of a girl was alive, she hardly ever traveled far from home, and she never went biking. She liked music, though.

"For fun I did meny different things like reading books which are interesting for me, play different games. I'm not calm)) I can't imeging me without adventurous too. And I also like musik," she writes.

He answers immediately.

"what sort of music r u into? i listen to mostly hiphop and rock n roll . . . some old stuff too. u like to dance?"

The skeleton of a girl bites the bone of her index finger, like she used to bite the knuckle of it when she was alive, which always helped her concentrate, and ponders over the abstract question: what dances would she like if she were alive?

"I like hip-hop, house, electro house, minimal and many old songs and popular music," she types. "I like dance very much, and what about you?"

He answers after a pause.

"cool and crazy. if the time and music (and perhaps the partner) is right, i really like to dance. but i am not always in the mood. sometimes i just want to chill when i am out at night. also, how old are you?"

She would turn seventeen in a month if she were alive. The perfect age. The best age to be.

Her dream to know English was inspired by her mom. Once, ten years ago, Mother had a chance to get a job in Canada and flee from her gloomy, dangerous homeland. During the interview, she was asked a question. "How many times have you been married?" But Mom didn't catch what was said. In her elegant handwriting, she wrote on the blank page "eighteen," because she thought the question had meant "how many years have you been married." No Canada, sorry. Those guys didn't need professors of chemistry married eighteen times.

The skeleton of a girl types the answer. "Am 17. I like spek to you."

She settles comfortably in the chair, but she is too fragile now, and even this small motion makes a couple of her ribs fall out. They rattle down onto the floor.

"i am 22 and a leo," the stranger writes. "leos i think are a bit crazy and very proud. but also dependable. always a bit in love. i dunno, cool. well i am certainly a leo. I even have the red hair something like a lion. you have a favorite sign?"

She doesn't know the names of the zodiac signs in English, and doesn't know how to say about it.

"are you sexy?" the skeleton of the boy suddenly asks.

Another rib falls down. Now it's lying in the back of her pelvis, where she used to have her perfect behind. Can it be called sexy, even in the remotest sense of the word? she thinks. She feels shy of the word 'sexy.' She's too young. She's stripped of flesh, but not of shame yet. She already kissed and was kissed hundreds of times, and she already had her first sex experience, but that childish shame still remains in her the way a snub-nosed piglet continues to exist in a link of sausage.

"Meny peoples seys that I look like a black panther," she writes, avoiding the direct answer, and adds, "you are big dangerous!"

You are *a bit* dangerous, she means. She hopes he understands.

"yes a leo is big and dangerous," he writes. "a black panther is a sexy animal in my opinion. a black panther is smart and fast and beautiful but also dangerous, all good things."

The clock on the wall strikes six in the morning. It's still so early. The last day in human history has just begun. She looks out through the wide window. At dawn, the city is black and white Guernica stretching to infinity and beyond, but the colorful Dali is already spreading in the sky. How can people do this? she thinks. Probably, no one can live without meaning in their lives, and political psychopaths suffering from nationalism and constipation try to find meaning in revenge, or territorial gain, in considering themselves better and nobler than other psychopaths suffering from constipation and nationalism.

The skeleton of a girl listens to the chime of the clock fading away, then hears footsteps in the kitchen. Her mom's skeleton appears in the doorway.

She moves the screen so that her mom cannot see what is on it. Mom has never approved talking about sex. She was a firm believer in the conventional things like love and marriage.

The skeleton of a girl squints to read a short question that has just appeared on the screen.

"u think i am too old haha?"

The skeleton of her mom wants to say something, but she doesn't have lips or tongue, so she just moves her lower jaw a couple of times. The jaw doesn't hold and falls down on the floor. The skeleton of Mom looks at it, shakes her skull, and leaves the room.

The skeleton of a girl listens to her retreating steps and types: "Why you said this?"

She is waiting for an answer. Somehow she knows she's just seen her mom for the last time. The clock on the wall counts away the sonorous seconds of loneliness. She feels a huge disconnection with the rest of the world. Perhaps this world doesn't exist and has never existed, she thinks. *Will it exist after I fall into bones and soot?* Perhaps it will. Or maybe not.

What about all people on earth? Will the world exist when there's no one to see it, to feel it, to think of it? If a tree falls in the forest and there's no one to hear its fall, did it fall at all? Will the rabid radioactive clouds eternally wander around, stretching downwards their cotton-wool fingers, hoping to find and kill the last survivors? Will the world be just switched off like a DVD player when there's nothing interesting to see?

The lines she sees on the screen make her even lonelier. She brushes aside this momentary feeling.

"i am almost 2m. like 183. 182 now without my scalp and skin on my feet. i like that you have all these dark features . . . like the panther. panthers have a wonderful body. i was just joking. but some girls like their guys older. u?"

She does not like the word 'body'. She prefers boys who look into your eyes before looking down at your bare knees. Perhaps such boys exist only in her imagination. No, she's not a panther. She's rather a kitten inside. Her idea of happiness is to cling to someone who loves you back and purr.

He writes to her again.

"i'm only teasing. i found you because i just joined kontakte and i was looking for another lynn, a girl who i was supposed to be working with when i teach english. but i found you instead, and i thought that maybe you would know some english so i messaged you. tell me some more about yourself though . . . u have a favorite thing to do if your whole day is free?"

The skeleton of a girl liked getting messages from her friends when she was alive. But she does not remember how to spell the word 'message'. 'A' or 'E'? She decides that does not matter much.

"If my day will be free I will go first to a library, than exchange massage with my friends. You?"

She hopes she wrote the word 'message' correctly. But the skeleton of a boy does not answer for a whole minute. Then he writes with pauses after every sentence, as if thinking about something.

"i would sleep late . . . cozy in bed. then i would get a huge delicious lunch. then go bmx biking at a skatepark in the late afternoon. then swimming to cool off. then out to party and enjoy some nightlife. then finally late to bed with a girl i like. then the massage. massage is a great thing . . . then sleep."

Very typical, she thinks. All they need is sex, bikes, and huge lunches. Five years ago, when she was only twelve, she spoke to a real, genuine English-speaking European. He had a beer belly, a motorbike, and oily eyes of a cat in the season. That European sat in a café in the marketplace every morning. He pawed waitresses but gave good tips to them. She had always wanted to test her English, and that day she had her chance. She had been preparing for three days, was very nervous, but at last she came to a real foreigner (to her, he seemed something like a white elephant—a rare thing and not a human being), introduced herself, and spoke about her attempts to master the language. He laughed and planted a playful kiss on her forehead, so she went away pleased with herself. The next day a waitress told her that after she had left, the foreigner scratched his balding head and asked: "Who the hell was that? I haven't asked for an underage whore."

"Cool, i like you day," she types.

The skeleton of a boy writes again.

"well i borrowed a bit from your day. i wouldnt have thought to get a massage in bed if you hadnt inspired me. it was your idea."

She imagines them in bed: naked, with their phones, exchanging messages. Hmm.

"I think instead massage you want some another thing with girl would you like in you bed, and you decided not to say it," she writes.

She reads the answer on the screen.

"maybe . . . maybe you are right and you caught me . . . or maybe a girl does all those other wonderful things first and then the night ends with a massage. or two massages. one for each person."

Perhaps he's different, she thinks. Actually, it may be so romantic to talk on the phone to a girl you love, even if she's in the same bed with you and has already done all the wonderful things she could. To use a telephone in order to tell her about your love. So touching.

"I never thought about it, but it is interesting," she answers.

He answers very quickly.

"exactly. especially with you by my side. we would be some scary fucking massagers."

It has become too personal for her taste. She likes unfashionable things, like dating, talking, thinking, proposing. Everything that makes the relationships sounder. Anyway, she does not want to discuss sex with a stranger any longer. Even with a skeleton of a stranger.

"My father is a military engineer," she writes. "He makes weapons. Good bombs that kill only people and leave things safe."

Weapons intended to kill millions of civilians. One day Lyn heard, out of the blue, that a girl from her school had died in a railway accident. They had never been friends. She did not even remember that girl's name. But days after hearing about her death, she felt as if some tender part of her nature, the skin of her soul, was bruised, which lent her a painful clarity of perception. She noticed that the world without one person had changed dramatically. The reality became thinner, like the air as you ascend the mountains. The days become clearer, more transparent. Every small thing lost its solidity, and some otherworldly sense showed through. She looked at the kids playing in a sandbox, at a man holding a smiling baby in his hands, at an old woman crossing the street and thought, if one death changes the world so much, what if millions die? Everyone die? Will all things explode and turn into vacuum?

"my fathers a lawyer," the stranger answers, "i like cars. i used to drive a bmw. but now i have no car. u have a car?"

"No, but I like Lexus," she writes.

"yes i do like it," he writes. "those cars are expensive tho . . . so it is a fantasy for me own one. if i did own one i would certainly take you for a drive with me. would u like that?"

She smiles, against her will, against the chasm separating them, against all those billions of deaths, logically possible, militarily justified, politically necessary, but impossible in some greater moral sense. She thinks she likes this guy, although she does not understand some of the words he writes.

"Yes, I would)))"

"id trade you a massage for a car ride if you had the lexus," he writes and adds after a pause, "only if you thought it was a fair trade of course."

This time she is sincerely surprised. There's something psychotic in it. Or is this just her imagination?

"Massage?" she asks.

He pauses, then writes slowly.

"it was a joke. i was saying that if you had a lexus i would love for you to take me for a ride as well. i would even give you a massage if u let me come in your lexus, if u thought it was a fair trade."

She thinks she cannot understand the point of this joke, if it was a joke. She opens a dictionary. "Trade: the act or an instance of buying and selling goods and services." It doesn't clear the matter up one bit. Why does anyone have to send a message to a person in the same car? Is this boy right in the head?

")))I wasnt anderstend what do you mean))) For what do massages in the car when we are close?"

But the answer she gets is even more puzzling.

"if just plain sex is everything you want"

Suddenly something idiotic interrupts his words.

"Hi, please help me win Hyundai Accent))

please send SMS with text 51_ 4135 to number1171. Price: $1. I need your help! As soon as I win I promise to send back $500."

"what does all this mean?" he asks.

She feels ashamed, though it is not her fault. She types as quickly as she can.

"Nothing, virus sent this massage."

She waits. He does not answer for a long while. Everything is so calm. The dead world is crumbling to pieces so slowly, so quietly. In cold polar seas, skeletons of whales try to sing their last songs to the skeletons of their wives with skeletons of their unborn babies inside, but no sound is heard. Skeletons of sloths fall from the branches like overripe plums. Skeletons of lions follow with the gaping stare of their bony eye sockets stumbling skeletons of zebras, still graceful in their disintegration. Skeletons of people burn slowly like sparklers, throwing the last sparks of their souls into the darkness around, trying to find the last word that will make the world resonate like a guitar body, but never finding it. It's ten minutes after six, still so very early. The next message unpleasantly surprises her.

"ok we can chat on there later. my computer is a bit fucked up right now anyways so i have to wait too. in the near future i hope though"

The bones of her fingers hit the keys.

"Don't leave. There is no future!"

He doesn't answer for a couple of minutes. Then,

"maybe it is too hard to explain here. anyways i have to go and say goodbye for the night. its night here in us. im glad i got in touch with you though. it has been a pleasure. anyways, hopefully you don't think i'm a creep or something."

THE DAY WHEN THE LAST WAR IS OVER

The screen is empty. *Oh my god, it's all over*, she thinks.

The skeleton of a girl comes out onto the porch. She's flaking like a plane tree. Her bones are off-white, the color of a full moon in a clear night sky. There's a nasal cavity, rather large, at the place where she used to have a small, freckled nose with a turned-up tip. She doesn't have her left hand now, and most of her rib cage is already gone. The landscape is steaming like a hot bath. She feels naked without her ribs.

She sees a heap of bones and the orange gas mask: all that is left from the skeleton of her father, the military engineer and creator of good bombs, who stood there some half an hour ago, looking at the skeletons of chickens digging the radioactive ashes. All that is left from his strong arms that used to toss his little daughter in the air and always catch her. All that is left from his shoulders she used to sit on when he was giving her piggyback rides in the central park.

She has never noticed before that his skull is so oblong and his eyeholes are so close together.

Her right leg falls off, and for some time, its toe bones jerk, neurotically. She keeps standing on her left leg, like an empty wine glass on its elegant stem. She does not find it difficult to keep her balance, probably because she is as light as a feather now.

When she hears a soft remote honking, she looks up at the sky, startled. But in the sky, there aren't any bombers anymore, and only skeletons of cranes are flying so high above the land, so smoothly, so strangely, that the skeleton of a girl smiles and understands that everything scary is already over, that everything is going to be good from now on.

MOTHER; MICROBES

H. V. Patterson

We are the microbes that ate your Mother;
we are what she became.

Lost at sea, drowning then dead,
her last thought was you, daughter.
Her bones so soft and fragile
we cradled them and fed like
a child feeds from a mother. We felt
you, her daughter, our daughter now,
your DNA imprinted inside
her very marrow

We pulled memories
from calcium and phosphate.
We knew you, and loved you
drenched in sunlight, hair corona flame around your head,
though we didn't yet know "head" or "sun" or "flame"
and had no "eyes" to see.
Still, we knew,
ingested love with your mother's bones

Lovesick for you, we crept from the depths.
It was lifetimes, generations dead and dying,
breathing poisonous air, but
as we divided, we passed along the memories:
her bones, her love.

MOTHER; MICROBES

You were our first awareness,
first understanding of hands
and grasping,
of pain
and yearning

We were your shelter, your milk, your Mother;
we will be your home once more

Why run from us?
We felt your feet-flutter, heard your scream
as you emerged from amniotic sea
to this oxygen-drowned world.
Now, we have come to take you back
to the loving depths
and slow, deep currents.
We have come, our daughter, to hold you
close, to take each fragment of you,
eyes like pearl, lips like coral, teeth cutting as shell,
your bones and their marrow,
within us

Then we will return
to the cold, dark waters and be, eternally,
Mother and daughter.
Trillions of hungry bodies, a million generations,
thriving in the crushing dark.
Loving and loved
even after the sun goes out.

THE MYTHOLOGIZATION OF TYMBER PRESCOTT IN FIVE SELECTED PHOTOS

Luciano Marano

IT HELPS THAT she's dead now, because we never thought of her as a real person anyway. She was an aspiration, the avatar of something we wanted or wanted to be. An attractive algorithm with a pretty face and keen sense of style, designed to be irresistible and sell us stuff. She was basically a brand, like any other. At least we no longer have to feel conflicted about what happened to her—the few of us who did, that is.

Her objectification was an achievement of sorts. She was everything to everyone, inscrutable but endlessly appealing. Mona Lisa in fair trade fashion. The girl next door with eyes full of unspoken promises, more followers than the Dalai Lama, and liked by absolutely everyone.

A true influencer, she made it easier for us with every post.

Tymber Prescott always looked good. She knew exactly what she wanted, was happier than we could ever understand. She was certainly not alive in the same way as lesser humans like us—people with desperate hopes and bitter disappointments, shame, regret, and secret thoughts we could never share.

Her perfection haunted us.

Her destruction obsessed us.

Now, her feed fascinates for very different reasons.

***

THE MYTHOLOGIZATION OF TYMBER PRESCOTT

Influence: the capacity to have an effect on the character, development, or behavior of someone or something; or the effect itself.

****

1. Cottagecore Cutie

Vibrant in a pink thermal shirt and white overalls against the crumbling interior of a ruined cabin, it was exactly this sense of personality—cute, cocky, perfectly posed—that shot Tymber from zero to 40,000 followers in her first year on the app.

Hands jammed in pockets, blonde hair flowing from beneath a black watch cap, Tymber laughs at us, rocking back playfully on her heels. She is incongruously at ease in such a place. You want to warn her away. It somehow doesn't feel right that she should be there, that anybody should. How much of that reaction is due to our knowledge of subsequent events is impossible to say. Still, the place is eerie.

Scorch marks on the splintered wall behind her seem less than random, an unsettling pattern of darker blacks beneath the char of some long ago fire. A stain, or perhaps weirdly intricate growth of mold, sends seeking tendrils upward from the ground beneath Tymber's tan boots. A moldering blanket of leaves and bristling patches of brown grass. Here and there small round beads of shiny black stone glint in the weak rays of light coming through what we imagine are holes in whatever remains of the sagging structure's roof. High on the wall, underneath the mold, a vague design of scratches can be seen. Curling lines within a circle, seemingly too deliberate to be the work of weather or wildlife.

Likely taken by Oliver Perkins, noted lifestyle photographer, the picture is the last of several Tymber posted from a weekend trip to a rural section of the Olympic Peninsula, where she and other models, influencers, and photographers from the Seattle area rented a house for a collaborative working weekend.

Investigators subsequently ascertained Tymber and Oliver went for a walk around noon and returned later than expected, nearly causing the group to miss their intended ferry back to the city. Others in the party said the pair were behaving strangely when they got back; "like they were high or something," said one witness.

211

"

In the case of Oliver, known to be a regular drinker and frequent user of drugs, this was not unusual. Tymber, however, did not often imbibe, and at least one witness expressed concern for her.

Searches of the area conducted after Tymber's death located no cabin. Oliver, of course, could not be asked about the image, as he was found dead just two weeks after the trip. Authorities assert he fell and struck his head in the kitchen of his Ballard apartment and bled to death while intoxicated by a combination of codeine and alcohol.

Initial evidence seemed to suggest another person was present at the time, but the investigation was ultimately inconclusive.

***

2. Sweaty & Ready

Tymber's athleticism was often a secondary aspect of her influencer persona. However, seeing her in workout clothes and holding a kettlebell, muscles flexed, we are reminded she initially rose to fame as a fitness model.

Wearing gray tights, white sneakers, a black sports bra, Tymber's hair is pulled loosely back in a playful pink band. She is standing beside a wall of windows in a large room with padded floors. The light is warm and clear. She is turned partially away from us, looking over her shoulder with a mysterious smile that is part challenge, part invitation. She wears no makeup or jewelry beyond a small gold stud in the visible ear. She is lightly sweating, as if having just completed a warmup she is ready to begin exercising in earnest.

On the skin of her shoulder is an area of discoloration. It might be a bruise, though it's almost perfectly symmetrical. The outline of the shape is more prominent, easier to spot. And within the circle are faint lines which seem to curl inward as if part of an intricate design.

Her eyes, previously a startlingly light green, appear different now, darker. A shade of brown so deep as to be almost black.

***

3. #nothappy

Her expression is difficult to decipher. Tymber sits on the floor just inside a pair of slim white doors, one open to reveal a small balcony rimmed by ornate blue ironwork outside. The light is dull and gray, threatening rain. She sits on a plush rug in faded jeans and billowy yellow sweater. Her legs are not fully visible. The nails on the fingers we can see, on the hand not holding her phone, are unpainted, though the skin beneath each is slightly blue.

Again, she wears no makeup. The dark circles beneath her eyes are obvious. She is smiling, but it has the feel of habit rather than true expression. Despite the apparent chill of the day and open door, there is a thin sheen of sweat on Tymber's forehead. It is not difficult to imagine she will soon begin to cry. The image has the feel of a haphazard selfie more than staged photograph meant for posting. And yet, post it she did, without hashtags or explanation.

The location of the room in which the picture was taken remains unknown. When asked later, Tymber's friends and associates were unable, or unwilling, to provide authorities with any additional information.

In the wake of this post, and several likewise melancholic and ambiguous selfies shared shortly after, Tymber's number of followers leapt astronomically.

***

4. The Infamous Mirror Image

Easily the most famous of her series of bizarre selfies, this picture is unquestionably more responsible than any other for the disturbing rumors that surround the influencer's sudden grisly and mysterious death just six days after it was posted.

She'd been avoiding friends, investigators later ascertained. She hadn't been seen in public for weeks. Essentially, Tymber did not exist beyond her increasingly strange postings to various social media platforms.

Here, Tymber leans forward, face close to the bathroom mirror. The hand of her raised arm is out of frame, likely braced against the wall, while the other holds a phone near her shoulder, lens forward. Though shirtless, Tymber's hair, wild and tangled,

213

clearly unwashed, is long enough to obscure her breasts. She is terribly pale, and looks even more so against the uniformly white tile of the bathroom. Despite the light source above the unseen mirror, her eyes appear entirely black.

There is a trickle of what may be blood coming down Tymber's forehead from somewhere within her hair, though the viscous liquid seems too thick and dark. She is very thin, with much of the lean muscle on display in previous photos seemingly wasted away. On her concave belly and boney hips can be seen a forest of harsh red scratches, the sort which may have been inflicted by the claws of a large cat or perhaps her own fingernails—those we can see have grown long and ragged. The waistband and visible portion of her light blue briefs look soiled.

Most disturbing of all, however, is her expression. Tymber's mouth hangs open, her discolored tongue lolling to one side, much longer than it should be. Milky drool slicks her chin. And although the edges of her cracked and bleeding lips are pulled slightly upward, as if in a smile, the young woman appears at the same time to be screaming. Looking back now, one cannot help but wonder if she was perhaps calling for help.

The image has received more likes and comments than any other Tymber ever posted. It has been shared countless times and remains a popular meme.

***

5. #whoiswithme?

Her feet, bare and dirty. The last photo posted to Tymber's feed, barely two hours before she was found dead. One imagines she was sitting with her knees up and apart, soles pressed nearly together.

Her skin is cut, deeply in places, and blood flows through the frosting of filth smeared across her soles. Dark blue veins bulge in small patches on her ankles and the portion of her calves we can see. Her toenails are black. Several have split apart and blood oozes from the ravaged tips of her toes. A small shard of glass can be seen, distractingly shiny amidst so much darkness, piercing Tymber's left heel.

She had clearly been walking without shoes, but for how long? And where? What is the meaning of her final hashstag? A siren call to would-be imitators? Encouragement to follow in the troubled icon's suicidal footsteps? Or is it simply the honest and desperate final question posed by a terrified young woman who was—or at least believed she was—in the thrall of some inexplicable influence?

These are just a few of the many questions that plague those who seek answers to the question of what truly happened to Tymber Prescott.

According to law enforcement, not long after posting the image, the 24-year-old influencer leapt to her death from the top floor of a commercial parking structure in Seattle's downtown business district.

She has since been the focus of several investigations, both written features and broadcast TV specials alike, along with countless YouTube videos done with widely varying levels of respect and production quality.

To this day, there are those who insist Tymber committed suicide while under the control of a supernatural force. Others argue it was true demonic possession, using her story to warn non-believers of the dangers of godless glory and vapid idolatry.

Most balk at such notions, however, maintaining Tymber was simply the victim of an undiagnosed, but decidedly non-supernatural, mental illness, nothing more.

Admittedly, members of the latter camp struggle to explain the state of her apartment.

In Tymber's home police allegedly found extensive writings carved into walls, written in numerous languages, none of them English and not one of which Tymber was known to speak. Also, several advanced mathematical equations were scrawled in human blood and excrement on her living room floor, apparently solved. Experts remain in disagreement as to the technical accuracy of her solutions, the math being of a reportedly highly experimental and theoretical variety, perhaps unprovable. But none of them can explain how a C-average student who hadn't completed a single hour of college instruction could manage even as much as she did.

And rumors persist of more macabre findings in the apartment—bottles filled with urine; dozens of watches, all broken; a mound of dead birds in one closet; bones that appeared to have been gnawed; and, perhaps most disturbing of all, several articles of shredded children's clothing.

No officials involved with the case have cooperated with outside investigators or journalists. Several, in fact, have died premature and mysterious deaths themselves, a fact which only strengthens the resolve of those insisting the ultimate cause of Tymber's condition to be supernatural.

Meanwhile, Tymber herself lives on after death, in a way.

***

Ascendancy: Occupation of a position of great power, dominance, or absolute influence.

***

Her photos are a ubiquitous presence on social media. She remains a popular choice for those seeking a Halloween costume both sexy and scary. The strange symbol on her shoulder is a tattoo favored by rising influencers and celebrity personalities. Her likeness has even been found painted on buildings in various cities around the world. A kind of new secular saint, Tymber's visage seems to mark scenes of similar, likewise unexplained, suicides. Of which, for whatever reason, there are many of late. And more happening all the time.

North American government health officials have persistently stopped short of calling the recent spike of suicides among young people an epidemic. Tech company representatives continue to be reticent to discuss the appearance among posts made by the deceased those including Tymber's now-infamous hashtag—#whoiswithme? Such posts are now typically flagged, if not removed, by company moderators, though critics and parent groups insist such action to be an insufficient response. Industry experts are in disagreement as to the connection, if any, between the proliferation of such content and national suicide trends, and free speech advocates rush to decry such censorship as both unnecessary and unethical. The debate rages on.

Meanwhile, independent research and multiple surveys conducted by mental health advocacy groups in the United States and Canada claim an indisputable correlation between these otherwise unexplained deaths and posts containing the image and/or famous last words of Tymber Prescott.

Of course, such evidence in no way proves those deaths are the result of a widening instance of some sort of mass possession, the work of supernatural or demonic forces, as many claim (some religious groups have gone so far as to encourage their members to avoid the internet altogether). But neither does it establish the existence of a lethal copycat craze among impressionable young people either, a kind of "lethal viral challenge" as mainstream media outlets and some prominent psychologists insist.

All that's certain is the continuing presence of Tymber Prescott, inscrutable and enigmatic as ever. Her story is somehow aspirational and simultaneously cautionary. What exactly about this figure continues to resonate with so many is a mystery.

Only her influence is beyond question.

BRAVE NEW WEIRDOS, CLASS OF 2022

Alex Woodroe is a Romanian writer and editor of dark speculative fiction, and Editor in Chief for **Tenebrous Press**. *Whisperwood,* her debut novel, is out July 2023 from Flame Tree Press. Her short fiction has appeared in *Dark Matter Magazine, The No Sleep Podcast,* and many more. Alex lives in the heart of the Transylvanian region of Romania.

Bitter Karella is the writer and horror aficionado behind the microfiction comedy account @Midnight_pals, which asks what if all your favorite horror writers gathered around the campfire to tell scary stories. When not writing Twitter jokes, she also dabbles in cartooning and text game design.

Cadwell Turnbull is the award-winning author of *The Lesson* and *No Gods, No Monsters.* His short fiction has appeared in *Lightspeed, Nightmare, Asimov's Science Fiction* and *The Year's Best Science Fiction and Fantasy 2019.* Turnbull lives in Raleigh and teaches at North Carolina State University.

Carson Winter is an author, punker and raw nerve, residing in the Pacific Northwest. His fiction has appeared in *Vastarien, Apex, The No Sleep Podcast,* and Dread Stone Press' *Split Scream* series. His debut novella, *Soft Targets,* is forthcoming from **Tenebrous Press**. Find him on Twitter at @CarsonWinter3.

Charlotte Ariel Finn is a longtime writer and critic; she has written at the Eisner-award winning website ComicsAlliance and currently reviews comics at *Shelfdust.* She also collaborates on the horror comic *Brand Echo.* Most of her work can be found at charlottearielfinn.com. Charlotte lives in Canada.

Colleen Anderson's poetry has been published in such venues as *Andromeda Spaceways, Lucent Dreaming* and the award-winning *Shadow Atlas.* Her fiction can be found in *A Body of Work* (Black Shuck Books). *The Lore of Inscrutable Dreams* is due for release in 2023. She lives in Vancouver, BC.

Emily Rigole is a software engineer and writer from Macon, Georgia. She grew up playing in red dirt and seeing strange things in the woods. She now lives in Atlanta, with a strange thing that claims to be a beagle, and enjoys writing about outsiders, curses, and horrible misunderstandings.

H.V. Patterson (she/her) lives in Oklahoma. Her work has been published by Sliced Up Press, Creature Publishing, *Horror Tree,* Dread Stone Press and more. When she isn't reading and watching horror, she loves baking, hiking, doing puzzles, and learning about the weird creatures we share the planet with.

Isha Karki is a writer based in London. Her short fiction has won the Dinesh Allirajah Prize, Galley Beggar Press Short Story Prize and Mslexia Short Story Competition. Her work appears in publications such as *khōréō, Lightspeed,* and *Best British Short Stories 2021.* Find her on Twitter @IshaKarki11.

Jennifer Jeanne McCardle lives in New York with her partner and an agent of chaos (her dog). She works in animal conservation, but previously she's taught ESL in Korea and Indonesia and also worked with nonprofits in Asia and the US. More info on her website: jenniferjeannemcardle.blogspot.com.

Joe Koch (he/they) writes literary horror and surrealist trash. A Shirley Jackson Award finalist and occasional editor, Joe is the author of *The Wingspan of Severed Hands, The Couvade* and *Convulsive.* Find Joe online at horrorsong.blog and on Twitter @horrorsong.

Jolie Toomajan is a PhD candidate, writer, editor and all-around ghoul. Her dissertation in progress focuses on the women who wrote for *Weird Tales.* Her work has appeared in *Death in the Mouth* and *Black Static,* among other places. You can find her on Twitter and Instagram @JolieToomajan.

jonah wu is a queer, non-binary, transmasculine writer and filmmaker living in Los Angeles. Their work explores their Chinese American upbringing and the intersection between gender, queerness, dreams, memory, and the existential complications of being. Follow them on Twitter & Instagram @rabblerouses.

Kirstyn McDermott is the author of two award-winning novels, *Madigan Mine* and *Perfections*. She produces and co-hosts *The Writer and the Critic*, a literary discussion podcast. Kirstyn lives in Ballarat, Australia with fellow writer Jason Nahrung and two distinctly non-literary felines. Kirstynmcdermott.com

Luciano Marano is an award-winning author, photographer and journalist. His work has appeared in *Year's Best Hardcore Horror*; *Monsters, Movies & Mayhem*; *Crash Code; Nightscript; PseudoPod*; and many more. A U.S. Navy veteran originally from rural western Pennsylvania, he now resides near Seattle.

Mae Murray a horror writer and editor living in eerie New England. She specializes in screenwriting and journalism, and has worked in the mental health field and film, writing, and publishing for a decade. She freelances full-time.

Matt Blairstone (he/him) is a writer, artist and indie comics creator; and the founder and publisher of **Tenebrous Press.** He lives in Portland, Oregon with his wife and son.

M.E. Bronstein teaches college composition, studies translation history in the Middle Ages, and writes horror and dark fantasy. Her short fiction has appeared in *Beneath Ceaseless Skies, PodCastle, khōréō magazine*, and more. You can find her at mebronstein.com.

Nikki R. Leigh is a queer, forever-90s-kid wallowing in all things horror. She reads her stories to her partner and cat, one of which scares easily. Her work appears in *The Dread Machine, The Book of Queer Saints* and more. Her short story collection, *Lessons in Demoralization*, is out now from DarkLit Press.

Sergey Gerasimov lives in Kharkiv, Ukraine, and has since the war started. He is a writer, poet and translator of poetry. His stories have appeared in magazines all over the world. His book of nonfiction about the war in Ukraine, *Feuerpanorama*, can be found on Amazon. NZZ, the Swiss-German newspaper, has published two hundred of his anti-war articles since the start of the war.

Sloane Leong is a cartoonist, illustrator and writer, engaging with visceral futurities and fantasies through a radical, kaleidoscopic lens. She is the creator of several graphic novels, including *Prism Stalker, A Map to the Sun* and *Graveneye*. She currently lives on Chinook land near what is known as Portland, Oregon.

Sonora Taylor is the award-winning author of seven books, including *Little Paranoias, Seeing Things,* and *Someone to Share My Nightmares.* She has been published by Rooster Republic, Cemetery Gates Media, Ghost Orchid Press and others. She lives in Arlington, Virginia with her husband and rescue dog.

Tania Chen is a Chinese-Mexican queer writer. Their work has appeared in *Unfettered Hexes* (Neon Hemlock), *Strange Horizons,* and many more. They are a graduate of the Clarion West Novella Bootcamp workshop. Currently, they are assistant editor at Uncanny Magazine. Find them on Twitter@archistratego.

Warren Benedetto writes dark fiction about horrible people, places and things. His work has appeared in *Dark Matter Magazine, The NoSleep Podcast, Apex,* and many more. His hobbies include sleeping, hitting snooze, sleeping some more, and naps. He is on Twitter @warrenbenedetto. warrenbenedetto.com

THE BRAVE NEW WEIRD SHORTLIST

A. P. Howell—*Dread Space*—Used Armor Smell

Alex Kingsley- *Radon Journal*—This Is Not A Place of Honor

Brian Evenson & Chris Kelso—*3-Lobed Burning Eye*—Jenny Longlegs

Briar Ripley Page—*The Book Of Queer Saints*—Therianthrope

Caitlin Marceau—*Phantasmagoria Issue 20*—Tabula Rasa

Christi Nogle—*Vastarien*—She Ain't Stoppin'

Ephiny Gale—*The Dread Machine*—Rewind

Erin Brown—*FIYAH Magazine #22*—A Brief and Hideous Scrawl

Eugenia Triantafyllou—*khōréō*—Tomatoes

Hailey Piper—*Cosmic Horror Monthly*—Parasites of Silver and Gold

J. C. Changmore—*khōréō*—The Scumbling

J.A.W. McCarthy—*Shredded: A Sports & Fitness Body Horror Anthology*—Our Perpetual Intention

James Bennett—*The Dark*—Ídolo

Jennifer Lee Rossman—*The Arcanist*—Darken The Corners Of My Mind

Karlo Yeager Rodriguez—*Pseudopod*—Got Your Nose

K.W. Colyard—*Seize The Press*—Those Who Forget and Those Who Perish

K. J. Shepherd—*206 Word Stories by Bag of Bones Press*—The Horror of Oz

L. Marie Wood—*Something Scary Podcast*—Hypnopompia

WEIRD PUBLISHERS OF NOTE

We discovered, while reading stories for this collection, that there are many publishers out there putting out great works of New Weird Horror despite not formally having anything to do with the Weird family. It just goes to show that Weird is always in the last place you look.

Here are just a handful of the places you should keep an eye on:

Apex Magazine
Seize the Press
The NoSleep Podcast
Wrongdoing Magazine
Nightmare Magazine
FIYAH Magazine
Ghoulish Books/PMMP
Shortwave Publishing
Cursed Morsels Press
Uncanny Magazine
Uncharted Magazine
Vastarien
Pseudopod
The Dark Magazine
Dark Dispatch
The Dread Machine
Baffling Mag
Flame Tree Press
Three-Lobed Burning Eye
Weird Horror Magazine
khōréō magazine
Something Scary Podcast
WeirdPunk Books
Tales to Terrify podcast
Wyldblood Press

X-Ray Lit Mag
The Antihumanist
Drabblecast
Dread Stone Press
Undertow Publications
The Arcanist
The Tentaculum
Mythaxis
Diabolical Plots
ParSec Publishing
Radon Journal
The Bear Creek Gazette
Ghost Orchid Press
Planet Scumm
Weird Tales
Malarkey Books
Neon Hemlock
StrangeHouse Books
Cosmic Horror Monthly
Orion's Belt
ergot.

WEIRD 2022 NOVELS & NOVELLAS OF NOTE

If you've made it this far into your Weird journey, chances are you wouldn't mind some further reading.** There's a world of books out there that deserve recognition, and half the fun is discovering your own gems, but the least we can do is give you a couple of places to start.

All **Tenebrous Press releases, past and future, would be a great place to start, but our goal with this volume is to celebrate everyone else.

No Gods for Drowning—Hailey Piper—Polis Books
   In the beginning, man was prey. Without the Gods, they'll be prey again.

Man, Fuck This House—Brian Asman—Brian Asman Books
   While the Haskins family might be the newest owners of 4596 James Circle, they're far from its only residents...

The Death of Jane Lawrence—Caitlin Starling—St. Martin's Press
   This Crimson Peak-inspired story will leave readers shaken, desperate to begin again as soon as they are finished.

Helpmeet—Naben Ruthnum—Undertow Publications
   It's 1900, and Louise Wilk is taking her dying husband from Manhattan to the upstate orchard estate where he grew up.

Mothwoman—Nicole Cushing—Word Horde
   *Mothwoman combines the style and playful dark satire
   of A Sick Gray Laugh with the grimness and quick pace
   of Mr. Suicide.*

Moonfellows—Danger Slater—Perpetual Motion Machine
   Publishing
   *One small step for man, one giant leap into the existential
   abyss.*

Unto the Godless What Little Remains—Mário Coelho—
   Solaris
   The internet is a lonesome god.

Blueprints for Madness:
10 Great Horror Comics of 2022

by Matt Blairstone

Ironically enough, I made a valid attempt to curb my comics-buying habit this year; the precarious TBR piles teetering in my bedroom, living room and office have grown unmanageable and are a serious hindrance to daily life. A vow was made to ruthlessly slash the quantity of titles I sub to at **Cosmic Monkey** and **Comic Cave PDX,** my two favorite Portland comics shops: (yes I have multiple pull boxes: no *you* shut up).

It worked . . . a little. Only thing is, less titles waiting in my box(es) meant more time to browse the racks and impulse-grab. And let's not forget the indie creators I stumble across on Instagram. Or numerous Kickstarters that light up my eyes. Or the copies of **2000AD** and **COPRA** that arrive in my mailbox. Or. Or. Or.

Sigh. I'll cut down next year, I swear.

So let's talk Horror Comics, shall we? Or at least, Horror-*adjacent*. Because we all know genre fidelity gets even blurrier and less important in the graphic medium. Here, then, are 10 Horror-y books from 2022 that I think are pretty keen:

Farmhand (Rob Guillory, Jean-Francois Beaulieu, Kody Chamberlain; Image Comics) returned from a COVID-related hiatus to begin its end run. I miss departed colorist Taylor Wells' punchier palette, but this dark-humored Eco/Body/Family Horror book, about a literal farm that grows replacement transplant organs, is as strong as ever. I can't wait to see what Guillory gets up to when this title wraps.

Tales from Harrow County: Lost Ones (Cullen Bunn, Emily Schnall, Tyler Crook; Dark Horse) is a fantastic Folk Horror return to form after a few lackluster arcs. Truth to tell, I had pretty much given up on the *Harrow County* universe, but this is the strongest the series has been since the original run ended.

If the book you wanna read doesn't exist yet . . . make it yourself. Harry Nordlinger has curated ***Vacuum Decay*** (various; self-published), a haunting, grotesque anthology series, for a few years now, and his gonzo indie spirit feeds my soul. Harry—and fellow ***Vacuum*** regular Michael Falotico—contributed to Tenebrous' inaugural ***Green Inferno,*** where I fell in love with each artist's slowly-unfolding-nightmare approach to comics. An issue of ***Vacuum Decay*** is discomforting in the best possible sense; it feels like it was made by aliens who observed humans for a few minutes and decided they should try human-ing too. This fifth issue is as fucked up and grimy as ever. Highest possible recommendation. www.vacuumdecay.com

Harry turned me onto the utterly warped ***Andi*** by creator Cameron Zavala. To my knowledge, ***Andi*** doesn't currently exist except on the creator's IG page (@cameron_zavala), where you can read it free; and you should, particularly if you dig an ending that, in the author's words, "is painful and awful and destroys all hope." Neat!

Across the room, budget- and polish-wise, but no less Horrific, is ***The Nice House by the Lake*** (James Tynion IV, Álvaro Martínez Bueno, Jordie Bellaire, Andworld Design; DC/Black Label) an apocalyptic tale that unfolds puzzle box-like, revealing its secrets across twelve impeccably illustrated issues. I'm only halfway through but its vibe is tailor-made for me. Tynion is the biggest name in Horror comics for a reason.

Technically ***Human Remains*** (Peter Milligan, Sally Cantirino, Dearbhla Kelly, Tim Daniel; Vault Comics) wrapped last year, but the trade released in '22, so that's reason enough to holler about this tale that evokes *The Quiet Place* on a global scale. Cantirino (who provided cover art for our own ***In Somnio***) has moved into the top tier of artists IMO, and Milligan is bona fide Comics Royalty if ya didn't know.

I didn't like Season One of Ed Piskor's button-pushing, voyeuristic, Dark Web torture-porn series **Red Room** (Fantagraphics), in the same way I don't like Rob Zombie films; I get the appeal, it's just not for me. I don't know what changed with Season Two—a few interlocking threads clicked into place, revealing a certain method to the madness, perhaps; and just agreeing to meet the comic on its own, very uncompromising terms—but I have officially shifted my perspective to all-the-fuck-in. It's an artistic tour de force, with a very specific vision, and Piskor is talented as all get-out and not afraid to test the limits of his skill set. I love that. Be warned, though; this one is subtitled **Trigger Warnings** for a reason.

Night of the Ghoul (Scott Snyder, Francesco Francavilla, Andworld Design; Dark Horse/ComiXology) is fairly straightforward, "lost cursed film footage encroaching on the modern world" material, but dear sweet god is Francavilla's art a feast. Check it out just for the tasteful nightmares his art elicits.

The creators of *Monstress*, Marjorie Liu and Sana Takeda, almost slipped the first volume of a new trilogy past me. **The Night Eaters: She Eats the Night** (Abrams Comic Arts) is gory as hell, supernatural and stunningly gorgeous to look at; I've heard it described as *Crazy Rich Asians* but Horror, and that tracks.

Finally, how could I not include the best modern *2000AD* serial, which is still going strong? **Brink** (Dan Abnett, I.N.J. Culbard, Simon Bowland; 2000AD/Rebellion) returned with its latest installment, **Mercury Retrograde**; 24 chapters of far-future Sci-Fi Horror aboard homicidal-cult-ravaged, claustrophobic, planet-orbiting habitats. **Brink** is a perfect comic series; I'm already impatient for the next volume.

ACKNOWLEDGEMENT OF COPYRIGHT

"Banhus" originally appeared in *khōréō* Magazine; khoreomag.com; original editor: Aleksandra Hill.

"User Warning" originally appeared in *Radon Journal*.

"The Bear Across the Way" originally appeared on *Pseudopod*.

"En el Patio de la Casa del Callejón" originally appeared in *Baffling* Magazine.

"In Haskins" originally appeared in *Apex* Magazine.

"The Imperfection" originally appeared in *Shortwave* Magazine (Shortwave Publishing).

"Blame" originally appeared on *The Dread Machine*.

"Low Tide Jenny" originally appeared in *Seize the Press* Magazine.

"Machine (r)Evolution" originally appeared in *Radon Journal #2*.

"Skin" originally appeared in *khōréō* Magazine.

"Paradise" originally appeared in *Death in the Mouth: Original Horror from People of Color*.

"There Is No Easy Way Towards Earth" originally appeared in *Los Suelos* Anthology.

"Blood Calumny" originally appeared in *Convulsive* (Apocalypse Party).

"Lemmings" originally appeared in *Weird Horror #5* (Undertow Publications).

"Water Goes, Sand Remains" originally appeared in *Death in the Mouth: Original Horror from People of Color*.

"The Mules" originally appeared in *Bear Creek Gazette* #10.

"Stage Five Clinger" originally appeared in *The Book of Queer Saints*.

"Notes on the Forum of the Simulacra" originally appeared on *Many Worlds*.

"The Day When the Last War Is Over" originally appeared in *Apex Magazine*.

"Eat Your Colors" originally appeared in *Chromophobia: A Strangehouse Anthology of Women in Horror* (Rooster Republic Press).

"Mother; Microbes" originally appeared in *Monstroddities* (Sliced Up Press).

"The Mythologization of Tymber Prescott in Five Selected Photos" originally appeared in *Nightscript: Volume 8*.

CONTENT WARNINGS

Brave New Weird contains scenes that may be triggering to some audiences.

This being a collection of mature Horror and Speculative Fiction, **some degree of violence, sex and/or gore should be expected.** For more specific concerns, please check the list of stories below for specific potential triggers suggested by the publisher and by the authors themselves:

"Banhus"—assault, misogyny

"En el Patio de la Casa del Callejón"—homophobia, misogyny

"In Haskins"—domestic violence, misogyny

"The Imperfection"—chronic illness, medical procedures

"Blame"—suicide, sexual assault (implied)

"Low Tide Jenny"—necrophilia

"Skin"—racism, misogyny, references to sati

"Lemmings"—suicide, self-harm

"Water Goes, Sand Remains"—animal death, depiction/description of historical genocide

"The Mules"—animal death

"Eat Your Colors"—eating disorders

"The Mythologization of Tymber Prescott in Five Selected Photos"—suicide (implied)

ABOUT TENEBROUS PRESS

Tenebrous Press strives to drag the malleable Horror genre into Newer, Weirder territory with stories that are incisive, provocative, intelligent and terrifying; delivered by voices diverse and unsung.

We welcome the esoteric; the unorthodox; the finest in New Weird Horror.

FIND OUT MORE:
www.tenebrouspress.com
Twitter: @TenebrousPress

NEW WEIRD HORROR